SINNER

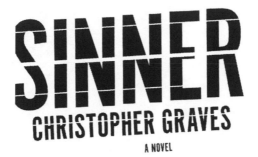

SINNER

CHRISTOPHER GRAVES

A NOVEL

This book is dedicated to the most extraordinary creative partner imaginable, my Rebecca.

"All wickedness is but little to the wickedness of a woman: let the portion of a sinner fall upon her."—Ecclesiasticus 25:19

PROLOGUE

"**F**OR THE LIPS *of a strange woman drop as a honeycomb,*" a man grumbles in the darkness. *"And her mouth is smoother than oil."* *That voice again.*

It is the last thing Minerva heard before the bottom of a boot stomped down on her face. She has slowly regained consciousness but doesn't dare move. Too afraid to even open her eyes, she lies as still as a corpse on what she can tell is a dusty patch of earth outside her billiard hall.

Miss Minnie's Place and its bevy of soiled doves are all Minerva has. She clawed through much of her forty-two years, fighting for every scrap, and is now the only female ever in Douglas County to own property. A strong woman with a fierce temper, she looks after the girls as though they were her own children. But she has failed them tonight.

There is a jangle of chains.

Horses, she thinks, picking up the smell of manure. *And there's something else. More voices.*

A group of men are mumbling words too quietly for her to understand. For a brief moment, Minerva wonders if tonight might have been a nightmare.

If I wake from this tormented slumber, I vow—

A powdery dust floats across her face as someone passes by her head.

It's not a dream. She remembers now.

The rumors circulating through Ava this afternoon are true. The Bald Knobbers have arrived. Accounts of the devastation they'd left in Chadwick reached town only hours before they did. At the time, Minerva kept a brave face, concealing her fear with a friendly smile. Inside though, worry swelled in her gut.

"But her end is bitter as wormwood, sharp as a two-edged sword," the scratchy voice continues. *"Her feet go down to death; her steps take hold on hell!"*

Minerva's ankles suddenly jerk to the side, startling her into cracking her swollen eyes. She immediately wishes she hadn't. Her feet are bound together with a long rope that leads to a body on her right.

Ethel.

Her first girl. Her mouth is agape, eyes glossy and lifeless.

A tiny moan works up Minerva's throat.

Behind the dead girl, a sea of muslin masks gaze back at her. Although each is unique, every one is topped with hornlike spires and painted with the terrifying faces the Knobbers are known for.

Monsters. Crusaders of God shouldn't have to hide their—

One man's face is uncovered. He is taller than the rest of the group, standing like a narrow sapling in the middle of an open field.

He's only a boy, she marvels, staring at the young man who cannot be more than thirteen or fourteen years old. *How could a child be so—*

"Git your mask back on!" a voice shouts from somewhere behind Minerva.

"It don't matter to me if'n they know who I am!" the young man yells, slapping his chest in defiance. "Paul Adison is gonna help send these whores to hell, and I'm proud of it!"

Several men cheer from beneath their disguises.

A horse neighs, tugging Minerva's ankles again. She lolls her throbbing head toward a pile of crying bodies that she knows are more of her girls. Tears cloud her vision.

It's almost over, she tells herself. *We will be with the loving, forgiving Father soon.*

Summoning the last of her courage, she drops her head and begins praying aloud, "*Yea, though I walk through the valley of the shadow of death, I will fear no—*"

"Oh, it's too late for that now, Minerva," the gravelly voice snaps. "*Now the body is not for fornication, but for the Lord; and the Lord for the body.*"

She ignores him, her hoarse voice rising to a growl. "*I WILL FEAR NO EVIL . . . FOR THOU ART WITH ME. THY ROD AND THY STAFF, THEY COMFORT ME!*"

Countless painted faces with horns on their heads and emptiness in their eyes begin to recite as a booming chorus.

A verse from Corinthians. Words from my own Bible.

The young man and another Knobber approach the horses. Minerva considers the face of the unmasked boy. His eyes are different from the others'. They are not vacant like those of a sheep mindlessly following its herd. There is a sparkle in his gaze, a glistening jubilance.

Paul Adison is savoring this moment.

"Miss Minnie," Paul taunts, crouching over her. "*Know ye not that the unrighteous shall not inherit the kingdom of God?"*

She clenches her burning eyelids, resuming her prayer in silence. *Surely goodness and mercy shall follow me all the days of my life.*

The words echo so loudly in her mind, she doesn't hear the hands slapping hide or the wailing of her girls. She gasps as her horse takes off, kicking dirt into her face.

And, as Minerva is dragged across the rocky field, she sobs her final words beneath the moonlit Missouri sky, *"I will dwell in the house of the LORD for—"*

She is gone.

ONE

THE SIGN ON the front window of Pizza Palace in East Stroudsburg, Pennsylvania, reminds diners it was voted Best Pizza in
Town, three years in a row. Ann Haut frowns at the browning
iceberg lettuce and clumpy dressings, assuming nobody voted on
the salad bar. As she pokes around the rest of the icy display, she
tells herself that, although grabbing a burger and fries would have
been easier, Weight Watchers has finally gotten her back into her
size twelves, so she's sticking with the plan.

A childish giggling interrupts Ann's self-coaching. She scans
the mostly empty dining area, quickly pinpointing the source in a
booth right next to the door where a frisky young guy is feeding
his date a piece of pizza. The adolescent girl, trying to seem older
than she is with a push-up bra and tight T-shirt, slowly pulls back,
stretching a long strand of cheese between them. The guy bites into
the same area of the slice so that they are linked by the hanging
thread. Their faces move together, each nibbling their end, finally

meeting in a cheesy *Lady and the Tramp*-like kiss.

"Ew," Ann mutters although she might feel differently if she actually had someone to cheesy kiss.

For the last few years, her love life has consisted of salacious novels and Chips Ahoy! cookies in a lonely one-bedroom apartment. It's not that she wants to be alone; she just doesn't like playing all the games that seem to come with dating these days. Besides, who could compare with the men in her books?

Ann's mind drifts back to her table where more of *Galatea's Secret* is waiting to be consumed. In the last chapter, Christos, a Greek drifter who works as a gardener on a grand estate, finally declared his love for Genevieve, the married lady of the manor. But the brutish count discovered their affair, and after locking Genevieve in a dark tower, he charged out into the stormy night, swearing to kill Christos with his bare hands. During their battle, the gardener overpowered the count, leaving him clinging to life on the massive front lawn. Then, using one of his landscaping tools, Christos freed his lover, whisking her away to his rustic childhood house in the Greek village of Oia.

The Greeks never put lettuce in their salads, Ann thinks, combing over the pile of sad, wilted shreds. *Or grass.* Pulling a chilled plate from the springy stack, she skips the lettuce, heaping on vegetables instead. *Of course, they probably wouldn't substitute their fresh feta for these processed cheddar bits either, but whatever.* She sprinkles some slivers of cheese stuff over her veggies and continues down the bar.

As Ann assembles her salad, she hears the bleeping of a video game. Across from her, the dim purple glow of a black light bulb illuminates the small arcade. Just inside an alcove, a shiny metal crane sways from within the glass box of a U-Grab-It! game. Next to it, a frightful clown face grins eerily from the backbox of a lit pinball machine.

"God, I hate clowns," she mumbles, slowly sliding out of its eyeline.

Grateful she's dining on the other side of the restaurant, Ann drives a spoon into the bucket of croutons that are dusted with what she hopes are dried herbs.

Clowns are the most terrifying things ever, she thinks until she notices the black hair floating in the bucket of Italian dressing.

"Oh, come on," she scoffs, opting for the olive oil and balsamic vinegar.

As she reaches for the cloudy bottles, movement from the game room grabs her attention. She sees the Ms. Pac-Man game first, its signature yellow orb pulsing behind the glass. But another motion pulls her gaze down, and she realizes the dark shapes wagging at the base of the console are shoes. As she squints for a clearer view, a man's shadowy face floats in from the darkness and locks eyes with her.

"Oh, shit!" She drops the vinegar bottle, clinking its glass against the metal cradle. "Jesus!"

Ann grabs the corner of the salad bar table, still a bit startled but mostly embarrassed. She chuckles to herself, reaching for the vinegar again. As she splashes her salad and gingerly replaces the bottle, she tells herself it was probably not that big of a deal.

Maybe he didn't really notice, she thinks, finding comfort in both her delusion and a bucket of seeded breadsticks. Snagging a few of the sticks, she starts toward her table but stops. *A fork. Perfect excuse.* As Ann casually rifles through the metal cylinder wedged in ice, she peeks back into the arcade.

Damn.

He's staring right at her.

After a moment, the corners of his mouth rise. As Ann returns the smile, the man dissolves back into the shadows.

Okay, not as creepy, she thinks, slinking off and almost forgetting to grab the frigging fork.

Taking her seat again, Ann rummages through her overfilled purse for her book, excited to join her pals in Greece.

"Hello?" A lanky teenage boy with frizzy yellow hair appears next to her table, smirking, as though he were standing there for hours.

"Sorry, I didn't see—"

The waiter cuts her off, "Drink?"

"Uh, sure. I'd like a Coke and—"

"We only have Pepsi," he interjects again, uninterested.

Ann forces a smile, telling the cornstalk of a boy that Pepsi's fine. He scribbles on a warped little notepad and starts to ask for her food order, but she cuts him off, "And I'm just gonna do the salad for dinner, thanks."

He stares at her, either confused by the complicated order or unhappily tasting his own medicine. Either way, Ann feels a little vindicated. She gives him a quick blink, dismissing him.

After a moment, he shoves the pad and pencil into his soiled apron pocket. "Help yourself if you want seconds," he huffs, nodding to her full plate before lumbering off to the kitchen.

Across the room, the oh-so grown-up girl squeals again as she leans in, whispering something into her guy's ear. He growls, sparking a little more chatter about what they plan to do to each other tonight.

Well, they're off to create another statistic, Ann thinks as the couple stands and gathers their belongings. *And it's not even prom night.*

The guy pulls his date in for another kiss and cups her breast.

"Don't," she squawks, pushing his hand away. "Wait till we get outside."

"What are you talking about?" he replies, coyly reaching out for another attempt.

The girl snickers, swatting at him. As he jumps back, dodging her swing, his hand knocks a half-empty cup off the table.

"Oh, shit." He laughs, ushering her out the restaurant door as another dark spot forms on the stained carpet. "Hurry up!"

Oh, that's nice. Ann watches the couple bolt around the side of the building, cackling like they're the only two people in the world. *Did we act like this when we were teenagers? Were we—*

"Assholes!" the waiter yells, hurrying across the dining room. At their booth, he fumbles through the dishes, looking for some cash. Realizing he's been stiffed, Cornstalk storms to the front door and flings it open. "You fuckers had better not come back here, or I'm calling the cops!" He stands in the doorway, hands on his hips, like some sheriff ready for a Wild West duel until a swarm of june bugs circling a light outside break away from their cycle and dart into the dining room. "Ugh, shit," he snaps, yanking the door closed.

Halfheartedly swatting at the bugs, the boy stomps back to the couple's booth. Clearly still fuming, he mumbles to himself as he tosses their plates on a tray and returns to the kitchen, bypassing the fallen cup.

"Fuckin' kids," he scoffs from behind the swinging door.

Settling back in, Ann pulls over the plate with her understudy to a Greek salad and finds the bookmark, eager to join the gardener and his mistress in Oia.

The sweaty couple lies on the kitchen floor, devouring a loaf of bread with the same ferocity they just made love with.

Ann chomps off the end of a breadstick, flicking seeds across her table.

Too exhausted from the journey, Christos doesn't bother to wipe his brow, instead allowing the beads of perspiration to slide down his chiseled, hairy chest.

A low-pitched mumbling breaks into the afterglow in Greece,

and Ann is reluctantly drawn back to Pennsylvania.

What now? More kids?

Dusting crumbs from her chest, she scours the room, like an old man ready to shoo somebody off his lawn.

Wait. When did he come in?

Across from her, a few tables away, a man is sitting in front of a tray of pizza. His head is bowed, fingers laced.

Has he been there the whole time?

Ann cannot see his face, but he's dressed nicely enough—khaki pants and a navy polo shirt. Noticing the frayed soles of his sneakers, she decides he must be wearing a uniform. Probably works some-place that keeps him on his feet a lot, like the hardware store next door or the new Best Buy that just opened on Route 611.

Maybe he's sleeping over there, and the mumbling is a snore. He must be exhausted.

She unintentionally clinks her fork against her plate, and he stirs.

As the man's head rises, his eyes sweep across the stained carpet toward her table.

Okay, so I guess he is not sleeping.

His gaze lands on Ann, and she realizes it's the guy from the arcade.

Don't you do it again, she warns herself, stifling a gasp.

His face shifts into another kind of bashful, closed-mouth smile. Ann attempts to be polite, but as she awkwardly bobs her head in acknowledgment, she's sure she looks more like a Parkinson's patient than a cordial fellow diner.

Oh, forget it. Get back to Greece.

The man murmurs something she can't quite hear and then dramatically clears his throat.

"Sorry?" Ann asks, glancing up with a sheepish grin.

"Amen." He smiles at her again.

"Oh, yes, you, too," she fumbles. "Um, amen."

Ann reads the same sentence about the enchanting scent of the Aegean Sea several times, unable to focus on the words.

Is he flirting with me? Can an amen be flirty?

Staring at what might as well be a blank page, she hears the rustling of a paper napkin being tucked inside his collar.

You're being ridiculous.

"Good salad?" he asks.

Wait. Maybe not. Ann feels her cheeks flushing as she lowers the paperback and returns the smile. "Yes, thanks. It's very good," she lies. *Nobody likes a Negative Nancy.*

From this distance, she can't determine if the man's hollow face is ruggedly handsome—like Charles Bronson, whom she's always found very attractive—or maybe . . . just rugged. He's definitely a little older than her but appears to be in good shape, so age isn't a deal-breaker.

"How's the pizza?" she flirts back, munching on another breadstick and deciding to roll the dice on Bronson.

"It's real good." With a mouthful of cheesy dough, he blots his greasy hands on his napkin and reaches for his large drink.

Ann notices a simplicity about him, a vulnerability. *Maybe he was also awkward in school,* she imagines, *and was forced to eat by himself every day in a lonely cafeteria crowded with the cool kids.* She feels chills coming on. *God, high school sucked.*

The man's eyes float from the pizza to Ann. "Want some?" He gulps down more soda.

Oh gosh, he's offering me his pudding cup, so I'll be his friend. She giggles inadvertently. "Oh, no. Thanks though—"

His plastic cup slaps down on the tabletop. He wipes away a cola mustache as his eyes seem to narrow a bit. "What's funny?"

Ann's smile quickly fades. "What? Oh, nothing. I'm just happy with my salad, is all." She shifts in her chair, confused.

Oh no, he thinks I was laughing at him. Great!

"Hmm," he says, rattling the ice in his cup. "Okay."

She sinks back behind the book, mortified. *Well, looks like you screwed that one up, Annie!*

As the silence thickens in the room, Ann's mind darts to a clump of the eleventh grade *It* girls standing outside the restroom. She hears what she's sure is her name, followed by a burst of haughty laughter. Her neck itches, as though she were trapped in a horrible wool sweater several sizes too small.

Apologize, you bully, her inner voice cries.

"Listen, I'm—"

"What is that?" The man seems calm again, like nothing happened.

Maybe the whole thing was just in her head. Puzzled, Ann studies him more closely, careful not to smile at all. "Uh, pardon me?"

He shrugs. "Maybe. What are you reading?"

"Oh, it's nothing. Just, you know, a romance novel. It's called *Galatea's Secret.*" Stifling a self-conscious snigger, she blurts out, "You read it?"

His deadpan stare tells her he's not understanding or at least not enjoying her stupid attempt at humor. He's also probably not read the damn book.

"*Whoso findeth a wife, findeth a good thing, and obtaineth favor of the Lord,*" the man says, sternly.

Ann considers the novel's plot. "Well, what if they findeth somebody *else's* wife?" she retorts with a playful smirk. *Well, that's great,* she thinks, immediately judging herself. *Now, you sound like a slut. Just eat your friggin' salad, you idiot!*

"Can I see that?" His chair scoots back from the table, its legs hissing across the carpet.

Startled into silence again, Ann glances around the restaurant. Although the man and she are the only diners left, they're not alone. The waiter slouches against the wall next to the arcade, chatting on a phone. And it sounds like someone is listening to music while washing dishes in the kitchen.

Ann relaxes. *This guy is probably just one of the socially awkward types, like Rain Man or Lennie from* Of Mice and Men.

"Um, yeah, sure," she says, extending the paperback.

He stands, grabs the tray with his remaining pizza, and joins Ann at her table.

As he is sitting across from her now, their age difference is a little more obvious. *Probably early fifties*, she guesses, noting the gray coming in at his temples. *But what's ten or fifteen years really?* She considers the thin-looking skin around the man's eyes and a crease leading from his furrowed brows to a heavily lined forehead. *There's something kinda dangerous about him,* she thinks, a little excited by the confidence of her peculiar dining mate. She imagines the deep scar stretching from the middle of his top lip to the base of his nose is the result of a wild bar fight or some other manly event.

He dabs his oily fingers on the napkin at his collar and reaches for the book. While his tongue works to dislodge food from his back teeth, he inspects the cover art.

On the bow of a great ship, an exotic, tan man holds his porcelain-skinned lover in a tight embrace. She peeks over her shoulder with passionate eyes as wild blonde hair drapes down her naked back.

"You're not married," he says matter-of-factly.

Oh God, Lennie, please don't ask to touch my hair. Ann pushes a cucumber chunk around her plate, considering how to respond. She has been fielding the why-aren't-you-married-yet balls from her parents for almost half of her life now.

"Guess I just haven't been *foundeth* yet." She winks, deciding not to be offended.

The man nods to her hand. "No wedding ring."

As if he didn't hear her, he continues with another bite of pizza, ripping at the crust like a wolf tearing meat from a carcass.

Wow, he eats like—

Ann freezes at the sight of his jagged, discolored teeth. The rocky crumbles are so jarring, she actually flinches a bit, spattering salad dressing on her white tank top. "Damn." She recovers quickly, shifting her focus to the drips of balsamic over her breast.

Okay, that mouth is a deal-breaker.

Blotting her napkin at a spot, she feels his gaze and glances up, expecting him to avert his eyes in shame. Instead, he stares carnivorously at her chest as chewed pizza circles in his open mouth like a Laundromat dryer.

"Dirty," he says, his eyes finally breaking away. Without emotion, he tosses her book down, tapping its cover. "Isn't it?"

The waiter passes their table, carrying a tray of salt and pepper shakers.

Ann waits until he's out of earshot before allowing a grin to creep across her face. "Well, I hope so, but I'm not that far into it yet."

"Anything else?" the waiter asks from across the room. He is not even looking in their direction, but Ann can only assume the question is for them.

"Not for me, thank you." She smiles, trying to sound perky. *I've lost my appetite. Maybe forever.*

The man shakes his head, still lazily chewing his gross mouthful of dough, as the waiter passes them with a variation of his previous overburdened scowl. When he disappears behind the swinging kitchen door again, Ann figures enough time has passed.

Surely, he's swallowed it by now.

"That's sinful," the man says, shaking his head. He shoves the book back to Ann, his eyes drifting up to hers, as if waiting for a response.

Unsure of how to answer, she concedes with an awkward half-shrug of her shoulders and hopes the waiter will bring her check soon. His conversation appears to have wrapped up.

Thank God.

As the man lifts his napkin from his collar, wiping his face, Ann notices a Buy-and-Save name tag dangling from his shirt pocket—*My name is ZEKE. How may I help you?*

He slowly traces her eyeline to the tag. "Beelzebub," Zeke mutters, quickly dropping the napkin back into place.

A sudden chill covers Ann's body. *Okay, this is getting uncomfortable.* "What was that?" she asks in the most unaffected voice she can muster. When he doesn't respond, she eases back in her chair, casually glancing toward the kitchen. "That guy is taking forever with our checks," she says, attempting to mask her anxiety. "Maybe it's free."

A knocking on the table yanks her focus back to Zeke, who is locked on her eyes. Her pulse begins to race as, in what feels like slow motion, he lifts a single finger to his lips.

"*Nay, but, except ye repent, ye shall all likewise perish,*" he whispers, dropping the crumpled napkin on his plate and rising to his feet.

As he moves toward the door, adrenaline sweeps through Ann's body. She feels like a mouse that's just dodged a snake's strike, like she has evaded the fangs but might still have a heart attack at any moment. She watches Zeke leave the restaurant and round the corner of the building to the parking lot. As he passes the side window, she notices his head bobbing from side to side, as though keeping rhythm with some catchy song in his head.

What the hell—

"You gonna eat that?"

Ann jumps in her seat, almost tipping it over, but is quickly relieved to see her apathetic waiter standing there. "Sorry, you scared me," she exhales. "So glad you're back though."

"Well? Do you want that to go?"

"Oh, no. That's not mine," she says. *I might not ever eat pizza again.*

She checks the window for Zeke one last time. He's gone.

The waiter rips a page from his pad, tosses it on the table, and begins gathering up the dirty dishes. "Well, your date already paid for it when he ordered. So, if you want—"

"I don't. Thanks." *And definitely not my date*, she almost adds. "God, that was so weird. Wasn't it?"

"Huh?" Another blank stare.

Ann rifles through her purse and sets a twenty-dollar bill next to her check without looking at it. "That guy, uh . . . with the pizza."

"Hmm. I didn't really notice," he says, giving the table an uninspired wipe with his filthy rag. "You need change?"

Ann's brows furrow at the idiot. *How could you not have noticed? We were the only people in this place!*

She considers waiting for her change but decides to get the hell out of there. "No, it's fine. I'm all set."

Across the room, the lights go out in the arcade, and a man's voice shouts from the kitchen, "Night!"

The waiter yells back as he shoves the cash into his apron pocket and walks off. From over his shoulder, with no trace of sincerity, he thanks Ann for dining at Pizza Palace and requests that she comes again.

Outside the restaurant, Ann hesitates on the sidewalk. It's only been a few minutes since Zeke left, and she's still a little freaked out. She peeks around the corner of the building, spotting her car in the back right section of the empty parking lot. As she wonders if she should maybe ask the waiter for an escort, the lock on the restaurant door clicks. She spins just in time to see the vapid boy flip over a We're Closed board and walk away.

Well, it's not like he'd have been a lot of help anyway, I guess, she thinks.

A hanging sign for the hardware store rattles in the wind above her. Ann steels herself. She grips her keys in her fist, like she saw in a YouTube self-defense video, and hurries into the dark lot. As she reaches her trunk, movement in a pickup truck grabs her attention.

It is parked in the shadow of a huge tree in the opposite corner of the lot, so she didn't see it before now.

Frozen in place, Ann strains for a glimpse into the cab. *It's empty? I swear, I saw something move inside it.*

Suddenly, its horn blares, and she jumps, screaming, as she scurries around her car. She dives in behind the wheel, yanking the door closed. The truck's engine roars to life. In her rearview mirror, she spots the contorted face of the frisky young guy from inside the pizza joint as he howls out his window. He and the girl wave at Ann as the pickup speeds off, kicking up shaly pieces across the lot.

ANN PULLS INTO her garage, still a bit shaky from her night. As she gathers her purse and an empty Starbucks cup, she realizes she can't see her garbage container. It usually sits right outside her back door. She slides out of her car and peers over the hood. Sure enough, the large rubber bin is on its side again, rank trash spilled out across the garage floor.

Raccoons? Cats? Whatever it is, how are they getting in?

She taps a button on her visor and heads over to start the clean-up. The automatic garage door jostles down its track as Ann rights the bin.

In a flash, a rat bolts out of the can, its claws prickling across her arm. Ann's had enough. Screaming the whole time, she flops onto the car hood and then hurls herself over the trash can, crashing against her back door. She dashes inside, leaving the garbage exactly where it is.

Hurrying to wash her hands, Ann hopes the rodent is gone. She didn't actually see it run out. She also didn't see the man who slid under the garage door before it closed.

TWO

ANN BOLTS UPRIGHT, her breathy yelp bouncing off the bedroom walls. As she subconsciously pulls the blanket up her chest, she scans the darkened doorway, trying to process what she sees. The large form of what looks like a person slouches in the shadow of her partially closed door. She strains to hear past the clicking tail of her Felix the Cat wall clock.

What is that? She locks on what could be the head of a tall, stocky body. *Is it moving?*

A car engine revs outside.

Ann jumps, huffing the breath she didn't realize she was holding. As she whips her head to the window next to her bed, headlights pop on, beaming through the mini blinds. She checks the door again. In the hallway outside, the car's lights reflect on the polished wooden surface of a bookshelf she recently bought. Clearly, she isn't used to it yet. An exhale of equal parts relief and annoyance flutters from her lips as the light beams slide across her bedroom walls and disappear. When she hears the tires squeal off, Ann decides she can release the death grip on her covers.

She flicks on the overhead light, swings the door fully open, and stares out at the bulky piece of furniture. Because her living room is so tiny, she thought placing the shelf in the hallway would make sense. She could use it as extra storage for linens, toilet paper, maybe seasonal clothes. Truthfully, it probably is too big for her apartment, but she had to buy it. At twenty-five dollars, leaving the exquisite sandalwood piece at that church yard sale would have been an absolute tragedy.

Although having a heart attack in the middle of the night because you didn't recognize a strange new shape at your door would also be a tragedy.

She gently taps the wooden side, as if consoling a runner-up in a kids' potato-sack race, and commits to rearranging things in the morning. But a pungent, musky odor assaults her nostrils, and she pauses halfway to the kitchen, turning back to the shelf.

Wow, that really stinks.

She's heard that sandalwood is famous for its earthy scent, but this is more like sweaty, soured gym clothes. She definitely picked up on a smell initially but assumed it would dissipate. It actually seems to have gotten stronger.

Maybe some stray cat also thought it was a great deal and claimed it first. Could be why it was so cheap.

In the kitchen, she throws back a swig of water and sets the glass in the sink as she assesses her living room. She wonders if moving the couch and television to opposite walls could work. *Although they're probably too heavy to handle by myself, and the damn thing still might not fit.*

As her buyer's remorse kicks in, Ann considers finishing off the tin of cookies she avoided earlier tonight.

No! a responsible voice shouts in her head. *You're out of points.*

Just go back to sleep!

Ann finishes in the kitchen and heads back into her bedroom. She shuts the door this time, hoping to prevent any more panic attacks while also restricting that terrible odor. She flicks off the light and hops back into bed, adjusting her pillows. Staring at the popcorn ceiling, she tries to remember what she was dreaming about as she starts to drift off.

Oh, yeah, the puppy and that sweet old couple.

Something clicks from beyond the foot of her bed.

Ann's eyes spring open, darting around. *I definitely heard something.*

As she reaches for the bedside lamp, there's another click. She bumps the shade, sending the lamp crashing to the floor with a quick blue spark. Her eyes whip to the bedroom door, focused on its twisting knob.

Before Ann can utter a sound, the door is open, and the overhead bulb is shining brightly. Her eyelids flutter, adjusting to the rings of light eclipsing her vision. She cannot scream or cry or even breathe.

The figure of what Ann now realizes is a man steps into the doorway and casually slouches against the frame. Dark clothing covers his body from the neck down—a bulky sweatshirt over faded black slacks. A painful tightness swells in her chest as he leans into the light, revealing his horns. Her body feels paralyzed, but her mind is racing.

What the hell is THAT?

Two curved, asymmetrical goat horns poke through the top of the man's hood, which conceals the upper half of his face. Between them, a set of demonic eyes painted in a brightly glowing orange glare back at her. The intruder shifts his weight from side to side, his head slowly wagging, as if he were swaying to the rhythm of some nightclub ballad. He seems completely unconcerned with

Ann until she gasps.

His arms fling out, gripping the sides of the doorframe with gloved hands, as he addresses the wall above her head. *"Guilty, vile and helpless, we,"* the man speak-sings, lowering his eyes to hers. *"Spotless Lamb of God was He."*

Ann shuffles up against the headboard, open-mouthed. She tries to scream but only produces a sort of soundless stutter.

"Full atonement," he continues in a throaty tone, *"can it be?"* As he jerks back and forth, the hood shifts up, revealing more of his emaciated face.

Ann flinches, spotting his cracked yellow-brown teeth. She recognizes this guy.

"Zeke?" she blurts.

The man lunges forward so swiftly, he almost loses his balance, having to grip the dresser top to stay on his feet. "NO!" he hisses, stomping across the room as he plunges his hands into the sweatshirt's front pocket.

Ann's full voice returns as she retreats against the headboard, kicking her feet beneath the covers. "Oh God! Please, no, don't—"

Two darts penetrate her neck, and the crackling of a Taser gun overpowers her scream. Her body flails for a few moments, bucking with electric current, and then slumps across the disheveled bed.

Staring at Ann's twitching body, Zeke extends his arms, as if offering a big hug. *"I say unto thee, except a man be born again, he cannot see the kingdom of God."*

He catches sight of his reflection in a mirror hanging over the dresser. Tilting his head like a dog that hears a high-pitched whistle, he gazes at the curled horns and painted eyes. His lips slide into a crooked smile. "I do the Lord's work here," he whispers to the glass.

Zeke stretches out a long length of duct tape, biting through it as the music starts up in his head again. And, working at the pace of someone unburdened by time, he binds Ann's hands and feet, simultaneously performing for his stained- and rocky-toothed re-flection. *"Hallelujah! What a savior!"*

THREE

Missouri, 1958

DEEP WITHIN THE Ozark Hills, it is almost noon when Sylvia peeks through the tattered curtains of her small wood-paneled bedroom. In the distance, a rusty barbed wire fence sways in the late fall wind as yet another station wagon carrying unwanted wedding guests moves up the dusty driveway toward her father's house.

Her gaze drops, landing on a trail of ants marching across the warped board outside her window. At the end of the line, a large spider flails its legs as the mass of soldiers attacks.

You will never get away, she thinks, tracing the pane, *even with all those legs.* She watches as the tiny army surrounds its target, overpowers it, and brings it down. *There's too many of them, biting and tearing.*

The fight on the rotted windowsill is over quickly. What was just a bubbly black knot has separated into an organized line of workers, hauling torn pieces of the dying spider.

Sylvia's eyes drift back to the caravan of arriving cars as a pang of despair kicks in her gut. *And there will always be more waiting.*

The doors will open with parishioners flooding into the modest den at the front of the house. They will bring love offerings of coffee cakes and crocheted satchels of dried flowers, but she knows they are not coming for her. Oh, they must briefly acknowledge her, but then the wives will file off to a corner somewhere while the husbands move to congratulate her father. After all, at twenty-two, Sylvia is practically antique, so he must be a hell of a salesman.

A leader of the Apostolic Church of Christ, Elder Paul Adison is a revered man. He holds weekly assemblies with the men of the Pentecostal parish, emphasizing absolute devotion to the word. On meeting nights, his voice booms from the crowded front room. He cites passages from his Bible, warning the group of the dangers of temptation. Many nights focus specifically on the inherent evilness of women.

Down the hall, Sylvia often prepares coffee for after the meetings, entranced by her father's condemning words. She knows he is right; she's seen it for herself.

Elder Paul was fifty years old when he married her mother, Elvira, who was only fifteen at the time. Although rather innocent at first glance with a frail, boyish-shaped body and unremarkably featured face, she had the mind of a much older woman. It was her eyes that gave her away—small, dark spheres constantly shifting, like a cornered rat calculating its next move. She was a cruel young woman, jealous and conniving, whose sickly, lethargic nature only improved when she was provoking trouble.

Elvira toyed with her sons and their father like tattered, expendable dolls she'd grown tired of. She would ignite tiny embers of disorder solely for her own entertainment and then stand back and fan the flame until a full-blown brawl blazed through the house. The brothers would scrap with the old man for hours while Sylvia, safely concealed in the shadows, watched her mother revel in the chaos.

As another form of manipulation, Elvira would pretend to be dying from a new malady every few months. She'd have the boys carry her from room to room, claiming to be too weak to move on her own, although Sylvia would see her walk just fine when she thought no one was watching. And, more than once, she'd be spotted dipping a rag into her hot tea and holding it to her forehead long enough to generate a temporary fever. So, when the woman did actually die several years ago from a violent influenza, nobody believed it until the body was removed. There was no grieving.

"The Lord sees and knows all," her father said. "That woman's soul was corrupt, and God took his vengeance."

Sylvia leaves the window and delicately opens the buckskin bundle on her bed. Goose bumps rise on her arms. As she removes the neatly folded cotton gown, she hears herself whisper, *"Of the woman came the beginning of sin."* Her knees buckle. She claws at the bed quilt as she slides to the floor.

While clenching the dress in her fist, her mind jolts to that afternoon ten years ago when she met a Bald Knobber.

———————

Sylvia fumbles with the door of her father's wardrobe, trying not to drop any of the clean laundry in her arms. She probably should've made two trips, but she hates this chore and wants to get it over with. She snags a corner of the door with her pinkie finger and flings it open. She pulls the top drawer, shifting her load forward. As the avalanche of clothes tumble in, something in the back corner catches her eye. She sifts through the new pile of rolled socks and lifts a mysterious leather package.

You shouldn't be touching this, a voice in her head warns. *It's probably hidden for a reason.*

She runs her hands over the package's velvety pelt. *What could it be?*

When she finds that the binding strings are already pretty loose, her curiosity wins out. Sylvia has to know what's inside. Besides, there is enough washing to keep her mother outside for another couple of hours.

Just a quick peek.

She tucks the bundle under her arm as she hurries down the hall.

She settles herself on the far side of her bed and carefully slides the knotted string off. As the pelt unfolds, Sylvia marvels at the whitest piece of clothing she's ever seen.

"What in tarnation?" Her mother's voice sends a sudden jab of fear into her gut.

Sylvia lunges to the window.

Elvira is staggering in a cursing fit between several heaps of damp laundry as she wrestles to pin a seemingly possessed bedsheet to the clothesline.

With a quick glance to her closed bedroom door, Sylvia decides to return to the package.

A ceremonial gown.

The snow-colored garment almost glows against the gray bed quilt as she unfolds it for a better look. The girls in church say this is what women—*pure women*—wear for their marriages. She considers the words while her fingertip traces across the soft cotton.

It's so pretty though, she thinks as she tugs the dress over her head.

Her transformation is immediate.

It's so white. So clean. Sylvia curtsies to the wall, feeling fancy, even a little pretty.

But, after a moment, that voice in her head interjects again,

Prideful feelings are a sin.

She ignores the nagging idea, sliding her palms along the dress's sleeves, as she wanders around her little bedroom. The cool fabric brushes against her knees, and she pictures a different life for herself.

This dress is too beautiful for chores, she thinks, daydreaming about a place where she could wear it all the time without soiling it. In her heavenly place, she wouldn't have to cook or sweep the dusty floor. *There'd be no chickens or scrounging through their filthy nests for eggs.*

Prancing back to the far side of her bed, Sylvia sits down against the wall and sighs at the best part of the fantasy. She'd be alone in that place. There'd be no screaming and fighting. No beatings either even if she did deserve them sometimes. She closes her eyes, peacefully submerged in her new world, and drifts to sleep.

The sting from a palm jolts her awake.

Sylvia thinks her father is towering over her, but she can't be sure. The side of her face throbs; her vision is too blurry to see. She squeezes her eyes shut, trying to focus. Another slap knocks her head against the metal bed frame. She immediately remembers where she is. A whimper escapes her throat as she shuffles against the wall. Her eye catches a flash of white from her flailing arms, and her heart sinks. She's still wearing the dress.

With a fistful of hair, the old man yanks Sylvia from the floor, flinging her across the room like a sack of walnuts. "Get it off," he roars as she crashes against the wall. "And you'd better not have soiled it."

The taste of metal rises in her mouth, but she quickly swallows it down before it has a chance to dribble out. He would surely kill her.

Someone scoffs from the other side of the room. Sylvia knows who it is without looking. As she works the dress up her body, her eyes land on Elvira standing in the doorway. A proud smirk stretches across the woman's face. It dawns on Sylvia that her mother probably discovered her sleeping long ago but decided to wait for the excitement her husband would bring.

Sylvia flounders to get the gown over her head, avoiding her pulsing mouth. She offers it to him, extending one shaky, frail arm.

His head flips toward the bedroom door. "Give it to *her*," he grumbles.

Sylvia scrambles to the doorway, passing off the dress like it's on fire. She wraps her arms around herself, attempting to cover her naked chest. Locking eyes with her mother, Sylvia quietly begs for mercy, but as the woman's glassy dark eyes sparkle with delight, she knows it's pointless.

"Now, leave us alone," her father says.

With a final inciting sneer, Elvira steps back into the hall. Sylvia watches the latching door, praying it will miraculously open again. It doesn't. She lowers her gaze to a knot in the wood-paneled wall, waiting for the storm.

A strangling silence fills the room. Sylvia cannot imagine what is coming. She's been getting whippings and switchings from her father since she could walk, but somehow, today seems different.

Her mind strays back to the moment she first found the bundle. *Why didn't you just leave it alone?*

She suddenly notices the heavy breathing, like the panting of a caged tiger. As the floorboards pop behind her, Sylvia huddles against the wall, too terrified to look.

He's coming.

"Turn around," a garbled voice says.

Steeling herself for his wrath, Sylvia slowly turns to plead with her father. Her words catch in her throat, erupting as a terrified shriek when she sees the masked man in front of her.

For years, fears of the Bald Knobbers have plagued the people of Missouri. Tales of the masked men charging through the night on horseback, burning down houses, and abducting townsfolk are countless. Everyone in the area knows of the brotherhood and their commitment to enforcing God's will. And, even though the law forced the group to dissolve many years ago, most folks suspect some of the members still meet secretly, that some Knobbers are still alive and active. Now, Sylvia is certain of it.

Furious eyes pierce through the two jagged holes in the mask painted with a wicked face. Twine cinches the top corners of the muslin, forming pointed horns that extend several inches off his head. As the rage bubbles through his gritted teeth, Sylvia knows her father is gone.

"*They conceive mischief, and bring forth vanity, and their belly prepareth deceit,*" he bellows, vaulting toward her.

Sylvia clenches her eyes shut, bracing herself against the wall. As the house rattles with his approaching charge, she fights with all her might not to pee. She loses that battle with the first blow. And, as a warm pool forms around her crouching body, Sylvia prays for salvation.

The Bald Knobber teaches her a lesson that whole night, armed with pious certitude and the thick cord from a broken electric percolator.

For hours afterward, through swollen, bloodied lips, she dutifully repeats from Ecclesiasticus, "*Of the woman came the beginning of sin, and through her we all die.*"

———

Sylvia breaks out of the memory and pulls herself to her feet, clutching the gown in her fist. Terror is still coursing through her veins. She makes it back to the window and cracks it. Heaving in the fresh air, she watches two ants struggle to drag away the last remaining bits of the spider.

FOUR

A SLOPPY, WET cough snaps Sylvia back into action. Elder Paul is coming.

Over the last two years, she's watched her father go from walking with a shuffle, aided by an old black cane, to clumsily wheeling around in a chair. And a curvature in his spine causes his head to slope so far forward that his eyes are barely visible. However, like an old timber rattler, his venom has gotten more potent with age. A strike could kill.

Sylvia recognizes the sound of his wheels creaking up the hallway floor.

I'm not dressed yet!

Rushing back to the bed, she fumbles with the clasps on her blouse, panicking halfway down. The last three buttons soar across the room as she jerks the gown over her head.

Damn. There's trouble at her shoulders.

Sylvia's been so skinny her entire life, she assumed the dress would still fit, but it's tighter than she remembers. In a self-hugging maneuver, she snags the dress beneath her shoulder blades and frantically wrestles it down her back.

HURRY.

She hikes up the worn gray skirt that she doesn't have time to change. Just as she flattens the ceremonial gown over the top of it, the bedroom door squeaks open.

Elder Paul wheels into the doorway, his glassy eyes darting around the room. He ponders the disheveled quilt on the edge of the bed. "Come on, girl," he wheezes. "It's time."

Sylvia nods. Tightly pressing her hand against her thigh, she squeezes into a pair of borrowed shoes. *Please don't let this skirt drop.* "Yes, sir. I'm just fastening my—"

His black cane smacks against the door. "I don't want no excuses," he says, poking a twisted, scabby finger in the air. "Got folks waitin' on you."

Her father pulls his chair back, but its front wheel catches on the doorframe. He rolls back into the room a bit and tries again. The chair is still caught. He begins rocking his slumped body back and forth as frustration beads across his forehead, like a steaming kettle. Finally, with a stiff prod of his cane, the wheel scrapes past the frame, flicking chips of old paint to the floor.

From the hall, the man tips his head back as far as he can, locking eyes with Sylvia. *"A continual dropping in a very rainy day and a contentious woman are alike,"* he barks. Steering his chair back down the hall, he shouts a final warning over his shoulder, "NOW, GET THE LEAD OUT!"

"Yes, sir," she calls, tearing off her skirt.

Sylvia prepares herself with a deep breath and leaves her room, but as she rounds the corner, the noisy voices coming from the front of the house overwhelm her. She has to stop again. Her legs can't be trusted. Bracing herself against the wall to keep from crumbling, she works her way down the hall again, forcing her clenched fists to relax.

The scent of the clove-infused pouches of potpourri nauseates Sylvia as she makes her way into the bustling den. A wave of quiet rolls across the room, drowning out the gossipy guests. She keeps her eyes on the floor as she continues to the center of the room. Shuffling feet clack their heels over the wooden floor. Sylvia slowly lifts her head. The church members have formed a wall around her, the smell of hair tonic and aftershave hovering above.

Just breathe.

"Move it," her father snaps, spearing the tip of his cane into her back.

With a half-stifled gasp, she staggers forward another few steps. The line of bodies begins to part, revealing an older man Sylvia has not seen since she was a child. He steps into the circle, and for the first time as a grown woman, she is face-to-face with her betrothed.

Ezekiel Woods is a wiry man in his mid-forties although his bald head and the glow of his budding white whiskers make him look older. Sylvia saw him often when she was younger since he regularly attended her father's weekly meetings. They never spoke, but she always noticed him; he has a memorable face. As a result of a childhood injury involving an iron railroad nail, his left eyeball has been replaced with a glossy artificial orb that seems too big for its socket.

Sylvia studies his face, unsure of where to look. The thick lens of his glasses magnifies his fake eye, giving it a frozen, startled appearance, but his right eye doesn't seem to be looking at her either. Fearing the consequences of getting it wrong, she settles for focusing on the bridge of his nose and forces a smile.

Ezekiel's father and her own had a long history. In addition to being two of the original founders of the Apostolic Church of Christ more than fifty years ago, they both were also two of the youngest members of the Bald Knobber brotherhood. The men shared an unwavering devotion to its creed of enforcing God's law—at all costs.

During one late-night raid, back when the boys were just teenagers, Paul got shot in the leg. He lost consciousness from the bleeding and flopped off his horse. He lay, dying, in a cornfield for more than an hour. When Elder Woods spotted Paul's horse on the road, he hurried back to the burning farm and rescued him. From that night on, the two men were as close as brothers.

Several years ago, issues arose between Ezekiel and some parents in the church. The rumor was that he had shown a less than virtuous interest in some of the young girls. Afterward, he moved away for a while, and no one really talked about it again.

But, when Elder Woods died two years ago, leaving Ezekiel the sole survivor of the family, he came back to town. However, he discovered his father had bequeathed the house, land, and all personal effects to the church, passing on nothing to his son. So, penniless, Ezekiel reconnected with Elder Paul, appealing to the sense of brotherhood the man had had with his father. A week later, Sylvia was told she would be Ezekiel's wife.

The circle opens again on the opposite side of the room. Sylvia cranes her neck to see past the shifting bodies. One knee buckles beneath her dress when she spots the pastor and surprise officiant of the ceremony—her uncle James. Desperate to stay on her feet, she clings to Ezekiel's arm. Her eyes plunge to the floor as lightning flashes in her mind.

———

Nothing scares Sylvia more than thunder. She knows all the verses from Genesis, how God's wrath destroyed the world once and just might do it again. So, when bad weather blows in, she always hides under her covers, praying the rain will stop, that she won't drown in another great flood.

Tonight's storm is the worst one yet. Each crackle of lightning makes her want to break into tears, but she won't. She can't. Her father says only babies and weak-minded people cry. Neither of those is welcome in his house. A strong November wind howls outside her window. She sinks a little further into her pillow. As another clap of thunder explodes, Sylvia clenches the covers in her little ten-year-old fists and wonders what has angered God tonight.

Being wasteful is very bad, she thinks, remembering that she tossed her moldy sandwich in the garbage can at lunchtime today. *Could that be it?*

Or maybe it's her brothers. Sylvia has bad thoughts about those horrible boys all the time because they're so mean.

And the Bible does say to love thy brother.

With chills suddenly rippling across her skin, her body stiffens. *It's the mirror.*

A week ago, she was wandering behind the schoolhouse and found a large shard from a broken mirror.

He knows all, a voice whispers in her mind.

Her eyes start to tingle as it all becomes clear. If God knows she hid the mirror in the barn, then He also knows she's been using it to look at her body, her private parts.

Vanity is a sin, the voice whispers louder.

Something pops from nearby.

Sylvia peels down the covers and looks around, careful to only move her eyes. The furthest corner of her bedroom is very dark, but she can still make out the bottom of her wardrobe. Its door is definitely closed. She spots the small chest of drawers that splits the wall across from her bed. There is nothing on either side of it.

Maybe it was the rain, she thinks, scouring the rest of the room. *Or maybe I just thought I heard some—*

Sylvia freezes. Her bedroom door is open.

Didn't I close it? She strains to remember.

The storm was raging so loudly that she burst into the room and leaped to the safety of her bed, flinging the door closed behind her. She thought it had latched.

Sylvia's head whips to the rumbling thunder outside her window. A tree branch has gotten wedged in the frame and is flapping against the glass.

Oh, that's what it was.

Relieved, a rush of exhaustion spreads through her tiny system as she slides back down in the bed. Flipping her pillow to the cooler side, she tries to get comfortable.

Pop.

Sylvia is certain the sound came from inside her room.

Another *pop.*

It's beside her, getting closer. She wants to scream but doesn't dare. Waking up her mother or father would be worse than whatever monster might be in her room. She slowly leans to the edge of her bed, forcing herself to peer over. Another floorboard pops as a man slides out from beneath her bed and whips his head toward her.

"Shh," he warns. "It's okay, darlin'."

Sylvia's held breath escapes with a flutter. "You scared me, Uncle James."

"Oh, I'm sorry, honey," he whispers, scrambling to his feet. He tiptoes to the door and glances into the hall. Satisfied, he gently closes it and sneaks back over to her. "I think everyone is asleep, so we have to be quiet."

James is fifteen years younger than her father. And, because his birth came as such a surprise to their parents, he was considered a miracle from the moment he took his first breath. But, as he got older, even more people took notice of the special blessing he possessed. Uncle James can speak the sacred language. Over the years, tales of his holy ability spread throughout their entire community. And, now in his early fifties, James is a coveted prophet. He travels throughout much of Southern Missouri, counseling and performing marriages and baptisms.

Out of all the children, Sylvia knows she's his favorite. When he visits, he spends much more time with her than the others, taking her along on errands, just the two of them. Last summer, he brought her some caramel candies and told her she didn't have to share any of them with her brothers.

"Don't tell a soul," he whispered, patting her backside.

He touches her a lot more than her mother or father ever does. It feels different somehow, too.

"It's our secret," he always tells her. "Just between you and me."

Most of the time, she feels invisible, so having secrets with Uncle James is wonderful.

Sylvia sits up in her bed. "Okay," she whispers. "Hey, how come you were under there?"

"Well, this storm's a bad one," he says, climbing onto the foot of her bed. "I wanted to be close by just in case you got scared. But, if anyone knew I was in here, they'd say I was babyin' you."

"Oh." She knows he's right. *Those boys are so jealous.* As she turns to the rainy window, the joy she feels at being chosen fades. "Uncle James, God's angry with me," she whispers, wringing her hands. "And I know why."

"What?" James rubs her leg through the quilt. "Now, why do you think God is angry with you?"

Sylvia cannot face him. Instead, she stares at the missing button on his pajama shirt. A strip of his white-haired belly peeks out from the gap. She tells her uncle about the sandwich situation, admitting she lied to her teacher about eating it. She also confesses that she stole a piece of hard candy from the gas station yesterday when nobody was watching.

"And, Uncle James"—she quivers, a lump rising in her throat—"I was looking at my body!"

"Shh! Quiet, sweetie." He squeezes her thigh through the covers as he eyes the crack under the bedroom door. "Now, what do you mean, looking at your body?" he asks, studying her face.

Sylvia's crying dissolves into a series of gasping whines as she reveals her secret about the mirror. She finishes her story and slowly lifts her gaze, guilt flooding down her face. It's worse than she feared. James is staring back in silence. The kindness is gone from his eyes, replaced by disgust, anger.

"What you've done is very bad, Sylvia." His voice is different now—cold and stern. "Pride is a sin. It's a *cardinal* sin. Very, very bad."

"I'm sorry," her little voice mewls.

"You are a dirty little girl. Filthy! Don't you *want* to go to heaven?"

"Yes, I want to," she cries, unable to control herself anymore. "I do. I want to go to heav—"

"Shh, shh, shh."

James presses a finger to her lips. He's pushing so hard, it hurts, but Sylvia doesn't move. She knows she deserves this.

"Well, if you want to get into heaven, you're gonna have to repent, darlin'," he says with a warmer tone. He pulls his finger back from her mouth and brushes it down her cheek. "I can help you, Sylvia. Do you want me to help you?"

"Yes," she squeaks, dropping her hands to her lap.

"Okay, then no more crying." James lifts her hands, slowly

drawing back the covers. "Now, why don't you show me how you looked at yourself?"

Sylvia's legs stiffen. As she slides up her nightgown, the sense of shame comes back along with new tears she promised she wouldn't cry. James lowers his head before her, his warm hands resting on her knees.

He's praying for me, she thinks, closing her eyes to join him.

"I know what God wants," his breathy voice snaps.

James whips his head up, startling Sylvia back against the wall. His eyes roll up under fluttering lids as his voice erupts into snarling hisses. She's seen others do this in the church, but watching her uncle's body tremble with the Holy Spirit is truly terrifying. Spittle flicks across Sylvia's face as his tongue clicks the air in a chaotic trance.

Suddenly, his hands lock on to her ankles, yanking her body flat on the bed. Her head smacks the wall as she slides, but she's too shocked to scream.

Instead, slamming her eyes shut again, she repeats the words in her mind, *I wanna go to heaven! I wanna go to heaven!*

She clings to the shifting bedsheets with both hands as James lunges on top of her.

The words race through her mind, coming faster and more frantic, until she realizes she's speaking them out loud, "I wanna go to heaven! I WANNA GO—"

The room goes dark as something covers Sylvia's face. She can't see, can't breathe. Thunder booms outside as the most excruciating pain imaginable shoots up her body. Her feet involuntarily kick out. Her fingers tear through the sheets. And, as she wails into her pillow, her body heaving under his weight, Uncle James helps Sylvia endure God's wrath.

———

"Man and wife."

Subtle prattle fills the den again where Sylvia is now a married woman. She scans the room, moving from one blank face to the next.

Ezekiel moves off to a corner with her father. As most of the men head out to the front porch, the women cluck down the hallway toward the kitchen. A young girl from the church is already coming through with a tray of lemonade. She stops at Elder James.

Another favorite.

As Sylvia watches them from across the room, she wonders if her uncle knows.

James was ministering so much during the past decade that they hardly heard from him. But he became a widower earlier this year and decided to move back from Dent County to live out his days serving the folks around here. He and his wife never had any children of their own. He always says the church is the only child God saw fit to give him.

Uncle James is wrong about that.

When he arrived at her father's house a little more than a month back, he told Sylvia he'd received a message from God.

"This will make you pure," he said. "It's what God wants."

So, James *counseled* her again that night.

Within a few days, her body started to feel different—sore and tired. Sylvia told no one.

Ezekiel tugs her arm, startling her. "I'll have some of that cake now, *wife*," he says snidely, nudging her toward the kitchen. Without waiting for a response, he leaves her, following Elder Paul's rolling chair out the front door.

Sylvia starts down the hallway, breathing through the nausea, and silently thanks God for sending her a father for this baby.

FIVE

ANN CANNOT OPEN her eyes yet, but she feels the groan vibrating in her chest. Everything hurts. Her neck burns, as if she maybe bumped it with a hot curling iron. *Did I?*

She tries swallowing but cannot get past the pain of what feels like two sheets of extra-coarse sandpaper scraping flesh from the back of her throat. Each cottony inhale seems to add to the smothering dryness in her mouth.

Ann clamps her lips, forcing a snorting breath through her nose. The foul stench of old blood and bleach invades her nostrils, and she winces, whipping her face to the side. As her forehead smacks against something solid, Ann forces her eyes open.

It's as though she were looking through a dark storm cloud, a veil of gray and white blurring everything in sight. Squinting, she identifies what appears to be a table a few feet away. And, above it, a yellowish glow is waving against a wall.

What is that?

She closes one eye, following the shape to its source, somewhere beyond her feet. With the light much brighter there, she realizes the flickering dots must be candles. Still, nothing makes sense.

Where am I?

Ann squeezes her eyes shut, focusing her mind. Her hands fidget up her thighs, working across her body, as she tries to make sense of this.

Wait. She cracks her eyes again, glancing toward her feet. She pinches at the fabric, her heart racing. *These aren't my clothes.*

Alarms go off in her head as she cranes her neck forward, taking in the dingy white dress that extends the length of her body.

What the hell?

Jolting up, she rams her face against another cloudy barrier. A thunderbolt explodes in her nose as she collapses. Tingling throbs of warm blood bubble from her nostrils and drift down her cheeks. She gasps in a few moaning breaths, struggling to see through her watery eyes.

As the moist heat from her exhale falls back into her face, she jerks her hands in front of her head, palms flattening against the murky surface.

What is this?

Eyeing the transparent streak beneath her hands, she throws her elbows outward, fully conscious now. There are barriers at her sides as well.

Holy crap! It's a box!

She shoves against the Plexiglas walls of the container, screaming with almost no voice. She grabs at her swollen throat, her fingers brushing over two small punctures on her neck. Panic surges through her as she slaps at the lid of the coffinlike box.

"HELP ME," she croaks. "PLEASE, HELP ME!"

Her breath fogs the glass again as she frantically explores the lid's edges. She finds a row of quarter-sized holes along the top of both sidewalls and jams her fingers through. Feeling the cool air outside triggers a wave of hysteria.

I can't breathe. I CAN'T BREATHE!

Pounding at the lid again, Ann rasps out a scream, "SOMEBODY HELP ME!"

"Shh!"

Ann jumps, startled into stillness. "Hello?" she asks with as much voice as she can.

There's no answer.

"Oh, please. Hello?" She holds her breath, listening to the silence, as she wipes the fogged surfaces.

Something moves near the candles.

"Hey! I hear you!" she wheezes, slapping the lid. "I know someone's there. Help me! PLEASE, GOD, HELP—"

"But you do *NOT* please God," a voice snaps back.

Not please God? What the hell does that mean?

As Ann considers the words, a man emerges from the darkness beyond her feet and glides into view. Her eyes move up his body, fixing on the bottom half of a creviced face peeking out from beneath a black hood. Ann's head collapses against the floor of the box, mind racing. As a stream of tears mixes with her nosebleed in a pool behind her head, she remembers the gnarled horns, the glowing eyes of the hood, the Taser. And, as a volt of terror flashes through her mind, Ann remembers Zeke.

He stands at the foot of the box, like a preacher at his pulpit, lowering his head in prayer.

She strains to hear what he is saying but realizes the sounds are coming from her.

"Please"—her voice crackles—"Zeke, don't—"

His head flips up as he grabs ahold of the box. *"Now the works of the flesh are manifest, which are these,"* he shouts, punctuating each word with a thrust of his pelvis. *"Adultery, fornication, uncleanness, lasciviousness, idolatry, witchcraft, hatred, variance, emulations, wrath, strife, seditions, heresies, envyings, murders, drunkenness, revellings and such like."*

Gazing at the air above the box, he shakes his head, as though addressing someone else in the room. *"As I have also told you in time past, they which do such things shall not inherit the kingdom of God!"*

Who is he talking to? Ann's eyes shoot to the space above her. *Are there others?* She tries not to imagine a group of these hooded maniacs.

"Please, just let me go."

Zeke grumbles as he moves alongside her, still addressing the empty air, *"But every man is tempted, when he is drawn away of his own lust and enticed. Then when lust hath conceived, it bringeth forth sin."* He stops at her head, tracing a finger across the lid of the box. *"And sin, when it is finished, bringeth forth death."*

Ann gently touches the Plexiglas, and a quivering whine rises from her gut. "Oh, please don't, Zeke."

He starts to speak but pauses, contemplating something. His shadowy face softens. He heard her.

"Please, Zeke. Please—"

His head plummets, eyes peering directly into Ann's. He mirrors her hand against the lid with his own as his lips slowly dip into the kind of exaggerated frown a mime or clown might present. *"Be not deceived; God is not mocked."* His smirk returns. *"For whatsoever a man soweth, that shall he also reap."*

"Please, no. Please, just let me—" Her voice breaks as she realizes he's mouthing along with her.

Oh my God, she thinks, clenching her eyes shut as new tears roll down her face, *I'm gonna die in here!*

Ann hears a loud squeaking from somewhere beyond the room. She cracks her eyes and finds he is gone. More alarmed by his absence, she shifts her body against the side of the box, scanning the shadows of the room. She quiets her breathing, listening for any signs of him.

There is another squeak.

It's coming from above me.

"DON'T HURT ME," she pleads as loudly as her broken voice allows.

Old pipes clang from the ceiling with a gurgling sound. Just as Ann figures it out, cold water surges into the box from an opening above her head.

"Oh my God. No," she shrieks, shielding her face from the pounding torrent.

Zeke's voice rises like thunder over the gushing water as he appears at the box again. *"He that believeth and is baptized shall be saved; but he that believeth not shall be damned."*

Ann struggles to cover the water's source, but the pressure is too strong. It sprays through her fingers, surging in around her. She's blinded for a moment and as her hair begins floating in the bloody water, latching on to her face, she snaps. The realization that she might drown ignites a new passion. If she doesn't fight now, she will die. A tornado of flailing limbs erupts inside the filling tank. She pounds at the walls, her hoarse screams evolving into gargled yowls, as the water rises.

From above, Zeke pounces onto the box, aligning his face with Ann's convulsing head. His horns tap the plastic surface as he slowly scans her body, his eyes glimmering like they are seeing her for the first time.

In a gulping frenzy, Ann flops toward the row of airholes along the sidewall as pink water continues to rise, lifting her body. She crams her fingers through, yanking her face into the top corner of the box. Her head knocks against the lid, but the openings are too high up for her pursed lips to reach. Stealing a quick breath, she spins upward, thrashing at the man through the Plexiglas barrier.

As she turns, Zeke smashes his head down on the other side of the lid, now face-to-face with Ann. "I baptize you in the name of the Father, the Son, and the Holy Spirit," he intones, peering into her bulging eyes.

Water streams from the airholes of the full box like a fountain, splashing into a mesh grate in the floor. Ann's hair stretches across her submerged face as she punches at the lid with everything she has left.

At last, the pounding pressure at her temples is too great. She can't hold on any longer. As she releases her held breath in a swirl of bubbles, water rushes into her lungs.

Another screeching pipe clunks from outside, but Ann doesn't hear it. And she doesn't notice the water shutting off or where Zeke is either. The thoughts currently running through her mind seem removed from where she is at this moment, as if she were watching a movie.

So, this is what drowning is like. I thought it would hurt more, but I don't feel much of anything.

Zeke appears again, crouching at the side of the box. He considers Ann's body, now only slightly bobbing in the water. Tiny bubbles flutter from her nose, floating upward, as her ankle flaps to the side with a final violent spasm.

Tapping the lid as he springs to his feet, Zeke rounds the box. He shoves a large metal lever at the base of the container, which shifts a layer of the box's floor, revealing several baseball-sized holes. A crashing flood pours into the grate in the ground, the water line plunging to below Ann's mouth in seconds. Her head slumps against the sidewall.

Suddenly, she is back. Ann explodes in a coughing frenzy, spewing up the filthy brine. She's unaware that Zeke is standing at the end of the box. Clinging to the airholes, she strains to keep her head above the draining water, but her body is too heavy for her trembling arms. She collapses to the floor of the emptying tank.

A large hatch swings open above her feet, sending a gust of cool air rushing up her legs. Ann tries to draw up her knees, but her legs are too weak. As she lies there, still slurping the air, she realizes she can see through the side of the box now. Zeke is standing at the table, facing away from her. He lowers his hood, the horns clacking beneath his shoulders.

"*I say unto thee,*" he sneers without turning to her, "*except a man be born of water and of the spirit, he cannot enter into the kingdom of God.*"

Ann's eyes burn, and everything is cloudy, but she has to know what he is doing. She slaps hair out of her face, pulling herself up onto an elbow. On the other side of the wall, Zeke works with what looks like another glass box, but it's much smaller. In fact, she thinks she sees several other boxes. As she tries to make out what it is that seems to be moving inside of one of them, Zeke steps back.

He stretches his hands above his head, sending his loose sleeves sagging to his shoulders, revealing several scabby scars along his forearms. As he mumbles something Ann can't hear, his body starts to sway. And, with a series of spastic shudders, his mumbling shifts into a flickering gibberish. His head slowly rotates to Ann. His eyelids flutter as his tongue clicks and snaps in a language she's never heard.

"OH, JESUS!" Ann screams, thrusting herself back against the far wall.

As abruptly as it all started, the chaos stops, and Zeke's eyes spring open. A silence fills the room; for a moment, there is stillness.

And, as he spins back to the side table, fumbling with something she can't see, Ann summons the courage to speak, beg. "Zeke—"

"*Behold,*" he roars, stepping to the Plexiglas box.

As he moves, Ann gets a better look at the top of the side table. *Aquariums.*

Her head whips to Zeke, standing at her feet. He extends his arms, stretching a thick snake above the open hatch, its body jerking between his hands, tail rattling.

As the snake drops onto Ann's kicking legs, he slams the lid closed. "*I give unto you power to tread on serpents and scorpions and over all the power of the enemy: and nothing shall by any means hurt you.*"

She stomps at the snake, but its lightning-fast strikes are much quicker. The box quakes with her twisting body, the scent of fresh urine seeping through the airholes.

Zeke wanders back to the side table, smearing away the new trickles of blood on his forearm. He considers the collection of aquariums, his finger tracing along the walls and aggressively tapping. As he reaches the last box, a viper strikes at him through the glass.

"*They shall take up serpents; and if they drink any deadly thing, it shall not hurt them.*"

A massive pressure envelops Ann's chest as a fire spreads across her back and shoots down her left arm. Now unable to move her limbs, she lies, moaning like a wounded hound, as the life dissolves from her eyes.

SIX

Missouri, 1964

A LATE SUMMER storm pounds a scattering of pickup trucks parked outside a large glowing revival tent. The structure is set back in a clearing that's surrounded on three sides by tall hickories, ensuring maximum privacy for the Friday night service. Inside, raindrops spatter against the canvas roof, adding a percussive element, as a sticky crowd sways in one large wave.

Zeke's mother shifts his sister to her opposite hip and tries to see through the mob of lolling heads. Beside her, Ezekiel Sr. leans against a large tent pole, his good eye trained on the makeshift stage. At his feet, Zeke plays with a large acorn he got from the wrinkled old woman at the tent entrance. A tiny sliver of red fabric protrudes from a crack in the polished nut. As he pulls at it, a satin ribbon emerges, inscribed with a gold-lettered message.

For by grace are ye saved through faith; and that not of yourselves: It is the gift of God.

Zeke stares at the words for a long time, but understanding their meaning is beyond the scope of his young mind. Instead, he presses the acorn into a stream of rainwater running down the tent pole. He watches the sprinkling drops hit a small puddle at his feet and thinks the bubbles look like minnows snatching insects from beneath the surface of a pond. A new idea hits him. Shifting into a wobbly squat, he dangles the wooden toy over the water, bobbing it like a little fishing line.

His mother notices his game. "Knock that off, boy," Sylvia hisses, nudging him with her foot. "Stay outta that mud!"

It's too late. He loses his balance and tips forward, squishing one knee into the moist ground. He glances up, expecting a smack, but Sylvia's focus is on the pastor, who's stomping to the other side of his platform. Zeke scrambles back into his position on his heels, patting at the muddy spot on his pant leg.

His family comes to services like this at least once a month. There's always shouting and crying and carrying on. He usually gets to sit outside with the other children his age, but on account of the weather tonight, he has to be in here.

He hears shouting from the front of the tent and quickly forgets about the mud. Steadying himself with a hand against the wooden pole, he peers through the legs of the crowd, pretending he's in a giant cornfield.

A white-bearded pastor paces on a wooden platform, bellowing to the crowd, *"Wherefore lay apart all filthiness and superfluity of naughtiness,"* he says, eyeing three fidgety teenagers. *"And receive with meekness the engrafted word, which is able to save your souls."*

A skinny boy with the beginnings of fuzzy dark facial hair stares at the wall of the tent. Blood from an open cut above his eye trickles down the side of his bruised face. Next to him, a stout, square-jawed girl stands perfectly still. Wild strands of mousy-brown hair have been yanked loose from her long braid and cling to her damp brow. The girl's head is bowed toward the floor, her arms stiffly at her sides. The last boy is the shortest of the three with orange hair and a fat belly. One of his eyes is swollen shut, surrounded by a purple welt that fades down his freckled cheek. The three have been separated from the rest of the congregation, moved into a line closer to the pastor's stage.

"Now, you'ins have heard from these children. God's children," the holy man says. "Okay? And you'ins heard 'bout the evils inside 'em. Of the devil's breath seeping into their minds. And demons making 'em commit SINS."

A hum starts at the back of the tent, building as it spreads across the area. This part used to scare Zeke but not anymore. Now, it's his favorite. Several people begin shaking tambourines, and the swaying crowd breaks into smaller clusters, bobbing and jerking to the clanging rhythm.

"But I'ma tell you'ins somethin'. Tonight, God wants them demons shouted out!"

The pastor jumps off the stage, prancing toward the teenagers, waving his arms. At the same time, a woman screams, catching the Holy Spirit. As she slumps into the arms of some fellow believers, a mumbling ripples through the crowd.

Zeke glances up at his parents, who are murmuring along.

"I bind the enemy!" the pastor shouts. "And I cast him out!"

"Amen," someone shrieks.

The heavyset boy's knees buckle. The girl at his side tries to steady him, but his weight is too much for her. He crumples to the ground, his slack jowls slapping against the dirt floor. She shoots her gaze back to a pair of muddy black boots stopping in front of her.

Zeke edges closer to the pole as an old woman shifts aside, giving him a better view.

The pastor is now clutching the young girl's shoulder, pressing his mouth to her ear. "Out, fiend," he barks, shoving her backward.

Zeke jumps, too, almost falling over. He checks that Sylvia hasn't seen him and then finds the action up front again.

"Out, demon!" the pastor hollers, grabbing a handful of shirt at the skinny boy's collar and flinging him into the restless crowd.

Spinning back, the pastor sets his sights on the chubby teenager. He charges to him, sinking his boot into the boy's loose belly. "Out, devil!" he yells with a heavy stomp. "I say, go thee out!"

The boy jolts up, coughing as he scuffles to his feet. His big, watery eyes dart around, like he doesn't know where he is. As the pastor dances away, the crowd parts, allowing the boy's father to come through. Zeke watches the man approach his quivering son, recognizing the boy's fear more than anyone else in the tent.

Zeke checks on Sylvia again. She's still locked on the action up front.

Pellets of spit dribble down the pastor's flapping beard as his body gyrates back up on the stage. Crouching behind a knee-high wooden crate, he lifts his head toward the canvas roof. "Lord, God, lead us, and guide us in the way."

A groan swells from the crowd. And, as a tambourine bangs out a frantic rhythm, the pastor's face drifts downward, leaving his rolled back eyes aimed at heaven. His shoulders jerk from side to side, as though he were receiving an electrical shock from a wire no one could see. With a series of quick facial spasms, his teeth clack together, biting at the air, and he's speaking in tongues.

Zeke squeezes himself against the pole, struggling to see past the swaying bodies. Finally, another hole opens, and he again finds the pastor standing behind the crate, which is now open. It's impossible to hear beyond the moaning voices, but as the man lifts out a yellow-colored rattlesnake, Zeke's whole world goes silent.

He's seen people take up lots of snakes at church but never one like that. The pastor stretches the serpent between his shaking hands, raising it above his head, as he staggers to the edge of the platform.

Still snapping out words of the sacred language, he whips his gaze to the three teenagers again, who have moved into a tight huddle. The pastor jumps from the stage, swinging the thick snake.

He stops at the skinny teen first, extending his hand. The boy's head tips back, and his shoulders begin to tremble as the Holy Ghost moves through him. He lurches toward the pastor, seizes the writhing snake by its thick belly, and swings it above his head. Consumed, the young man bounces in place, jerking the rattler back and forth through the air.

Fully entranced, Zeke watches as the pastor bobs over, retrieves the serpent, and considers the other two teens. He picks the redhead, starting toward him with the snake dangling at his side.

The boy's pupils immediately shoot upward, and as his mouth gapes open, he passes out again. His large body plunges into the first row of worshippers, slipping to the ground. As his grumbling father emerges to drag the boy away, the pastor's gaze slides over to the girl.

An old man shifts positions in the crowd, blocking Zeke's view, so he shoves off the pole. Dropping to his knees, he lowers himself to his elbows, carefully avoiding the mud. Beyond the stretch of moving bodies, he spots her skirt again.

The girl pauses before the pastor as he completes another twirl. At first, it looks like he is going to continue the service, bouncing over to her, the snake flailing above his head. But he stops short. Instead of passing off the serpent, the pastor raises his other hand, wagging his stubby finger.

"If the Lord don't move on you to take up the serpent," he shouts over his shoulder, starting back to the stage, "then you ain't *worthy* of the salvation yet."

The sole of another man's boot pounds into the girl's backside, and she yelps, tottering after the pastor.

"No, my daughter's ready." The man takes a step, ushering her forward, as he shouts over the crowd, "God has moved on her!"

The pastor pivots around, examining the girl's face again.

Her father closes in behind her, jabbing a finger into her ribs. "You'd better tell him."

"He has moved on me," she blurts.

The girl's shoulders shoot up as her head jerks to the side. "GOD HAS MOVED ON ME!" she yells, flinging up her quivering hands.

Zeke loses sight of her as she whirls behind another pole near the stage, but her voice reaches to the back of the tent.

"I MUST TAKE UP THE SERPENT!"

"Amen," her father encourages her from somewhere Zeke can't see.

As the pastor frolics toward the girl, an old woman near the side exit shrieks. She's caught a new wave of the Holy Ghost. Dancing herself off her feet, she collides with the canvas wall and slides to the dirt, her rickety frame still quaking with the Spirit.

Several folks up front hurry over to the woman, giving Zeke a direct view of the teenage girl.

The pastor prances up to her again, still sweeping the incensed snake through the air. Just a few inches from her face now, he cocks his head, narrowing his eyes. "You say God has moved on you and wants that you should take up this here serpent?"

The young girl exhales, nodding tentatively.

Giving her father a quick glance, the man waves the rattling snake in a large circle, exciting the crowd. And, as he slowly lowers it, he signals to her with a bob of his head. She extends her shaking arm toward—

The serpent strikes out!

The young girl's shriek startles Zeke into the belly of the man behind him, but he can't look away. The scream must have surprised the pastor, too, because he drops the snake as he jumps off to the side. At the same time, the girl hurls herself backward into the crowd, leaving the rattling serpent in a pile on the ground.

"DECEIVER," the pastor hisses, rage flushing his face. "Guide me, oh Lord!" he shouts, shaking a fist toward the roof. "Move on me so that I may cast out this deceptive demon!" His body starts to flop around again, his head popping from side to side.

As the congregation begins to cheer, vibrating the tent with their volume, they shove the girl back toward the stage.

The pastor pounces, his left hand clutching her shoulder. "Out, demon," he roars, wildly shaking her. "In Jesus's name, I command you to let loose of this girl."

The girl wails as his right palm wallops against her face, re-splitting a tear on her swollen mouth. "I CAST YOU OUT, DEVIL!" he shouts, slapping her again. "OUT, I SAY!" His final blow collapses her to the floor, her glazed eyes staring back through the shuffling feet of the crowd.

As the pastor lingers over the girl's prone body, a rail-thin man rushes forward, swinging a stick. He guides the rattlesnake into a large burlap sack and returns it to the wooden crate on the stage.

Zeke imagines he hears more rattles from inside the box although it's far too loud to be sure. Looking for a better view again, he drops back into a squat, suddenly locking eyes with the fallen girl. He was so excited about the snake, he forgot about her. He considers her blank stare for a moment, wondering what she did to get in so much trouble.

"And these signs shall follow them that believe," the pastor booms. "In my name shall they cast out devils; they shall speak with new tongues!"

Something shifts in the girl's face and she begins shaking. Rolling over to her back, she flops against the ground. A string of flapping, nonsensical words bursts from her lips.

"Heal her, Lord!" someone yells.

As she flounders in the dirt, her father appears at her side and drags her off.

The pastor calls for quiet as he returns to the stage. He drags his sleeve across his sweaty forehead and begins the closing prayer. "Father God, we know that, at Jesus's name, every knee must bend, and every tongue must confess," he says. "I just ask, Father God, that you forgive this entire flock of worshippers for the *secret* sins they done. Sins that their brothers and sisters and wives and husbands might not know about but have offended you. Forgive them, Father, and move on them to do better. We give all the glory to you today and every day. Amen."

As the celebrating dies down, the congregation separates, forming several smaller chattering clumps. Sylvia, still toting Faith on her hip, follows her husband into a line of people leaving the tent.

A bald man with thick horn-rimmed glasses joins them. "We're not gonna yield much of nothin' this year, I don't believe," he says. "Just been too wet."

Zeke's father responds with something about the weather, but he doesn't pay much attention. He's focused on navigating through the crowd.

"Well, we'll pray for you," Ezekiel Sr. finishes, guiding Sylvia into the procession.

As the mass of people excited to talk with the pastor flows outside, Zeke finds himself caught in a current of bodies that sweeps him away from his parents. He tries to follow them, pushing against the endless wall of slacks and shuffling skirts, but he can't keep up. Spotting a sliver of canvas, he darts through a break in the crowd and reaches the side of the tent. He leans against the moist wall, considering whether to yell out for his mother. But then he remembers the time he got lost at the grocery store. Although he found her a couple of aisles over, the beating he got on the way home for embarrassing her is not something he wants to face again.

Deciding he ought to wait for all the people to clear out, Zeke wanders along the wall to the front of the tent and follows his curiosity up onstage. He dangles the toy acorn by its ribbon as he climbs the steps and shuffles over to the large crate. No one seems to have noticed him.

He mashes his ear to the side of the box. It's silent inside, but he notices a row of small airholes along the top of the wooden wall. He pokes his finger into the darkness for a second and then presses his wide eye against the opening. Several rays of light are beaming in from the holes on the other side but not enough to see anything clearly. Disappointed, he steps back and circles the crate, absentmindedly dragging the acorn along the line of airholes.

As Zeke reaches the opposite side, he thinks of the girl again, wondering if she was actually bitten. It was hard to tell from where he was. He didn't see any blood, but—

The toy slips out of his fingers, disappearing into the box.

Zeke panics, his eyes darting to the back of the tent. A few people are standing at the entrance, bottlenecked by the others outside. There's no sign of his mother or father.

He can't remember what else the old woman said when she gave him the "little gift from God," but the smack he got for swinging it around too much earlier is still sore.

"That is a *gift*," his mother said. "Put it in your pocket, and you'd better not lose it!"

With a desperate grunt, his shaky little arms force up one of the two top doors. Zeke peeks into the crate, immediately forgetting what he's looking for. In the corner, across from him, the albino timber is wedged under a large mound of other bodies. He scans the shiny lumps and locates several heads. A couple of feet away, a smaller snake stretches across the center of the box, lifeless.

Oh, yeah, he thinks, remembering his acorn as he spots the red ribbon near its tail.

He thrusts himself up, pushing the side of the box into his belly and clutches for the toy, but it's too far away. He tips further into the crate. Just as his fingers reach the ribbon, he sees the others. Concealed in the shadow cast by the second door, another lumpy pile of serpents tracks his every move.

"Ezekiel?" His mother is calling from somewhere outside the tent.

He knows he's going to be in trouble. He has to hurry.

A warning rattles from the dark half of the box as Zeke quickly rakes his hand across the floor, shoving himself backward. Like a flash of lightning, a viper's fangs sink into his fleshy wrist. His momentum lifts him back off the box, and he stumbles down onto the wooden stage. He stuffs the acorn into his pocket and rushes back to the crate, noticing the marks on his arm.

It was so fast.

He doesn't quite understand what happened. He knows he heard rattling and then felt a tap, but it doesn't hurt. Two glossy dots of blood are rising from his skin, but he only feels a slight itch, like from a mosquito bite.

"Zeke?" Her voice is moving closer to the entrance.

He swings the door shut and springs off the stage, heading to the back of the tent. As he approaches the huddle of people in the entryway, Sylvia steps in, snatching a tuft of his hair.

"Where you been, boy?" she hisses through gritted teeth, dragging him through another small crowd. "Didn't you hear us calling you?"

Afraid of getting into more trouble, Zeke clasps his hands behind his back, concealing his wrist. They reach their idling car just as the rain picks up again, and Sylvia slings him through the back door. He slides in behind the driver's seat, quietly waiting for his mother to take her spot up front.

As the car drives off, Zeke relaxes into the shadows of the backseat and empties his pocket. He darts his tongue out at the little dead snake he took from the crate, licking at the air as he pretends it's still alive.

SEVEN

SOUNDS OF CHIRPING registers and gossipy prattle fill the checkout area of the neighborhood Buy-and-Save. Its location, just minutes from I-80, means the store is always busy. Zeke secures the bow at the back of his apron as today's late afternoon rush begins with a crackling voice from an overhead intercom system, reminding shoppers of this week's special price on family-pack pork chops.

A short, stumpy man wedges a cell phone against his double chin as he thumbs through his wallet. "Well, now, look, Roy, that ole dog ain't gonna hunt." He snags a bill, passing it to the cashier, as he continues his conversation, "Okay? So, I need a check by Friday, or I'm done."

At the end of the conveyer belt, Zeke tosses a Milky Way bar into a plastic bag, offering it to the man.

"That's not my prob—" He lowers the phone, scowling at Zeke. "I don't need a damn bag!" he yaps, snatching out the candy. "It's a chocolate bar, for cryin' out loud." He goes back to his phone call, flicking the plastic bag so that it flutters onto the conveyer belt, as the cashier hands the man his change. "I don't give a shit, Roy!" he barks, walking off.

Zeke lifts the empty grocery bag from the belt. "Have a nice day, sir."

The man tears back the candy wrapper, chomping into his bar. "Yeah, whatever," he scoffs.

Zeke isn't sure whether it is to him or the phone.

As the angry shopper totters through the automatic sliding door, someone calls out from the other end of checkout, "Need a sacker down here."

Zeke wanders to the last register, pulling a wire stand to the end of the counter, snapping open its plastic bag. A lumpy older woman on a motorized shopping cart pulls up, swatting tight lavender-tinted curls out of her face. She nudges a pair of thick glasses up her nose as she digs through her purse.

"Here you go, honey," the woman says, sliding a stack of coupons onto the counter.

She jerks a few grapes from a produce bag, winking at the cashier, as though it were their little secret. "These are just so delicious," she whispers, tossing them in her mouth. She shifts her attention to Zeke. "Listen, I want all this in paper," she garbles. "I hate those plastic bags."

"Yes, ma'am."

"And double bag them, please." She turns back, scolding the cashier, "You guys have very thin bags here. I don't know why you don't get stronger ones."

An assortment of frozen dinners, ice cream cups, and cat food drifts down the belt. Zeke layers a couple of large brown bags as he watches the sliding pile of groceries, his mind on his real work.

Wretched sinner. He didn't expect the woman from the pizza parlor to live; they never do. But this one was particularly resistant, her demon defying the rite much longer than the others had.

Killed the serpent, too, he thinks, reminded of the cleanup waiting for him back at the house.

"What are you—now, don't put too many of those cans in one bag," the old woman whines. "I'm not as strong as you, fella." She drops a pack of spearmint chewing gum on the conveyer belt. "I'll take that, too, honey."

A high-pitched squeal pierces through the idle chatter. Zeke's eyes snap to the fiery-haired cashier at the next register. Cindy's laughter is infectious, like the luring song of a siren calling a ship of sailors to their deaths. She hasn't even been working at the store for a full year yet, but she is Checker of the Month again—for the fourth time in a row.

The store manager, Ron, a blondish stick figure of a man in his forties, runs a tight ship. But he keeps a particularly close watch on Cindy, seduced by her trickery.

Twisting an end of his wispy handlebar mustache, Ron whispers into Cindy's ear. His free hand brushes against her upper arm as he reaches around her. "Let me just grab those real quick." He snickers, his fingers latching on to a ring of keys on her register.

"You'd better behave," Cindy says, playfully bucking into him.

"Oh, sorry, I didn't mean to do that."

"Uh-huh." She smirks, tapping her employee number on the keypad as her next customer approaches.

Ron snatches one of the bow-tied strings of her apron. "I meant to do this." He tugs the cord, pulling it with him as he backs away.

Cindy whirls around, grabbing for his hand, but he's gone. She flips a sheet of red hair out of her face, calling after him, "You're so bad, Ronnie."

A leathery-faced older man in camouflage coveralls steps into Cindy's lane.

As he passes the large magazine rack that shielded the flirty scene from view, Ron grins from his podium. "Aw, you know you love it."

"Ha. You wish." Aware she's being watched, Cindy glances to the next register.

Zeke gazes back at her. *I see you*, he thinks. *And I know what you are.*

She gives him a quick wink and returns to her keyboard, retyping her employee number.

The weathered customer sets his six-pack of longnecks on the conveyer belt and tucks a cigarette behind his ear, ogling the Checker of the Month.

She smiles with another wily giggle. "Hope you found everything all right."

"Oh, *I* did," Ron chimes in, pretending to be on his phone. His pale eyebrows applaud his joke with a couple of bounces as he flips the pages on his clipboard.

Cindy finishes the transaction and rustles through her drawer for a free book of matches for the man. Zeke notices the loose apron strings swaying at her lower back. He can't look away. As he packs the bags at his station, drifting into the shadows of his mind, he remembers his mother cooking at the stove.

———————

A plump teardrop splatters down on Sylvia's King James Bible. Zeke dabs his little finger, wiping it away, as he quickly turns the page. He glances across the smoky kitchen to see if she noticed. His mother is working at the old stove, her back facing him, as she fries breakfast. After a moment, she leans forward, pressing a sizzling link with her spatula. He quietly exhales. She didn't hear him.

The wisp of a woman pushes back the sleeves of her oversize dress, fanning smoke out of her face. As she moves, the sagging strings from her apron slowly untie themselves and dangle at her back. Zeke's eyes move up her skinny neck to the dirty-blonde bun lolling at the back of her head. It kind of looks like a dandelion, like a big gust of air might blow it clear off her head. He remembers picking dandelions with Faith last summer. They made bracelets from the little wiry stalks. A tiny sniffle escapes before he can stop it, and he checks on his mother again. The spatula clinks against the surface of the stove, and he knows he hasn't been so lucky this time.

Sylvia whips her head to her whimpering son. At seven years old, he doesn't understand everything that has happened over the past few years, but he knows it has changed his mother. Her face looks so hollow now with worry lines covering most of her forehead. And the creases surrounding her permanent frown remind him of the cracks in a patch of dried out soil. Her eyes lock on to Zeke. He holds his breath, too afraid to move.

"I told you to dry up," she snaps, gritting her teeth. "Didn't I?"

"Yes, ma'am." He swallows back the lump in his throat. *Don't cry!*

"Now, get to it," she says, returning to the cooking.

Safe for now, Zeke flips back to the previous page. He finds his teardrop has almost dried but gives it an extra wipe just in case. Taking a big breath, he begins the passage. "Ecclesiasticus, twenty-five, nineteen. *All wickedness is but little to the wickedness of a woman: let—*"

"Twenty-one!" she shouts, banging the skillet. "Read twenty-one!"

Zeke quickly drags his finger down the page, searching for the start of the verse. As he recites, Sylvia peers over her shoulder, mouthing the words with him.

"Stumble not at the beauty of a woman and desire her not for pleasure."

"But you did, *didn't* you?" she sneers, waving the spatula at him. Drips of hot grease fling across the flimsy kitchen table. "DIDN'T YOU?"

Zeke darts to the side to avoid the spray as Sylvia turns back to the stove.

"Yes, I know you remember." She slides the links onto a plate, setting it on an unused burner. "Filthy little sinner."

A cracked egg hisses as it lands in the hot skillet.

Her voice rises. *"Of the woman came the beginning of sin and through her we all die."* Sylvia slaps the side of the stove. "And *she* had to die!"

Zeke winces, bouncing the legs of his chair against the floorboards. New tears flood his eyes while an uncontrollable whine works its way up his throat.

In an instant, Sylvia is facing him again, fists clenched at her sides. "What did I just say?"

Paralyzed by fear, he stares back in silence, fighting the urge to even blink.

"Come here," she hisses, pointing to a spot on the floor next to her.

Zeke drags his dirty sleeve across his face, inadvertently shaking his head. "I . . . I . . . I'm not crying anymore," he promises, wishing to God it were true. "I'm not."

"I said, GET OVER HERE!" she shouts, stomping.

He jumps from the chair, tipping it backward. As it smacks to the floor behind him, he lurches forward, closer than he meant to. Instinctively, his tiny arms extend into a defensive posture as he carefully approaches his mother. "I'm not crying," he mumbles to himself.

"Ezekiel, we do not cry for doing the Lord's work," Sylvia says, shaking her head at him. "Do we?"

Her voice is quieter now, almost soothing, but Zeke keeps his distance. He knows better.

"No. We are proud to be his warriors," she whispers as she slowly turns back toward the stove.

Her head continues around, stopping at the thunderstorm raging outside the kitchen window. She stares at the pounding rain as it muddies the grassless area behind their house. Her voice begins to rise again. *"For every one that curseth his father or mother shall surely be put to death—"*

Zeke bursts into uncontrollable hiccups.

The Sylvia he knows is back. She spins around, grabbing the frying pan, and lunges at him, sending a half-cooked egg to the floor. Zeke shuffles up against the kitchen wall, but it's too late; his mother is already on him.

"There's something to cry about!" she roars, smashing the skillet into his face.

Knees buckled, Zeke collapses to the floor, cupping his bloodied mouth. Tiny fingers flutter over his broken nose, terrified sobs filling the room. He chokes down blood, swallowing some sandlike bits as his tongue brushes against newly jagged teeth.

Sylvia, still panting, throws the pan into the kitchen sink, ignoring her son's wailing. She yanks the apron over her head and wads it into a ball, looming over him. "Yes, you cry about *that*," she mocks, tossing the apron in his lap. "And clean yourself up. You're getting blood everywhere."

————————

"Uh, Earth to Zeke." Ron chuckles, playing to an audience of employees and nosy customers. "Hellooo?" He leans in, jabbing Zeke's arm. "Hey—"

Zeke flinches, seizing the guy's finger, bending it backward until the knuckle pops. His face is frozen, fear glistening in his eyes, as they dart around like a trapped animal ready to tear apart anything that gets too close.

"Ah!" the manager howls, dropping to one knee. His clipboard slips to the ground and slides across the floor. "Hey, take it easy, man!" he shouts, his free hand flailing behind him like a crazed water hose.

A mother standing two registers down pulls her little boy close, gasping at the commotion. "Oh my God!"

Zeke's head snaps toward her voice. He spots the frightened child clinging to her legs, and the terror drains from his face. He releases his grip on Ron. Zeke is now back in the Buy-and-Save checkout area.

"Jesus Christ, Zeke!" The manager shuffles back to his feet, rubbing at his tweaked finger. "Uh, welcome back."

A curly-haired young sacker wrestles the clipboard from beneath a gumball machine by the front door and brings it over.

Taking in the sea of eyes, Ron snatches the rustling papers and plays to his crowd. "You take your pills today, buddy?"

Ignoring the man, Zeke returns to his register. Whispery giggles flutter up from a group of employees gathered in a nearby aisle. The purple-haired old lady has her purse clamped under one arm and is waving frantically from the motorized shopping cart.

"Um, 'scuse me, sir!" she shouts to the manager. "I want someone else to help me with my bags."

"That's no problem, ma'am. Jerry will take care of you," Ron answers, calling over the curly-haired sacker. "And, Zeke, you go take your fifteen now."

He doesn't respond. He is distracted by the old lady's hand fumbling with something on her lap. His eyes narrow, considering her purse. As she shifts in her seat, raising her hand a bit, Zeke spots the red tab of a small pepper spray canister. His gaze rises to her face.

"Now, Zeke," the manager orders, stepping up to him again.

"Okay," he replies with a nod.

As the curly-haired sacker lifts the woman's bags into a cart, Zeke starts toward the break room. He studies the bewildered faces at each register, pausing briefly when he reaches the woman and her son. The little boy peeks around from behind his mother, his face expressionless.

"And get some coffee or something," Ron calls.

Zeke glances back at him with another nod and then returns to the boy, who's now sticking his tongue out.

His mother notices him and palms her son's face. "Hey, now," she scolds, shoving him behind her again with a scowl.

Zeke continues on.

"Okay, folks, the excitement's over!" Ron shouts from his podium. "Let's all get back to work."

The chaotic atmosphere resumes—people chatting over beeping registers, rattling grocery carts. Someone echoes from the overhead speaker, requesting a price check.

Cindy flags Ron as he passes. "Wow, are you okay?" she asks, handing change and a receipt to another customer. "That looked like it hurt."

"Nah, it's nothing." He winks, leaning into her. "I like things rough."

"Oh my God!" she squeals. "You're so ridiculous." Cindy bursts out laughing, giving her hair another unnecessary flip, as she glances across the front of the store.

Zeke is standing in the open doorway of the break room, glaring back at her.

"Y'all sell stamps?"

Cindy jumps. A perky blonde woman with thick glasses has

appeared at her register.

"Oh, sorry." She chuckles nervously. "Um, yes, we do. How many do you want?"

EIGHT
TWO WEEKS LATER

A BOX FAN pushes stale air around a cramped parlor, fluttering the old newspapers on top of a large wooden-framed television set. The TV has been running so long, the tube has started to go. Wavy lines occasionally tremble across the picture. Doesn't matter though; it's just for noise.

The channels change sporadically.

A morning talk show switches to a courtroom debate over an unfinished paint job. The judge repeatedly bangs her gavel. The station flips again. It lands on a commercial for a local car dealership where a lumpy blond man in a tight suit promises guaranteed financing.

Crook.

The remote control clatters onto a folding snack table.

In the kitchen, the burner on a gas stove clicks to life. Bottles clink in the opening door of the refrigerator. As a tea bag drops into a chipped mug, the commercial in the parlor is interrupted by the agitated tempo of a breaking news segment.

Zeke steps into the doorway between the two rooms, popping open a bag of corn chips. Cold eyes watch a bright red banner move across the bottom of the screen.

Another Body Discovered in Delaware Water Gap.

An Olan Mills–style family portrait appears on the television. In it, a middle-aged man with thinning hair and thick glasses stands next to an elderly woman sitting in a large upholstered chair. On the other side, Ann's cheerfully bookish face stares uncomfortably. The picture enlarges until her awkward smile fills most of the screen.

A news anchor's voice promises more information on this developing story as the monitor flashes to the live coverage of a muddy riverbank crowded with people.

Several Stroud Area Regional Police Department officers wrangle a group of bantering reporters behind the yellow line of tape that forms a perimeter extending from the water's edge up to the tree line. As two more teams of newspeople arrive and stake out their locations, the picture wobbles, shifting to a clump of men standing over a large white bundle. In the distance, a man wearing a sheriff's jacket speaks into a small microphone at his shoulder as he regards the crowd.

Zeke slouches against the doorframe. *Looks like they found it.*

The picture finally steadies as a crisp, buttoned-up reporter with perfectly coiffed salt-and-pepper hair steps in front of the camera. He adjusts his bright pink tie, giving a nod.

"Hi, Karen. Well, as you can see"—he gestures over his shoulder—"this is a very active scene here at the Delaware Water Gap where a body has been found." He pauses, restraining a flipping page on his notepad. "Now, although no formal statement has been given yet, we've spoken with a law enforcement source who's given us some exclusive details on the case." A thick band of the reporter's sprayed hair breaks free, fluttering in the wind. "Our source tells us that the body back there is believed to be that of the missing Stroudsburg woman, Ann Haut, who disappeared a little over two weeks ago." He steadies his flapping tie, continuing, as the breeze picks up, "The body was discovered early this morning by a local woman walking her—"

A huge gale surges through, ruffling the white tarp in the background. Someone shrieks as Ann's naked torso is revealed.

"What's happening?" the reporter asks. The picture zooms in, capturing congealed lesions on the splotchy, bloated body. "Oh my God."

A team of uniforms dives into action, wrestling the tarp back down over the body, as the sheriff spins to face the crowd. He spots a clump of newspeople who have snapped through the ribbon barrier, jockeying for a closer view.

"Rivas, get those bastards outta here," the sheriff roars.

The salt-and-pepper-haired reporter whips back to the camera. "Ladies and gentlemen, apologies for the graphic nature—"

"Hey!" A burly officer storms up the bank toward the camera.

"Of . . . of what you might have just seen," the reporter continues with urgency. "We will, of course, get back to you with more details when we get them." The officer charges up behind the flustered reporter, sending him scurrying out of sight. "Uh, back to you, Karen—"

The bobbing camera plummets to the ground as the officer's muddied black boots stomp into the frame.

Offscreen, the reporter yields to the officer. "Okay, okay!"

"You gotta go," the cop grumbles.

"We have First Amendment rights to be here."

"Ha! Not today, fella."

"Officer, we're just doing our job—"

"Yeah, right. Go. *Now!*" The officer's boots step in closer. "And turn that thing off. I can still see the red light!"

"All right, all right."

The video of the transmission goes black, but the audio continues.

"Friggin' parasites," the officer huffs over the sound of his retreating footsteps.

In the darkness, the reporter's voice whispers, "Did we get that, Arnie?"

With a quick static puff, the audio cuts out.

The picture flickers to a display of colored stripes, a blasting high-pitched tone pinging around the parlor. Just as the remote rises toward the television, the screen flashes black and then returns to the broadcast.

"Ready," a muffled voice announces from the TV.

The stunned salt-and-pepper-haired reporter stares blankly into the camera lens from a new position much further from the scene. He smooths his tousled hair, unaware that the transmission has started again.

"Hey, we're back," a hushed voice urges from offscreen.

"Oh!" The reporter snaps to the camera. "Well, as I said before, we apologize for the graphic scene you all might have just witnessed. But, um, to continue, Karen," he says, easing back into his groove, "police believe this to be yet another victim of what some are now referring to as the Rattlesnake Killer. It seems that this body, like the last two, is riddled with snakebites."

Another red banner slides across the monitor with an update.

Woman's Snake-Bitten Body Discovered. Authorities Warn of Possible Serial Killer.

The teakettle screams from the kitchen.

Blasphemy.

A moment later, a deep cough honks through the parlor as Zeke sets a cup of tea on the crowded tray next to his BarcaLounger. He picks up the remote control, flipping to a new station where a beet-faced televangelist is slapping the side of his podium.

"Your wickedness makes you, as it were, heavy as lead," the man preaches.

I'll have to weigh the next one down better.

NINE

THE LIGHTING IN the expansive Buy-and-Save break room is murky under the twitching overhead fluorescents. Shane, a teenage cashier with a complexion like the underside of a Nestlé Crunch bar, stands in a short line of employees waiting to clock in. He chomps on some French fries while slouching against the glowing front panel of a Coke machine; the plastic crackles under the chunky boy's weight.

"Ooh, you broke it again," Shane taunts with a mouthful of fries.

"No, I did *not*." Barb, a gangly woman with a ratlike face, spins around from the time clock. "It locked up after I typed in my number," she scoffs, her two enormous front teeth sinking into her lip.

A few other employees step away from their lockers. Aprons in hand, they file out of the break room, starting their afternoon shift.

"Ah, must've thought it was your phone number." Shane chuckles. "I know that'd make me lock up."

"Shut up, Shane. Nobody thinks you're funny." Barb scans the room to be sure. It seems no one has really been listening to the exchange. Her nostrils flare when she notices his Arby's bag. She softens her tone. "Hey, can I have some fries?"

Shane shakes his head in silence, staring into her narrowed dark eyes.

As he loudly guzzles from his large shake, a series of short beeps confirms Barb has been punched in.

"Whatever." She double-checks the clock, striding over to a locker on her storky legs. "By the way, you shouldn't eat those; they're fattening."

"Well, yeah, to a stick figure, I guess everything's fattening." He snickers, entering his employee number. "You're probably full now just from smelling my fries!"

The time clock beeps again.

Shane steps aside, cramming the last of his lunch into his mouth. "What's up, Cindy?"

Cindy opens her locker and grabs her apron. "Hey, Shane. How's it going?"

"Whole lot better now," he says, tossing his empty cup into a garbage bin. He starts out the door but pauses. "Hey, the time clock was freezing up earlier, FYI, so give yourself extra time."

"Oh, shit. I forgot to clock in. Thanks."

"Yeah, think Matchstick Maggie might've broken it." He sniggers, continuing out the door.

"Oh, that's hilarious," Barb snaps, slamming her locker. "He's such an asshole."

"Don't let him bother you. He probably just likes you." Cindy giggles, tapping at the time clock.

"Oh God, no way. He's such a pig!" Barb ducks into the employee restroom, shouting around the corner, "I'll just wait till you're done with Jim."

"Ha! Well, have at him. We broke up a few days ago."

"What? What happened? Wait, I'll be out in a sec."

Back at her locker, Cindy checks her face in a magnetic mirror on the door, reapplying lip gloss to her shimmery mouth. Her head nods to the beat of Shania Twain's "Man! I Feel Like a Woman!" playing quietly from a ceiling speaker. She throws the gloss back into her purse, tousling her wild hair. As she mouths the song lyrics to her reflection, the locker door drifts fully open. She wedges a napkin between her lips for a quick blot and pulls at the door, bringing the mirror back to her face.

Zeke is standing just a few feet behind her.

"Shit!" Cindy spins to face him. "You scared the hell outta me."

"I doubt that," he mumbles.

"Seriously." She laughs awkwardly. "Sorry, I didn't hear you come in."

"I was over there," he says, pointing to another row of lockers across from the restroom. "I saw *you*."

Cindy smiles, scanning his blank face. He doesn't move.

After a moment, she winks at him. "You okay?"

"I'm okay." He nods, still frozen in place.

"Uh, well, that's good." She closes her locker. "Guess I'll see you out on the floor."

A toilet flushes.

"So, what happened with Jim?" Barb shouts over the water running in the restroom sink.

"Cindy, I have a question I want to ask you," Zeke says.

The restroom door opens, and Barb rounds the corner, pausing when she sees Zeke. "You know what? Tell me about it later, Cindy." Cinching her apron, she ties the strings behind her back. "Hi, Zeke."

Zeke glances over at Barb but doesn't speak.

"Oh, by the way, Cindy, I asked for next Saturday off, but, of course, they screwed it up. I'm gonna see if they can switch my shift, but if not, you wanna work it?" Barb notices Zeke's eyes are locked on her now. "What's wrong with you?"

"Yeah, I'll take it," Cindy interjects. "Just tell Ron."

"Awesome, thanks! I'll call you tonight to let you know for sure. Is your new number on the schedule board?"

"Yep."

"Okay, great." Barb checks on Zeke once more as she heads out the door, whispering to herself, "Such a weirdo sometimes."

"I said, I have a question," Zeke repeats, moving in closer to Cindy, now blocking the path out of the room.

"Okay," she says, backing against the lockers. "What's your question?" She casually unwraps a stick of chewing gum.

"You want to go get food sometime?"

"What?"

"Eat. Do you want to go get supper with me and talk?"

"Um, well . . ." Cindy glances around the empty break room. "Sure. Maybe after work some—"

"After work is good."

As Zeke moves to the schedule board, Cindy hurries toward the door.

"Wait," he says.

She freezes, glancing over her shoulder. "I have to get out on the floor now."

"That Italian restaurant across the street smells good," he says.

"Okay, uh—"

The break room door opens, tapping Cindy's arm. She shrieks, startling an older porter as he wheels in several buckets of cleaning fluid on a hand truck.

"Oh, sorry," he yelps, mussing his silvery hair.

Her eyes dart to Zeke, who's still trained on her face. "I've gotta go, Zeke," she says, bolting out into the store. "Can't be late."

Zeke stares at the closing door for a moment, oblivious to the porter.

"She almost gave me a heart attack, man," the guy says under his breath as he unloads the supplies. "Young folks are so jumpy nowadays, ain't they?"

Zeke doesn't hear the man. He turns back to the schedule board. *"Now is she without, now in the streets, and lieth in wait at every corner,"* he mumbles, running his finger down the list of names and phone numbers.

TEN

THE CRINKLED CELLOPHANE wrapper just misses the waste-basket under the desk where Dani Caraway sorts through tiny slips of paper.

Her face is more striking than conventionally pretty with a strong jawline and sparkling eyes the same turquoise hue of an Arctic glacier. Her dark hair sits in a tightly coiled bun, which, when combined with her cat-eye reading glasses, gives the appearance that she might be older than her thirty-two years. While the silk blouse and navy skirt are not mandatory for the conservative office, they are certainly expected. And she needs this job.

Dani tosses a golden piece of hard candy into her mouth, and wedging the telephone handset against her shoulder, she gets back to work. Her desk is covered with the expenses from one of her boss's recent business trips, a small stack of copy paper, and a tape dispenser. She's separated the receipts into various piles—hotel, taxis, meals, and so on. Snagging a small piece of Scotch tape, she attaches a chit for a client lunch to a crowded sheet of paper and gives in to her curiosity.

"So, have you heard from your brother lately?" Dani garbles, still sucking on the butterscotch.

A round little man with a rebellious comb-over wobbles out from the back hallway and into the reception area. He tugs up the waist of his pants under his bloated gut and adjusts his snug pin-striped suit jacket. "Good night, Larry!" he shouts over his shoulder, flipping his sun-bleached hair from his face.

As a faint reply comes from a distant closed-door office, he approaches Dani's desk with several envelopes clenched in his fist.

"Hang on a sec," Dani whispers into the phone. "It's one of the partners." She sets the receiver on the desk, turning to face the stout man. "Hi, Frank. Done for the day?"

"Yeah, I think so." He scans her face, pursing his lips. The tiny smoker's lines around his mouth seem to glow against his overly tan face. His squinty eyes slowly drift down, settling at her breasts.

"Frank?"

"Uh-huh," he mumbles, as if someone offered him a second serving of warm cobbler.

Dani drums her fingernails along the desktop and considers staring at his crotch to make a point. *Ugh, too gross,* she thinks, afraid the move could backfire. She forces a smile, waiting for him to feel the silence.

Frank glances up, realizing he's been caught. He tosses the envelopes on her desk, fluttering a few of the taped receipts. "These have to go out tonight," he snaps petulantly as he crosses to the front door. He drapes his lightweight trench coat over his arm. Reaching behind the coat stand, he straightens a framed Monet-style poster hanging on the wood-paneled wall.

"And let's try to be a little more buttoned-up, okay?" As he scolds her with his deep-set forehead crinkles, his gaze returns to Dani, as if he were waiting for an explanation.

She studies the tiny reception area, taking a mental inventory. Two dusty synthetic ferns flank a half-empty Poland Spring water dispenser that's been unplugged for months. Against the far wall, a floral-printed sofa, stained from countless coffee spills, sits opposite a chipped black-lacquered coffee table. Its cloudy glass top is covered with last year's *People* magazines.

Oh, yeah, it's like an Architectural Digest *cover photo in here,* she thinks, almost saying it. She also considers flinging the tape dispenser at him. But, remembering that rent is due in a week, she simply nods, accepting the responsibility for the crooked art piece and the tragic impact it has had on the room's aesthetic.

"You'll need to get stamps on those before you mail them," Frank reminds her. As he drives his doughy arm into a coat sleeve, he sneaks another peek at her bosom.

Dani glares back at him, letting her furrowed brows and frozen grin do the talking.

When she doesn't speak, he finds her eyes again. "Well, uh . . . have a good night then."

Frank totters out the door, piling into his bright red convertible Mazda Miata, as Dani lifts the handset to her ear.

"Hey. Sorry. Fat Napoleon had to say good night to my boobs. Hang on a second." Putting the handset in its cradle, she hits a button on the phone base. "Still there?"

"Yeah, I'm here." The scratchy voice of her childhood best friend, Jess, blares from the speaker.

Dani quickly lowers the volume.

"Well, okay, so maybe we put Napoleon at the bottom of the list then." Jess snickers. "But, hey, a lawyer's a lawyer, you know?"

"Ugh!" Dani grimaces as she gets back to her receipts.

"I mean, he's probably got a big—"

"DON'T YOU EVEN SAY IT!" Dani snaps.

Jess's cackle rattles the phone's speaker. "Bonus! He probably has a big *bonus* coming to him! *What?*"

"You're disgusting," she says, spitting the half-dissolved candy disc into the garbage. "So, have you heard from Mike or not?"

A cough that sounds like an argument between geese booms up from the phone. Dani assumes her friend has started smoking again.

"Not really," Jess croaks. "I saw him at my mom's birthday party a few weeks ago, but that's it."

"He still dating that Hooters girl?"

"*Mandy,*" she sneers. "Yeah, she was at the dinner. And it's Chili's. She was his manager at first, but I think they work at different locations now."

"Wow, so that's lasted more than a year."

"Yeah, right when you left, I guess. And you've been gone—"

"Uh, actually, *before* I left," Dani corrects her. "Technically, before we even *broke up.*"

"He's such an asshole. They got pregnant a few months ago."

"Seriously?"

"Yep. They almost split up, too, I think. Mike said he just wasn't ready to be a dad yet. But then she miscarried, and I guess they worked things out. Like I said, she was with him on my mom's birthday, so I'm pretty sure they're still together."

"Unbelievable," Dani mumbles, remembering that time *they* had a scare.

She had switched to a new birth control pill one month, which delayed her period a couple of weeks. When she told Mike she was late, he got pissed, blaming her for not being more careful. He ignored her for the next few days, playing video games and sleeping on the couch. Then, one morning, he found the pair of negative

Dani settles in for a lengthy call.

A few minutes later, having jotted down the pertinent details and doodled a sizable family of stick figures, Dani promises to have someone get back with the woman ASAP.

Like, first thing in the morning, she thinks. *Not sure how many more sunrises this one's gonna get.*

Wishing the lady a nice evening, she tears off the message and slides it into the desktop-organizer slot labeled *Frank*. She tosses the message pad back into the drawer while tapping the speaker-phone button.

"Sorry. You still there?" Ambient silence rises from the speaker as Dani loads a new ring of Scotch tape into the dispenser.

A moment later, the slapping of a game-show buzzer, followed by enthusiastic audience applause, echoes from a television in one of Jess's distant rooms.

Dani leans closer to the phone. "Hey, Jess! I'm back. Are you—"

"Yeah! Hold on. I'm coming, I'm coming." As a door slams, Jess orders a dog out of the kitchen. "Go get in your bed, Charlie." A collar jingles as long canine nails pitter-patter away. "Idiot dog." Jess's voice gets closer to the phone. "Sorry, Charlie found a possum in our backyard and thought it might be fun to corner it."

"A possum?"

"Yeah. This one happened to have babies with her, so I know it would've been bad. And I really didn't feel like running to the vet hospital tonight."

"Jesus! I think those things are so freakin' scary."

"Uh-huh. It was still hissing, even after we reached the house!" she shouts as she washes her hands. "Don't you miss Texas?" Jess sniggers, killing the water. "Okay, let's get back to your sad dating life."

"Oh, that's nice."

"Now, what do you mean, the guys aren't like their profiles?"

"Ugh, I don't know. Like, it will say he *loves* reading, but then he can't name any books when I ask for his favorites. Or, like, the guy I met last week got hammered after two drinks and admitted that his roommates were actually his parents. He was thirty-five." Dani finishes the cola. "And then there's Brett, whose profile talks about how rewarding it is to work with animals. He does freakin' *taxidermy*, Jess!"

They both erupt with laughter.

Dani crumples the Diet Coke can, flinging it into the basket under the desk. "I mean, he *stuffs dead animals*, Jess, but damn, is it *rewarding*."

"Oh my God, that's amazing," Jess squawks. Her face accidentally hits a button, and a shrill tone rings out. "Ah, sorry. Wait, does he do possums?"

"Not funny."

"Yeah, you might be right. Maybe it is time to stop trying," Jess says sarcastically. "Just buy a rocking chair and get some cats instead."

"Please, you think I haven't considered it? Could I move in with you and John?" Dani whines. "Maybe over the garage?"

"Well, I'd love to help, but, uh . . . I'm allergic to cats—"

"Oh, *there's* a good best friend. Hey, guess who just fell off the Christmas card list?"

"Come on, Dani." Jess sobers up a bit. "This is supposed to be your year of *yes*, remember? You can't give up."

"I know, I know."

"And at least you get great material from the dates."

"Seriously. No, I actually have a date tonight with this guy from Right-Connection.com."

"Great! See? Say *yes* to every opportunity. You never know where it'll go, you know? What's his deal?"

"Well, it *says* he works in the metals industry." Dani titters. "So, that probably means he collects soda cans."

Jess explodes again, and Dani can't help but join in.

As tears flood her eyes, she struggles to speak. "You laugh, but this is *my life.*"

"Okay, okay, okay," Jess shrieks. "I'm not laughing any-more . . . well, hang on, I'm almost done." She inhales loudly, trying to regain control.

Dani wipes away smudged mascara from under her eyes, still giggling in spite of herself. "You gonna be okay there, Jess?"

"Yeah, I'm good now. So, you're seeing a guy tonight? What time are you meeting him?"

"We're meeting at—" Dani bolts up from her chair, staring at the clock on the phone display. "Oh, shit! It's already after six. I gotta get going. I'm meeting him at some Italian restaurant in New Jersey. I still need to get home and change—"

"Jersey? What? Are there no restaurants in Pennsylvania?"

Dani shoves the loose receipts into a large orange envelope, sliding it and the taped pages into a file folder marked *Expenses.* "I don't know. I think he lives there. It's not bad. Just a few miles over the border."

"Okay, I'll let you go. But, Dani," Jess says as sternly as she can, "do *not* fall in love with this guy and move to Jersey!"

"Ha! Okay, I promise. Gotta go." Dani switches off her monitor and shoves her chair under the desk, yanking her suit jacket off its back.

"Call me after, okay? And have fun. And say *yes!* Unless he doesn't pay for dinner."

"*Byeee.*" Dani smirks, grabbing her purse as she taps the speak-erphone button. She hustles to the front door and snatches her raincoat off the rack. "Good night, Larry."

No response.

With her car keys in hand, she gives the reception area a quick glance. She calls out again, "I'm heading home, Larry. Good night."

A moan from the back office replies this time.

Dani switches out the lights as she steps out of the office. Before the door closes, she ducks her head back in. She taps the Monet-style poster into a crooked position again.

Fuck you, Fat Napoleon!

She smiles, locking the door behind herself, and hurries out to her car.

ELEVEN

DANI RAISES HER crystal goblet, respectfully joining the rest of the diners in an anniversary toast for the couple across the room. She's never met them, but she felt obligated when the older gentleman who kind of reminded her of her father stood up and addressed the whole room.

Wow, forty-five years. Good for them.

As the applause dwindles, Dani takes in the beauty of the place. Tiny stars expand across a shadowy ceiling, fading into soft bands of scarlet and indigo. The deep colors drift down the dark wood walls, creating a remarkably natural-looking twilight sky. An enormous glass-enclosed fireplace divides the dining area in half, its dancing flames serving as the ornate centerpiece that Del Reno's Italian Bistro is famous for.

Dani learned this when she Googled the restaurant for its dress code. She was nervous about overdoing it since this would be a first date, and she couldn't really tell how fancy the place was from the website. But, after observing the other women in the room, she's happy she went with the black Calvin Klein dress although it shows a little more cleavage than she intended.

At a table near the front window, a violinist serenades a young couple with a delicate rendition of Henry Mancini's "Moon River." Dani smiles without realizing it.

Wow, this place is amazing, she thinks, glancing around.

She catches the eye of a sharply dressed server across the room. He gives her a nod, which she returns, unwittingly summoning him over.

Discreetly peeking under the table, she checks her phone. *Seven fifty. Okay, this is getting ridiculous.*

"*Buongiorno, signora, cosa desidera?*"

"Oh," she exclaims, popping the table up with her knees. "Sorry?" She steadies the glassware, hoping her shriek was louder in her mind.

The man seizes the wobbling table with one hand while quickly lifting a vase filled with tinted water and a floating candle to safety. "*Non si preoccupi, va bene, va bene.*"

The table settles, and he returns the candle to its place. Battling a thick Italian accent, he tries again. "How may I help you, *signora?*"

Dani twists her napkin under the white-clothed table. Although embarrassed, she's grateful for the man's reflexes.

"*A damn bull in a china shop,*" she hears her mother say in her head.

She considers the wax sphere bobbing in its rose-colored liquid. *I mean, what's wrong with a nice, plain ole candlestick?* Chichi restaurants have always made her uncomfortable with their delicate tables and overabundance of utensils.

"Actually, I am fine right now." She grins. "I'm waiting for, uh . . . he should just be another couple of minutes." *I hope.*

"*Si, signora.*" The waiter fades away, gesturing for a busser to refill Dani's water glass. *"Portale il pane, per favore."*

Dani scrolls through an email on her phone, rechecking the details for tonight's date. *Yeah, this is the right night and the right restaurant. What is—*

It suddenly occurs to her that they could've somehow missed each other. She casually scans the dining room again. Everyone seems to be paired up. Her nervous anticipation shifts to insecurity as she observes all the happy couples chattering through their perfect dinners. It's not that she minds eating alone. She's been doing that every day since she moved up here. But scarfing down a quick burger at the pub on Main Street is different.

This place is like the Noah's ark of dating.

Another waiter drops off a basket of assorted breads as Dani taps a button on her cell phone. *Calling Jess's Home* appears on the screen. She adjusts the neckline of her dress, which somehow keeps shifting down too much. As she hears the second ring in her ear, the restaurant's front door jingles with a new arrival. Dani quickly hits *End*. She sets the phone on the table and takes a sip of water, trying not to look mad.

As the door swings open, a polished old man in his late sixties escorts his stunning and much younger Asian date to the hostess podium.

False alarm.

Dani dials again.

Jess answers before the first ring, "Hey. You hung up on me."

"Sorry. I thought it was maybe him—finally."

"Oh. Wait, he's late?"

"Yeah," Dani slurs. "He's late. Also, guess who rushed home to freshen up, change into a *very* cute dress, and is now sitting *alone* . . . in what appears to be a couples-only restaurant . . . in Jersey?"

"Wow. It's almost eight. What time was he—"

"Seven thirty," Dani interrupts. "That means, I'm already an hour in with these sexy three-hour heels!"

Jess chuckles. "And no call or text or anything? Maybe he left a message with the restaurant. Did you check?"

"Nope. Nothing." Snagging a crispy triangle of seasoned flat-bread, Dani shifts to her right, so she's facing the fireplace. "And, Jess, this restaurant is unreal. I mean, really beautiful. And it smells incredible in here. I should probably just get something to go. Place is too classy for me anyway."

"Oh, honey, I'm sorry. What a dick. Such a waste of time. Fuck him!"

Dani's eyes glaze over, entranced by a dancing flame. "Exactly. Maybe I should flag him on the site for *inappropriate behavior*," she scoffs. "What do you think he'd say to that?"

"I think he'd hate that," a rich, masculine voice answers. "I think he'd also say he's *really* sorry for being late and to please forgive him."

Dani's head whips back to her table. A tall, dark-skinned African American man is now standing across from her.

"These are for you." He smiles, offering a bouquet of flowers.

Keeping her eyes locked on him, Dani shuffles to her feet, almost gracefully. "Um, I have to go," she whispers into her hand. "Uh, yep. 'Kay. Bye!" She ends the call and lays her phone on the table. "Sorry, I—"

"No, no! *I* am really sorry," he jumps in. "I left my cell at the office, and then, of course, traffic was ridiculous. I . . ." He pauses, his eyes twinkling with confidence and humility at the same time.

This could go either way, but for some reason, she believes him. After a sufficient moment of silence, she smiles.

He sighs, still peering into her eyes. A single dimple emerges on his cheek. "I'm just really glad you're still here. I'm Eric."

"Oh gosh, I'm sorry," Dani says, straight-faced. "I'm waiting for someone named John."

Eric's face flushes. "Oh, sorry about that." He laughs awkwardly. "I thought, uh . . . sorry." He steps back from the table, turning toward the front door.

"But I'll give those to Dani if you want. I know she *loves* flowers."

It hits him. Eric spins back to face her with a wicked grin. He chuckles. "Wow."

Dani takes the flowers with a wink, deciding they're even now. "These are so pretty, Eric. Thank you," she says, extending her hand. "I'm Dani."

"That was, uh . . ." He smirks to himself with admiration. "Okay, yeah, I guess that was fair." He lifts his palms in surrender. "You still feel like eating?"

Dani pretends to feel dizzy as she takes her seat. "Sure, if I'm not too weak to hold a fork. I do feel faint."

"Uh-oh," he says, nodding to the crumbs in front of her. "Better have some more bread then, I guess."

She dusts off the tablecloth with a giggle. "What? No idea what you're talking about."

"And how about some wine to wash it down?" he asks, taking his seat. "You like red?"

Their eyes meet again, and they mutually agree to a truce.

"Sure. Wine would be great," Dani says coyly.

Their chemistry is off the charts already.

As Eric scans the selection, she examines him further. His large eyes combine with a strong nose and full lips to create a definite contender for any *GQ* cover she's ever seen.

Um, this guy's profile picture did not *do him justice,* she thinks, struck by his perfectly white smile.

He politely signals the server over and orders a bottle of the Willamette Valley Pinot Noir. As the man heads off to the bar, Eric folds his hands on the table, slowly shaking his head. "Your eyes are incredible."

"You have really beautiful teeth."

"Teeth?" He snickers. "Uh, thank you. I've never heard—"

"Okay, wait, that was definitely weird," she blurts. "I wanna do mine again!"

DANI TAKES THE last bite of her salad. "So, you were born in Philly, but then your family moved, and you grew up here?" she asks, laying her knife and fork across her plate.

"Well, yeah, kind of." Eric dusts a few stray crumbs off the table. She can tell he's a bit uncomfortable.

"I had a . . . a sort of complicated childhood."

"Oh, I'm sorry. I didn't mean to—"

"No, it's okay. It's just kind of heavy, is all."

He seems to be debating on whether to continue. Dani studies his eyes, wondering if perhaps she overshared. The wine has certainly helped to soften some of the walls she usually hides behind on first dates.

But he's so easy to talk to.

It's only been a couple of hours, but she feels like she's known this guy for years. She's already told him about going to a small college back in Texas where she picked up a daily journaling habit. And that, although she got a degree in English, she still had no idea what she wanted to be when she grew up. How her parents were really supportive while she bounced from job to job, searching for herself.

Then, somewhere between the buttery veal marsala and second

glass of pinot, she brought up Mike . . . *and that slut Mandy*. How, when she'd discovered them together, in her own bed, she felt like killing them. But the universe, or God—although she's not really religious—intervened. And, when an old college friend whom she'd recently reconnected with mentioned he was renting out his vacation home in the Pocono Mountains, she decided she needed a change of scenery.

Dani basically vomited horrible bits of her life all over this poor stranger, which was totally unlike her. And possibly rude.

Eric just smiled, nodding occasionally in a way that made her feel he was really listening to her.

But what if he's just been uncomfortable the whole time? Maybe he's actually wondering why in the world I brought up my-cheating-ex-boy-friend-and-whore-face-Mandy baggage on a first date.

A server steps in, removing the plates from the *insalata* course, so Dani takes the opportunity to gulp down some water. She dabs her lips with the silky napkin as another set of hands appears at her side to replenish their wine.

The man pulls back the empty bottle, turning to Eric. "*Signore, vuole un'altra bottiglia?*"

Eric glances at Dani, who subtly declines. "No, thank you," he says, dismissing the waiter. "I think we're all set with the wine."

"*Molto bene, signore,*" he replies, fading off toward the bar area.

Dani speaks first, "Sorry. We don't have to talk about your family. I didn't mean to change the vibe."

"No, no. You don't need to apologize. I just didn't want to scare you away with all the drama from my childhood." He takes a sip of wine. "But I guess, if I had to hear about the Mike-and-Mandy circus, you should be subjected to some of my insanity, too."

She beams. "Lay it on me." *Shit, I might already love this guy.*

"Uh, okay. So, when I was two, I came to New Jersey to live

pregnancy tests in the bathroom. He apologized to her for being *distant*, saying he had just been scared.

What a fucking child.

"You're better off, D," Jess says. "Trust me."

"Yeah, I know. Although, if I'd known just how hard it would be to date up here," Dani scoffs, taking a swig of a Diet Coke, "I might have fought for him."

"Look, I'm sure it's annoying, but you've just gotta hang in there, you know?" Another series of honking coughs. "I mean," Jess recovers, picking up where she left off, "have you gotten online yet?"

"Yes! Seriously, Jess, I'm signed up on, like, four different sites."

"Four? Oof, can you say, *desperate?*"

"Bitch," Dani spits with a snicker. "And stop smoking!"

"I *don't* smoke . . . very often." Jess laughs, clearing her throat. "Anyway, listen, you've gone out a few times, right? You've met some guys—"

"Yes, but when I see them, they're *nothing* like their profiles," Dani interjects. "And I don't just mean how they look."

A red light flickers on the phone base with the shrill beep of an incoming call.

"I mean, personality, too. Hang on a sec." Dani grabs the handset, pulling a message pad from her top drawer. "Tarvin and Partners. Hello?"

The phone is silent.

She checks that the line is active. A glowing green light indicates it is.

She tries again. "Hello?"

When the caller finally speaks, Dani feels certain the slurred words are coming from either a very old person or someone halfway through a Percocet-and-vodka martini. The monotone thrumming ends with name and a case number, so realizing it's the former, with my foster parents. I've never met my father, and I've seen my biological mother only a couple of times since I moved. She's struggled with drugs her whole life. Having me while she was still a kid herself—I think she was only fifteen or sixteen—was more than she could handle. So, the Lambs adopted me and raised me as their only son. They're who I consider my family."

Dani reaches for her water again, feeling so lucky to have gotten her mom and dad for parents. Her eyes rise from the shifting ice cubes. "How often do you get to see them?"

"Well, my dad was killed in a car accident my senior year of college."

"Oh my God."

"Yeah, it was really horrible. He was such an amazing man. My mom was completely devastated. She ended up getting really sick with pancreatic cancer, and she passed away a year later. I just don't think she could bear to be without him." Eric swishes the last of his wine in its glass. "So, I graduated school and immediately took over my dad's company. We manufacture metal storage buildings."

Dani sighs, not sure of how to respond. "Maybe we should've ordered some more wine."

"Told you it was a little heavy," he says with a short, self-conscious laugh. "But, look, things have gotten better. Now, I own the company, and even though I have to work crazy hours most of the time, it does afford me evenings like tonight every once in a while." He raises his wineglass toward her for a toast. "And I have Gus."

Dani smiles, clinking glasses. Her mind races. *Who the hell is Gus? Does he have a kid?*

"My big, fat tabby cat, Gus," Eric clarifies, noticing her wheels turning. "He's a rescue."

A three-tiered cart stops beside their table. The server reviews the various dessert options, ranging from a towering nine-layer tiramisu to the delicate trio of pistachio, amaretto, and black cherry tartufo. *"Cosa posso portale?"*

Dani shakes her head, unable to imagine eating even one more thing this evening. "No, thank you."

"Magari un caffè o un liquore?"

"Really?" Eric smirks at her. "Maybe a coffee then?"

"I am stuffed."

"Have an espresso with me. I don't want this to be over yet." His eyes chip away at her.

Dani cracks. "Okay," she moans with a faux-labored tone, turning to the server. "Two espressos, please."

As the dessert production wheels off to its next audience, Dani places her interlaced hands on the table. "You know, we *could* get together again. If you wanted to."

"Wait, are you asking me for a second date already?" he asks coyly, mirroring her hands. "Is that what I'm hearing?"

"Hey, I'm just saying, I could think of worse ways to spend an eve—"

A fist pounds on a table on the other side of the glass fireplace. "I don't think you're coming," a deep voice blusters over the rattling silverware. "I think you lied to me!"

Eric and Dani both whip their heads to the fireplace directly across from their table. Through the opening above the flames, a man furiously shouts into a flip-top cell phone.

The restaurant's jovial ambience dissolves as startled chatter rises at the neighboring tables.

The violin music gets louder, attempting to mask the disturbance, and an older server hurries toward the man's table. *"Signore, la prego di tenere la voce bassa.* You are, eh . . . disturbing our other guests."

"You said, 'Sure, Zeke. After work.' And we both got off at eight o'clock today," he fumes. "I put that note in your locker, and I saw you reading it on your break, Cindy. I saw you."

"*Signore, per favore!*"

"You *promised*, but you lied. You lied, Cindy."

Zeke spots the approaching server and quickly shuts the phone, waving the man off. As he considers the startled faces at the adjacent tables, his hands curl into fists again. The server steps away, positioning himself against a nearby wall. He gestures for another waiter to deliver the check, but the man shakes his head, indicating that Zeke hasn't ordered anything.

The StarTAC snaps open. After redialing, Zeke mashes the phone against his lips as he eyes the older server. He grumbles into the device, leaving another seething voice mail, "*The lip of truth shall be established forever: but a lying tongue is but for a moment!*"

From the other side of the fireplace, Eric and Dani stare shamelessly.

"Poor guy. That's rough," he whispers, entranced by the scene. "Hope she's just running late . . . and that she brings flowers."

Dani snorts, unable to peel her eyes away either. "Uh, or not."

"*Mi dispiace se ho disturbato,*" their server says, delivering the espressos. "Eh, so sorry for dat."

"Ah, we've all been there, right?" Eric asks, lifting his tiny coffee cup. "It's no problem. Actually, I feel bad for the guy . . . kinda."

"Um, I'm gonna go with *no*." Dani contorts her face in judgment as Eric sips. "She probably realized he's the mayor of Crazytown—population one—and just kept it movin'."

Eric chortles, spraying hot coffee over the sides of his cup. A little splash flies into his nose, triggering a cough.

Dani bursts out laughing, knocking her demitasse spoon to the floor. "You okay?" she asks, trying to stifle her giggling. "You need a life jacket?"

"I'll live." He chuckles, regaining his composure. Eric mops a napkin across his face, clearing his throat.

As Dani leans down for her spoon, the neckline of her dress gapes again, revealing the ornately colorful wings of a butterfly tattoo above her breast. She inches the tiny rogue utensil closer with the tip of a finger, finally grabbing it. Her eyes rise to the fireplace, landing on a wavering reddish flame, but as she smiles, considering what a fantastic time she's been having, a bony face comes into focus just beyond the fire. That weirdo with the phone is staring at her. Dani's smile fades.

Zeke's eyes dart to her tattoo and then slowly drift up to her face. She jolts upright, almost tipping out of her chair. Following her movement, he spots Eric. Zeke leans closer to the fireplace, examining the couple, his confused stare bouncing between their two faces.

"Hittite," he hisses, locking back on Dani. *"And when the Lord thy God shall deliver them before thee; thou shalt smite them, and utterly destroy them."*

"Holy shit!" Her levity evaporates as she notices Zeke's closed cell phone on the table. *He's talking to me!*

Zeke bolts out of his chair, smacking it against the next table. The violin music halts.

He yanks the clip-on tie from his collar and shoves it into the pocket of his khaki pants, his eyes still trained on Dani. *"Thou shalt make no covenant with them, nor show mercy unto them."*

The Del Reno's manager rushes to the table as Zeke scoops up his phone.

"La prego di uscire dal locale!" the man shouts, pointing to the door. "Go out now!"

Zeke strides to the front of the restaurant as a tense silence blankets the dining room. He reaches the door and rips it open.

Someone squeals from a nearby table. Zeke's head whips around to Dani, sending a chill prickling across her body.

His finger wags in a slow, disapproving motion. *Thou shalt make no covenant with* them, he silently mouths.

"I calling *la polizia!*" the manager shouts, charging toward a phone behind the bar.

Zeke stomps out into the night, and the front door eases closed.

An intoxicated guy a few tables away breaks the silence. "What the hell was that?"

A collective sigh of relief gives way to nervous laughter, and the crying violin starts up again.

"Okay, you're right," Eric concedes. "Most definitely the mayor."

"Wow." Dani inhales deeply, trying to shake it all off.

As the restaurant's charming atmosphere resumes, their server appears tableside again, offering Eric the velvet-covered check holder. "*Quando yei é pronto. I'sa no hurry.*"

Dani starts for her purse but stops at Eric's shaking head.

He slides a credit card into the sleeve, passing it to the server. "Thank you."

"Thank you," she says as the server leaves them. "I get the next one though. Deal?"

"Well, we'll have to see about that." He winks.

"Oh, we will."

"And just when might that be?"

His playful banter hammers at her good judgment.

"How about you call me tomorrow, and we'll make plans then?" she asks, wrestling with her self-control. "Fair?"

Their eyes lock.

"Yep. Totally fair."

DANI AND ERIC stroll arm in arm through the parking lot that separates the freestanding Del Reno's restaurant from the neighboring storefronts in the strip mall. He nods to the glowing electrical channel letters above a grocery store. The bulbs in the N and S of the sign have burned out. "What do you think?" Eric chuckles. "You wanna Buy-a-Dave?"

Dani laughs as they arrive at her humble little two-door Honda Accord. "So, I was a little nervous when I reread your profile," she confesses. "It says you work with metals, and I thought that might mean you collected cans."

His brows furrow, a curious smile forming. "What are you talking—"

"But, wait," she interrupts. "After a dinner like that, I'll pick up cans with you anytime you want."

Eric stands across from her, grinning in silence.

She can tell he likes her, but she wants to hear it. "What are you smirking at?" she asks, poking his arm.

"Nothing. I was just thinking, it will *technically* be tomorrow in a couple of hours. So, maybe we could hang out a bit longer, and then I could ask you for that second date—in person."

She sets her purse and flowers on the trunk, considering his suggestion for longer than she means for him to see. "I gotta be at work early tomorrow." She smiles, pulling him closer. "I will give you an I-had-a-great-time hug though."

"I'll take it," he says, leaning into a tight embrace. "And sorry about all that family drama I laid out at dinner."

"No, no. I'm glad you told me." Dani pulls back. "I mean, not to sound patronizing, but I think it's really astonishing that you turned out so normal, you know? It takes a lot of strength to pull through those kinds of challenges."

"Yeah, well, I think most people are stronger than they think. It's just that, sometimes, they don't know *how* strong until something crazy happens." He guides her into another hug. "Thanks for a fantastic night, Ms. Caraway."

"Thank *you*, Mr. Lamb."

As they separate again, she gives him a peck on the cheek.

He steps back, still holding her hand. "I'm going to call you in just a little while, you know?"

Jesus, I gotta get out of here before I go home with him. She opens the car door, tosses her purse onto the passenger front seat, and smells the flowers one more time.

"I hope so." Sliding into the driver's seat, she closes her door and rolls down the window as the engine starts. "Have a good night, Eric," she says with a wink, backing out of the parking space. "And, by the way, you really *do* have beautiful teeth."

TWELVE

T HE BOUQUET OF flowers rattles to the floorboard as Dani
swerves her car, cutting across two lanes and barely making
the exit ramp. A horn from somewhere behind her wails its
disapproval. She's unfazed, still basking in the glow of what might
have been the best date in history. Her cheeks are beginning to
ache. She has been smiling since she left Eric.

Jess's raspy laughter fills the car as it approaches the Stop sign
at Route 115. "Nice *teeth?* Seriously?"

"Shut up! I was nervous!" Dani giggles, retrieving the flowers.
"The whole night was unbelievable, Jess. Like, I have *never* had a
date like that. He was so . . . I don't know . . . *normal.*" She gives
the bundle a quick sniff and sets it in the passenger seat again. "It's,
like, even now, I'm not sure it actually happened."

HONK-HONK!

Dani jumps, her eyes darting to the flickering headlights in the
rearview mirror.

"What was that?" Jess asks.

"Some asshole behind me is honking."

She leans up to the mirror, waving a quick apology. As she starts to accelerate, the growling vehicle behind her jerks around to the side, stopping at her passenger window.

She stomps on the brakes. *What the hell?*

A bearded man wearing a stained John Deere cap leans through the window of his light-blue pickup truck. He pinches the last inch of a cigarette away from his lips. "You okay?" he shouts, glancing around the inside of her car.

On the phone, she mouths, pointing to her cell. *Thanks.* Dani flashes an embarrassed grin.

The truck's motor roars again, whipping past her, its one working taillight speeding off to the right, toward Blakeslee.

Dani turns the opposite direction. She notices the neon glow from her dashboard clock. *10:40 p.m. Shit!* She guns it. "Sorry, I'm back."

"So, I was right then?" Jess gloats. "That's really what you're saying, right?"

"Okay, fine. You were a hundred percent right."

10:52 P.M.

Dani veers onto State Highway 903. Considerably slowing down, she scans the sloping countryside that flanks the dark road ahead. This particular stretch is one of many in the Pocono area that seems to attract suicidal deer and other car-damaging wildlife.

When Dani first moved here, the attendant at a local gas station warned her that, "Out here, it's not *if* you'll hit one, it's *when*."

Since then, she's had several close calls, but she has avoided joining the club of Bambi killers so far.

Tonight's been too perfect to have it end in tragedy.

"Well, he's supposed to call me tomorrow—or, actually, in, like, an hour, I guess," she says, crawling down the curvy blacktop. "If he does—"

"Oh my God. See? I told you!"

"Yeah, you might just have to come up to Jersey after all, Jess."

"Ah-may-zing," she sings. "Ooh, how many kids do you want?"

Jess squeals like a little girl who just discovered a puppy in a box on Christmas morning. Dani yanks the phone from her face.

Jess jumps back in. "Just kidding. But, seriously, we've obviously gotta start looking at dresses!"

"Obviously." Dani adds her own squeal, and they both erupt with laughter. "Hey, I gotta get into this store before it closes. I'll let you know what happens."

Having survived yet another journey through the deer straits of death, Dani sighs in relief and turns into the mostly empty parking area of Harris's Country Store. She stops her car under the fluorescent glow of a pole in the center of the lot.

"But, wait," she says, shutting off the engine, "did I mention how *fine* he is? I'm serious. His lips . . . I-I just—" She smacks the steering wheel, stomping her feet, as Jess cackles.

Dani notices a guy coming out of the store, and remembering she's got a deadline, she grabs her wallet. "Okay, I need some ice cream! Call you tomorrow. Love you. Bye." She tosses the phone toward her purse but misses. It slides into the crack of the passenger seat.

Ugh, I'll get it later, she thinks, springing from the car.

As she starts toward the store, Dani realizes the guy she saw coming out has changed his course. He is now heading straight for her.

What's with the creepers tonight? She picks up her pace, instinctively balling her fist, as he approaches.

"How are you doin', sweetheart?" he asks, flashing a cigarette-stained smile.

Dani bobs her head, passing the man without making eye contact. *Um, no, thank you.*

The beeping store door announces her entrance as she glances back over her shoulder. The guy gets into one of the few vehicles parked in the shadows along the edge of the lot. Cigarette smoke rises from his window as headlights pop on. A moment later, sparks flutter as his sagging muffler scrapes out onto the road.

The scent of a soured mop fills the vestibule of the store, like an intimidating bouncer at a closing nightclub. Dani tiptoes across the glossy squares of the gray Excelon flooring, attempting to avoid the older woman at a register.

"We're closing in two minutes," the old woman says.

"Okay. I'll be really quick," Dani assures her. "I'm just grabbing some ice cream."

The woman nods with a sigh, like she's been replenishing that candy rack for a hundred years. "Row five, honey," she says, tearing open a large box of Mounds bars.

"Thanks."

Dani dashes off, considering the various potato chip and soft drink displays along her path. An array of canned pumpkin pie mix and cranberry sauce catches her attention as she passes it, rolling her eyes.

It's barely September. Thanksgiving stuff already?

She rounds the corner of the frozen foods aisle, almost tripping over a beat-up mop bucket. Her leg grazes the old yellow tub, and bluish-gray water threatens to splash over the side. Dani recognizes this as the same scent that greeted her at the front of the store. She scrunches her face, trying to block out the pungent air, as she peruses the dessert options.

She stops at the single-serve ice cream freezer toward the end, peering through the windowed doors. Normally, her go-to flavor is Häagen-Dazs Coffee, but they don't seem to have it.

Ugh, you're killing me here, people.

She drums her fingernails against the frosted glass, deliberating between the Vanilla Bean and Chocolate Peanut Butter. As disappointed as someone can actually be when getting ice cream, she settles for the second one and yanks at the chrome handle.

Tonight is too special for plain vanilla.

She smiles to herself, releasing the large door. It slams shut, resealing itself, just as a shiny blue wrapper catches her eye.

"Ooh," she mumbles, eyeing the crunchy chocolate Drumstick. She pulls the handle, but it doesn't budge. "Oh, come on," she huffs.

"We're closing up now."

Dani spins to find a bony old man dragging a tattered rope mop at the end of the row. He plunges the filthy strands into the stagnant water, apparently oblivious to the odor.

"Sorry. Okay." She grins, trying the door again.

The tired man drops his head and continues his evening routine, steering the slopping tub in front of himself. As he disappears around the corner, Dani tugs on the door a little harder.

"I think it's stuck." She snickers to herself, realizing how desperate she must look.

The suction finally releases, flinging the door open, almost knocking her off-balance. She swaps the cup for the Drumstick and rushes up to the checkout area. As she passes the seasonal display again, she imagines introducing Eric to her parents at Thanksgiving. She's pretty sure her mom will love him. Her dad will be the tougher nut to crack.

Uh, I should probably have a second date before looking into flights though.

"Coming. Sorry!" she shouts.

The old woman jerks up from a stool behind the counter, training her alarmed gaze on the ice cream package. Dani notices her bloodshot eyes and assumes the woman must have dozed off.

"Thanks for waiting," she says, handing over the ice cream.

With a passive-aggressive grin, the woman taps a few buttons on the register. A shrill *beep* exclaims an incorrect code, startling the woman. She mutters something under her breath, scowling at Dani as she tries again. Another scolding *beep*.

"Ward!" she shouts, punching her hands to her hips. "This dern thing's locked up again."

"G'night, Liz." A chubby old man with silver hair and a bushy mustache eyes Dani from the store entrance. Tossing an apron over the arm of his stained white butcher's jacket, he unlocks the door and totters out.

"Good night, Owen," the old woman slurs. She tries toggling the power button on the cash register but gets another few piercing beeps. She gives up. "WAH-ARD."

God, it's like I've walked into the movie Cocoon, Dani thinks, glancing around the empty checkout area, as she pulls an entertainment magazine from its rack. *Ward's probably out back in a pool with Wilford Brimley and Jessica Tandy.*

The magazine's teaser line reads, *Online Dating: Clicking Your Way to Love.*

Hmm. Dani smiles to herself. *Maybe.*

"You getting that, too?" the old woman asks impatiently, still staring toward the rear of the store.

"Hmm? Oh, no. Just the ice cream, thanks." She slides the magazine back into place, returning to the counter.

"Well, just go ahead and take it. This stupid machine is busted, and we're closing up."

"Are you sure?" Dani asks. She snaps open her wallet, feeling a little guilty. "I probably have a couple of singles."

"It's fine, honey. Just go on now. Have a nice night." The woman doesn't wait for any more discussion. She slaps the register's power button with a grunt, reminding the machine just who the boss is, and walks to the front door.

Dani hurries after her. "Thank you." She passes the woman, stepping out into the parking lot. "Good night."

"Night, dear," she says, twisting her keys in the dead bolt.

Dani starts toward her car, carefully surveying the vacant parking lot. To the right, a rickety wooden fence separates the store from the playground of the neighboring mobile home community. Several of its boards look like they fell away or were kicked down by kids looking for quicker access to the store. Backed up against the fence, the carcass of an old sports car with a crunched front fender and no tires waits to be hauled off. A white cargo van with a numberless For Sale sign in the front window is parked next to it, perched like a predator guarding its recent kill.

The lights go out in the country store just as Dani lifts her door handle. She glances back, imagining the curmudgeonly old couple probably bickering about the cash register on their way home. *They get to go home together.* A sweet smile spreads across her face. *Eric mentioned that he likes to cook. Maybe our next date will be at his place. Oh, for crying out loud!* she yells in her head. *Wait till he calls.*

The door swings open, and Dani glides behind the wheel. She shoves the key into the ignition, quickly peeling back the ice cream wrapper for a bite. Her chomp sends an explosion of tiny nuts and cone pieces flying.

"Damn it," she garbles to herself, considering the chocolate bits on her dress. Stopping the closing door, she leans out and dusts most of the rogue crumbs from her lap.

Dani eyes the fence as a dog howls tirelessly from somewhere in the trailer park. She takes another bite that finishes off the nutty dome, pulling the door shut. Carefully navigating the melting cone as she drags the seat belt across her torso, she fastens it into place and twists the ignition key.

There's a short click, but the starter doesn't engage.

"Oh, come on." She flips the key back and tries again as she scans the console.

The icons behind the steering wheel light up, but there's no cranking and no motor. She had a problem with the car engine on her drive up from Texas, but her dad said that was because of the long distance.

It's been an hour maybe. This thing can't possibly be overheated.

Her gaze sweeps across the dashboard, landing on what looks like a little yellow block. A set of tiny prongs extends up from the plastic piece. As Dani cranes forward for a better look, something falls against her left calf. She springs back against her seat and spots the small plastic door. The interior fuse box has been tampered with. Inside the compartment, there are several rows of similar yellow blocks plugged into a panel.

She reaches for the piece on the dashboard. "What the hell is that?"

Something moves in her rearview mirror.

Dani whips her head to the backseat, coming face-to-face with a set of glowing orange eyes. A scream bursts up from her gut as she spins back around, dropping the ice cream cone. She yanks the chrome lever, kicking her door open, as the stranger lurches forward. The high heel of her shoe hits the pavement outside the car just as the man's arm slams across her throat, pinning her against the headrest.

Struggling to breathe, Dani doesn't notice the returning swing of the door until it smashes into her shin. As she grapples with his constricting elbow, a solid object thumps the side of her head. She claws at it, her fingers latching on to a twisted goat horn. As she wrenches it downward, the painted eyes in the rearview mirror stretch into slanted gashes. Suddenly, the tension breaks. The hood shifts to the side, revealing Zeke's contorted face.

His arm tightens at her esophagus as he fumbles for something on the seat next to him. A clapping sound of electric current sparks to life. Zeke jerks his head back to her, raising a flashlight-shaped stun gun to her face. Dani's fist collides with his nose and he explodes with a furious growl, dropping the fluttering strobe. As blood bubbles from his nostrils, his grip loosens at her neck. He sinks to the floorboard, groping for his weapon beneath the seat.

Dani seizes the moment. Shoving his arm over her head, she launches herself at the open door, but her torso jolts back against the seat, locked in place by the taut belt across her chest.

"Help me," she wails, frantically struggling to release the buckle.

Her thumb finds the edge of the button, and she jabs it, ripping off the tip of her nail. The clasp clicks, and she throws off the seat belt.

At the same time, Zeke's head pops up from the backseat, his eyes watering with rage. He thrusts his hand around the left side of the driver's seat, blocking her path, just as Dani lunges. The snapping stun gun connects with her rib cage, sending electric tremors rippling through her abdomen. The crackling shock takes her breath away, making it impossible for her to scream. A single yelp is all she can manage from behind her clenched teeth.

She flops her quaking body toward the windshield, smashing her palm against the center of the steering wheel. As the tinny horn blares across the parking lot, Zeke smacks down her rigid arm, wedging the stun gun deeper into her side.

His eyes cut to his bloody-nosed image in the crooked rearview mirror. *"It is joy to the just to do judgment,"* he softly whispers to the grisly man staring back at him. *"But destruction shall be to the workers of iniquity."*

Flashes of blue and white flicker in the dark car as Dani's convulsing body finally loses consciousness. She collapses toward the passenger seat, slumping over the emergency brake.

THIRTEEN

THE HEAVY BACK door of Harris's Country Store huffs, scraping across the concrete. Throwing her shoulder against the edge, the old woman drives it halfway open.

"Cheese and rice," Liz scoffs, giving up on the push.

She snatches up her grocery bags and continues outside, noting the door's bowed top hinge. Loosened by many years of use, it threatens to snap away from the frame at any moment.

"When you gonna get this door done?" she asks over the rustling plastic bags. "Just about popped my shoulder out on the dern thing."

With a grunt, Liz heaves the bags into the bed of a rusty Ford F-1 pickup. *I'm getting too old for all this.* She leans against the side of the truck, her head resting against the window, as she catches her breath. The late hours have been getting to her more and more lately. She massages the base of her neck, deciding it's probably time to bring up retirement with Ward again.

We can get some young folks in here to run the place for us. And then we can finally go on that Alaskan cruise. She stares into the dark store, assuming her husband has probably stopped to "fix something right quick" on his way out. *Ugh, but Ward'll never go for it. That man would go crazy without something to do.*

"Ward? Come on, let's go."

The howl from a dog across the fence surprises her. She bolts off the truck, opening the door. *Well, maybe I'll bring it up this weekend, over a nice chocolate cake.* She smirks, recalling how well that worked to get her a new dishwasher. "Hey, are you comin' or what?"

She listens for Ward, but the constant yowling is too loud for her to hear. "Oh, why don't you just hush?" she snaps at the fence line. "Ya dern jackal!"

Squinting at the frozen arms on her wristwatch, which appear to have stopped a few hours ago, she scowls. "Well, that ain't right." *These batteries just don't last as long as they used to.* She climbs up into the truck, shouting for her husband again, *"Wah-ard!"*

The old man emerges in the doorway, pausing for effect. *"Li-iz,"* he bellows, cupping a hand around his mouth like a megaphone. With a self-satisfied grin, he steps out of the store, carrying an open canister of Pringles. He tosses a few in his mouth. "Now, why are you out here, hollerin' like that?" he garbles, shoving the weighty door closed.

He glances toward the howling behind the fence as he pulls a large ring of keys from his pocket. "Somebody's gonna kill that damn thing," he mutters. "Decent people are tryin' to sleep."

"Well, come on then," Liz scoffs, reaching for her door handle. "Let's go home and be *decent people.*"

A car horn blares from nearby, startling Ward into dropping his keys. The sound stops as abruptly as it started, but its echo still hangs in the air. As he retrieves the keys, a chorus of new dogs joins the yapping frenzy from the other side of the fence.

"What in God's name was that?" Liz shouts, leaning out of the truck for a listen.

"I can't hear nothin' but them damn dogs," he snaps. "It's probably just some kids grab-assin' though." Ward surveys the area behind their store as he locks up and joins his wife in the truck. He tips up the canister, showering the remaining broken chips into his mouth, as he fires up the engine.

The old pickup wobbles out onto Route 534, continuing around the side of their store.

"Remember I gotta go see the doctor in the morning, so Gloria will be by to get me," Liz says, sweeping some crumbs off the seat.

He nods, gazing out the window.

"Then, she'll—" A yawn interrupts her. "Ooh, 'scuse me," she continues. "Then, she'll drop me by the store after I get done."

"All right then," Ward drones, veering into the left turning lane as they near the junction of Highway 903.

The truck pulls up, parallel to the store's front parking lot, and stops at the traffic light.

"Look at that," Liz says.

Ward shakes his head at a white cargo van speeding through the intersection in front of them. "I know," he replies, clicking his tongue. "Why in the hell does he need to go *that* fast?"

"No." She taps the side window, pointing to the store's lot. "Over here."

The traffic light goes through a full cycle as the couple stares at an abandoned car.

After a moment, Ward checks his rearview for any vehicles. "Well, shit," he huffs, crossing two lanes and turning into the store's front parking area.

"We should just sell it, Ward," Liz grumbles, searching the storefront for any movement.

As the Ford teeters across the lot, they notice the car's driver-side door is ajar. Ward parks at the edge of the fluorescent circle beneath the light pole. They appear to be the only ones around. With an exhausted glance to his wife, Ward kills the motor, stepping out of the truck with a sigh.

Keeping an eye on the strange car, Liz reaches beneath her seat, snagging the corner of a terry-cloth bath towel. "Be careful now," she whispers, sliding the Remington 870 Wingmaster up onto her lap, as her husband approaches the open door.

Ward meanders around the rear of the car, peering into the backseat. He stops at the passenger door. "Hello?"

He considers the perimeter of the lot again before peeking into the window. His gaze drifts from a bouquet of flowers on the floorboard to what he thinks is an overturned purse on the seat. A small bottle of nail polish and a pair of sunglasses are among a pile of loose change and chewing gum sticks just outside the bag.

"You find anything?" Liz asks, monitoring the missing boards of the fence.

"Noth—"

Motion in the front seat catches Ward's attention.

In the ignition, he spots a wagging keychain, shaped like the state of Texas. "What in the hell?"

He gives another glance to the empty backseat through the windshield as he rounds the front of the car. On the concrete, outside the driver's door, a partially wrapped sugar cone sits crushed in a tiny melted clump. He watches a thin trickle of clumpy chocolate ice cream slide across the lot's uneven foundation.

This just happened!

Ward spins toward the sound of the barking dogs behind the fence. "Hey, this is private property!" he yells. "You gotta move this damn car."

Liz sways nervously in the truck. "Who's he talking to?" she mutters, straining to see whatever he sees. *Probably one of them dopeheads again.*

No one responds to Ward. He turns back to the car's front seat, pondering if maybe there's some ID in the purse. He braces his arm against the door as he leans in, but something poking out from beneath the car stops him. Using the tip of his boot, he nudges a high-heeled pump into the light. His blood goes cold as he puts all the pieces together.

A cell phone notification chirps from the crack beside the passenger seat.

Ward jumps, tripping over his own feet as he whirls around and stumbles to the Ford's hood.

Liz kicks open her door. "What is it?" she shouts, cocking the Remington as she slides out onto the pavement.

"Get back in there, woman," Ward barks, still regaining his balance. He hurries around to his side of the truck and hops up behind the wheel. "Lizzy, this don't look right!" he says, out of breath. Firing up the engine, he locks the doors, giving the whole parking lot another worried scan. "We'd better call 911."

FOURTEEN

DANI SWATS AT a mosquito that keeps coming back to the same area on her arm, but it springs away again just before her slap connects. She's been walking down a shady path forever now, it seems, looking for a break in the long row of canvas tents that flank the winding trail.

Jess and Dani have gone to the Needville County Fair every single fall since eighth grade. It's their favorite time of the year and practically the *only* fun thing about living way out in the country.

She pauses, checking over her shoulder. *How did I even get back here?* She scans the endless rear walls of identical tents for a way out.

Adding to Dani's annoyance, an accordion blasts the hypnotic melody of "Beer Barrel Polka" from a speaker above her.

Ugh, Jess must be so pissed by now, she thinks, starting down the dusty pathway again.

They were supposed to meet at the funnel cake cart at seven and then go find Jess's boyfriend at the balloon animal booth.

The mosquito is back, prodding at her arm again. She smacks it, immediately checking her palm for the bloody carcass. There's nothing there.

What? She checks her inner elbow, certain she nailed the little bastard that time.

"Shit!" She forgot her watch. *I don't even know how late I am.*

From somewhere in front of her, a faint fizzing sound rises and falls in perfect rhythm.

Balloons. Someone's inflating balloons. Dani picks up her pace. *It has to be coming from one of these tents.* She considers trying to squeeze under one of the back walls, but imagining the embarrassment of potentially getting stuck, she abandons the idea. *Damn it, there's gotta be an opening here somewhere.*

The path seems to be getting darker, as if someone were slowly turning down the lights. She can't hear the polka music anymore either.

Wait, are they closing?

The hissing of a filling balloon is getting closer, and Dani lurches to a stop. She pivots around in the shadowy walkway, trying to pinpoint the source of the sound.

A beaming strip of light stretched across the ground just a few yards away catches her eye.

Another path! "Oh, thank God," she mutters to herself.

She rounds the corner, frantically rushing down the long alley between the tents. She's almost out.

A figure steps into the opening at the end of the path, chomping on a funnel cake.

Dani immediately knows her best friend's silhouette. "Jess! Oh my God, I'm so sorry. I don't know how—"

"We told you to be careful, Dani!" a voice shouts. "We *told* you!"

Dani recognizes that tone, but it's not her friend's. "Dad? What are you doing here?"

He hates crowds. Something must have happened. *Why else would he be here?*

"What's wrong, Dad?"

As she trots toward the figure, she feels the sting at her arm again and glances down at the pest. She swats at it, but this time, the insect floats up for just a second before driving its bloodsucking nose into her flesh.

What the hell? Dani looks up, knowing she should have reached the end of the path by now.

The figure is gone.

"Wait! Dad?"

What is going on? Panic booms in her chest.

"Dad? Hey, I'm right here! Where'd you go?"

Although she's running now, the glow at the end of the passage isn't getting any closer. In fact, the lights and sounds of the fair seem to be fading.

Except for the balloons.

The wheezing inflation is getting louder and louder with each step. It actually sounds more like breathing now, like huge, labored breaths heaving right next to her ear.

This is crazy, she thinks, breaking into a full-on sprint.

"Please, Dad! Don't leave—"

A waft of something like soured milk or sewage invades her nostrils.

Dani jerks her head back. "Oof," she spits, fanning the air in front of her face. "What the hell is that?"

Unable to escape the odor, she slowly raises her eyelids, revealing the man standing over her with a syringe.

Zeke's blurry head comes into focus. When he notices her blinking lids, his audible mouth-breathing stops. Between swaying goat horns, two neon-painted eyes stare down at her. She locks on the crooked row of rotting teeth gripping his chapped bottom lip.

Dani's chest expands with a scream she cannot release. She tries to punch out at him, but neither of her hands is responding. And, though she's kicking with all she's got, there's only a slight flick from her right foot. Her eyes flash to something in his hand.

What is that?

As her focus narrows, she spots the needle poking out of an arm she somehow knows is her own.

She is barely conscious as the mixture shoots through her bloodstream, paralyzing her body.

And, from somewhere inside her mind, a voice wails, *He's drugging me. I can't move!*

Zeke releases her limp arm. As it clumsily flops to her side, he dabs his finger over a tiny droplet of blood that beaded up at her punctured basilic vein. He stares into her eyes, watching as a tear swells over her lid. With a smile spreading across his lips, he moves off into the shadows behind her head.

A fog rolls into her brain. Dani fights not to pass out again. Somehow, she still has control over her eyes, and they wildly dart around, searching for identifiable objects.

She's in a dark place although a glow is coming from near her feet. Odd shapes are waving across the ceiling above her face; the whole room seems to be quivering.

There are lots of candles here. Her attention veers toward the lights at her feet. *What is this?* She doesn't recognize the dress she's wearing. *I don't understand.* She struggles to make sense of the dingy white fabric. *It looks like an old-fashioned nightgown.*

A little moan swells up from her belly, seeping out of her slack mouth. The thoughts are coming to her more slowly now.

Hold on, she tells herself. *Focus.*

To her right, another flame wags from behind some kind of glass barrier.

As she peers through the grimy wall, it hits her. *I'm lying in a box!*

The drug's effect finally reaches Dani's eyeballs, locking her frozen stare on the ceiling. Just as she starts to give in to the swirling clouds in her head, his septic breath falls into her face again. The horns bob into her sight line.

Zeke reaches across her, snagging the neckline of the cotton gown. He gently lowers the material midway down her left breast, revealing the vibrant turquoise-and-purple wings of Dani's large butterfly tattoo.

"Tsk-tsk." He sighs. *"Know ye not that your body is the temple of the Holy Ghost which is in you, which ye have of God?"* He traces his finger along the thin black border of a wing. *"And ye are not your own?"*

With a deep exhale, Zeke reaches under his hood and slides on a pair of safety goggles. He stares into Dani's petrified eyes, shaking his head at her, like a disappointed grandmother. *"Ye shall not make any cuttings in your flesh for the dead, nor print any marks upon you,"* he whispers. *"I am the Lord."*

His eyes sparkle with excitement behind the thick plastic as a squealing motor revs to life at his side. He lifts a whizzing Black+Decker palm sander into the box, hovering the tool over the vibrant artwork on her chest. Zeke bites down on his tongue as he presses the spinning tool against Dani's flesh. A wisp of smoke and the scent of burning meat rise above her vibrating body, particles of skin and blood whirling against the Plexiglas walls.

Although her eyes remain open, consciousness is suddenly too much to bear. And tears begin trickling down her temples as she succumbs to the swallowing darkness.

FIFTEEN

BEADS OF SWEAT cover the minister's crimson forehead like a simmering pot. With each word he speaks, more of his unnaturally black hair shudders free from its shellac, stretching up like the legs of a large spider breaking out of its egg sack. *"And I say unto you, my friends, be not afraid of them that kill the body,"* he cautions, wagging a finger at his parishioners. *"And after that have no more that they can do."*

A camera sweeps across the stage for a close-up. His hands meet at his brow, gliding upward to restrain his mane again. As he turns toward the lens, he sips from a fingerprinted glass. He glares through the television screen, as though somehow distracted by Zeke's messy parlor. His Adam's apple bobs with the last swallows of water. As he drags a sleeve across his top lip, his eyes drift back to the congregation.

He dusts off the top edge of his podium, continuing with his sermon, *"But I will forewarn you whom ye shall fear . . ."* The minister flings himself from the pulpit, bolting to the edge of the brightly lit stage. *"Fear Him, which after He hath killed hath power to cast into hell; yea, I say unto you,"* he roars, his fists pounding the air, *"fear Him!"*

The television speakers buzz from the crowd's massive praises.

"Uh-huh," a full mouth garbles from the BarcaLounger.

Loud, open-mouthed crunching in the parlor overshadows the exalting cheers; a half-chewed bit splashes down into the milky bowl of Fruity Rings breakfast cereal. As the sermon ends with a final bellowing crescendo, another heaped spoonful of colored loops is devoured with a sloppy bite.

The camera pans across the tearful crowd, capturing various desperate pleas for salvation. As the introduction for a new segment scrolls up the old tube, a remote control rises, changing the channel. The screen flips from station to station with the perfect rhythm of a grandfather clock.

FLIP. Some kind of herby broth sizzles as it hits a panful of julienned vegetables. Steam puffs.

FLIP. A pretty Asian newscaster promises more details as a red text box pops up in the top right corner. *Another Missing Woman.*

FLIP. Two Midwestern contestants nervously calculate on a Showcase Showdown segment of *The Price Is Right.*

FLIP BACK.

The channel returns to the newscaster, Holly Zhang, and then quickly switches to video coverage of Harris's Country Store parking lot. A shaky picture shows officers interviewing an elderly couple surrounded by police cruisers and news vans. After another long slurp of milk, a spoon clinks against the side of an empty bowl.

A red banner appears along the bottom of the screen, identifying the pair—*Wardell and Elizabeth Buddner, Store Owners.* The television volume rises. The old woman, shielding her eyes from the camera lights, points toward a rickety wooden fence as her husband speaks with police in the audioless clip.

The screen switches to a blown-up Texas driver's license with the annoyed smirk and piercing blue gaze of a young woman.

Holly Zhang's voice reports from off camera, "Officers responded late last night to a report of an abandoned car at this corner store near Albrightsville on Route 534. Police have been unable to locate the owner, Dani Caraway, but say her identification was found in the car. According to our sources, this ominous scene is remarkably similar to the recent disappearance of another eastern Pennsylvania woman."

Another photo pops onto the monitor, replacing Dani's. In the picture, a curvy redheaded woman wearing a sweatshirt that says, *Boas give the best hugs!*, is standing behind a checkout counter. She's holding a pair of baby Burmese pythons up to her face, each forked tongue grazing a dimpled cheek. Two large Rubbermaid containers labeled *Live Rats* are stacked against a pastel yellow wall beside her.

"Three weeks ago," Zhang continues, "Kristen Byrne, a manager at the specialty pet supply store Reptopia in Mount Pocono, went missing after closing up one evening. And, as with this new disappearance, Byrne's purse, wallet, and keys were all found in her abandoned car."

The screen snaps back to video coverage of the hectic grocery store parking lot where several policemen are combing over Dani's Honda.

"In light of yesterday's discovery of a woman's snake-bitten body over in the Delaware Water Gap, authorities are urging anyone who has seen Dani or Kristen or could possibly offer any information on their current whereabouts to call 570–555-TIPS."

Suddenly, the anchorwoman's somber face fills the monitor again. She shuffles through some pages on her desk. "We, uh . . ." Zhang searches for a good transition. "We sure hope these women are okay and will be found very soon." She closes a file folder, smiling into the camera as she switches gears. "And up next," she says with canned excitement, "we'll have last night's winning lottery numbers!"

The channels flick by again, returning to the evangelical station. The blistering minister has passed the torch to a younger brown-haired version of himself and taken a seat at the side of the stage. The spirited young man basks in the white lights, bellowing through another fiery section of Jonathan Edwards's sermon, *Sinners in the Hands of an Angry God.*

The old parlor floor creaks beneath rustling newspapers. A moment later, the cereal bowl clangs into the kitchen sink. A hissing faucet sprays cloudy water over the dish as guttural flatulence rips through the room.

From the blaring television, the young pastor barks another warning to his massive assembly of followers. "At any moment God shall permit him, Satan stands ready to fall upon the wicked!" he yells, wrenching the neck of an invisible sinner. "And seize them as his own!"

SIXTEEN

ZEKE'S FOREARMS QUAKE, as though he were handling a jackhammer rather than the loaded grocery cart with a deviant front wheel. Several clusters of cars are dispersed throughout the parking lot, making it appear more crowded than it actually is. In another hour or two, the store will be jammed with impatient city slickers popping in for a few things on their way home. Thankfully, he'll be gone by then. Ron had better not ask him to stay late today. He has work waiting for him at home. And she might already be awake.

As Zeke reaches the start of the last row, he checks back over his shoulder, realizing the lady is no longer with him.

HONK-HONK!

His head whips over to the store entrance where his very pregnant customer has paused in the middle of the crosswalk to examine her lengthy receipt. A low-riding muscle car leaking marijuana smoke and angry rap music is not pleased.

"Let's go!" a scratchy male voice shouts from his extremely reclined seat.

"Hey," the appalled woman snaps back. "Pipe down!" She shoves the receipt in her purse as she waddles across the walkway, scowling at the car. *I mean, c'mon*, she mouths to the tinted windshield, tapping her gigantic belly, *I'm going as fast as I can!*

The revving engine replies to the woman. And, as she reaches the other side of the crosswalk, the car peels off, leaving a puff of gray exhaust hovering in the parking lot.

She wafts smoke away from her face, continuing toward Zeke. "I'm comin'!" she shouts with a wave. "I'm in the white Corolla down that row."

As Zeke approaches the four-door compact at the end of the aisle, its clicking trunk pops open a couple of inches. He wrestles the unwieldy grocery cart to a stop against the car's bumper, raising the trunk lid. Inside, the rear wall has been lowered, and an ocean of stuffed Bed Bath & Beyond bags flows into the backseat. As Zeke unloads the groceries, the cart shifts, starting to roll off.

"It's gettin' away from you!" the woman warns from behind him. "And, hey, if you see the box of Fiddle Faddle, can you set that aside for me?"

Zeke yanks the cart back into place. Wedging the tip of his shoe behind its wheel, he goes back to work. He nods absently to the customer, checking the bags in the trunk for the blue box of butter-toffee-flavored popcorn. As she totters past him toward the driver-side door, he sets the box in the child seat of the cart.

"Now, why did they have to get so close?" she scoffs, eyeing the adjacent pickup truck. "This would be tight if I *wasn't* pregnant."

The woman snags a few dollar bills from her purse and opens her door. After tossing the bag over to the passenger seat, she returns to Zeke.

"Thank you, sir. This is for you," she chirps, passing him the rolled bills. She grins, grabbing the popcorn, as she pats her belly. "And this is for the boy." Hurrying back to her seat, she sinks in behind the wheel. "Goody, goody, goody," she mutters to herself, tearing open her snack.

Zeke crumples the bills with a two-fingered grip as he lifts in the last couple of bags. The lid to a Styrofoam carton shifts open, and several free-range eggs start to live up to their name. He leans into the trunk, gathering them. As he replaces the eggs in their container, he sees one is missing.

"How's it goin' back there?" the snacking lady garbles, plunging her hand into the box of popcorn.

"Fine," he responds, scanning the plastic piles.

He spots it. The egg has somehow made it all the way up to the seam of the rear passenger door. It's perched there, ready to plunge out to the ground as soon as the door is opened. Zeke grunts as he hunches further into the packed trunk. Clinging to a side-panel wall for leverage, he stretches his left hand toward the egg, twisting his head to the side to extend his reach.

A flash of red hair catches his eye.

That flirtatious hair flip is familiar. Cindy, the redheaded Checker of the Month, sits, intertwined with some guy, in the neighboring car. The couple hasn't noticed the pregnant woman and her heaps of groceries or Zeke. In fact, their passionate kissing has them oblivious to the world outside of their front seat.

Zeke follows Cindy's hand as it moves up the tattered leg of the guy's cargo shorts. She forces his head back with another kiss, causing his Lehigh Mountain Hawks cap to slide off and drop into the backseat. Zeke watches it land next to a half-dressed baby doll in a stained car seat. He stares into the dead gaze of the doll's marble eyes.

As Cindy's teasing giggle rises in the car, he hears his own voice whispering, "Whore. You little whore." The word echoes in his mind, growing louder and angrier.

And, suddenly, he's six years old again, racing a scratched up Hot Wheels car through the dirt.

———————

Strips of the sweltering August sunlight seep through the splintered boards of the playhouse wall. The beams stretch across Zeke's five-year-old sister, Faith, creating a jailhouse effect over her sweaty body. She sits, sprawled, in the center of the crude fort, tying a ragged cloth around the neck of her glass-eyed doll. Faith's tiny tongue dabs at her cheek in concentration as a string of drool trickles down, moistening her grubby T-shirt.

Across from her, Zeke wipes away a bead of sweat from above his eye as he gets back to his game. His lips vibrate with the revving engine of a speckled red sports car at the start of his freshly drawn racetrack. "On your mark . . . get set," he mumbles to himself, "go!" He lunges forward, ripping the tiny vehicle through the dusty course.

And, as the car sputters around a bumpy corner and lines up for the final stretch to the finish line, Faith ruins everything.

Reaching for a broken hairbrush, his sister has inadvertently brushed her foot over the dirt-floor speedway. Zeke gasps, noticing the bottom of her foot. The race screeches to an emergency halt.

"Hey," he complains, shoving her leg. "Look what you did!"

He assesses the damaged road and decides to create another track; the race must go on. As he starts to design a detoured route, he notices tiny chips of red paint on his fingers. Sitting back on his heels, he concentrates on picking at them. A couple of specks flit down, landing on his filthy shorts. The red bits seem to be multiplying. As he brushes a line of sweat from his shirtless belly, more fragments of the veneer smear across his skin.

After a moment, Zeke grows bored with the cleanup job. He goes back to his game where the race car is plowing along that destroyed track. There's no time to fix it; the driver's gonna have to jump. With an explosive sound effect, he rockets the die-cast car over the dangerous break in the road, flinging it into a plastic milk crate on the other side of the playhouse.

His sister's grunting grabs his attention, calling him away from the raceway. He scoots over next to her to investigate. She's gotten the brush entangled in her doll's ratty hair, and she is struggling to rip it free.

Zeke reaches out to help, but Faith pulls away. "Nooo!"

Her high-pitched voice pings off the boards above them, and even though he's not sure if it was loud enough for their mother to hear, Zeke backs away. He listens for movement outside the fort. There's nothing but a couple of old crows squawking from the neighboring cornfield.

She's not coming. Everything's okay.

A plan for a new game pops into his head, sending him crawling to the milk crate. "Hey, you're sick today," he says, digging to the bottom. "'Kay? And I'm the doctor."

Faith ignores him, still consumed with her doll's matted mess. She has its body wedged between her thighs and is tugging at the tangled knot of wax hair.

"Hey, I'm the doctor, 'kay?" He spots the toy he's been looking for.

"No, because I have to fix Sharon-Beth's hair," Faith explains. Finally yanking the brush free along with a small clump of synthetic strands, she pops off the cap of a brown marker. "Has to be ready for church," she says, coloring the doll's plastic blonde hair.

Zeke pulls on a flimsy tube, drawing a toy stethoscope from the milk crate. The rubber medical kit was a treasure he secretly took from a Christmas donation box last year. When he realized the carrying case was too big to hide, he just snagged a couple of items from inside, leaving the rest of the kit behind some bushes in the school parking lot. He slides the stethoscope around his neck, grabs a plastic doctor's hammer, and wriggles over to his sister.

"You might have a fever or the measles," he says. "So, you need a checkup."

Faith concedes, adjusting herself onto her belly, as she applies more layers to her makeshift dye job. "What's measles?"

"A disease." Zeke slides the rubber toy under her T-shirt, moving the chest piece down the trail of sweat on her back. "Might die if you catch it."

"Don't, Zeet," Faith says, swapping her K for a T, as usual. "That hurts." She plucks the neckline of her T-shirt away from her throat and goes back to Sharon-Beth.

"Hey, take your shirt off," he says, flipping it up her back.

She sighs at the interruption but sits up, pulling the soiled shirt off. She tosses it aside as she flops back down to continue her work on the doll. Zeke skims the device down her spine. He stops at the top edge of her flowery panties, getting an idea for a new procedure. Trading his stethoscope for the tiny reflex hammer, he begins tapping her buttocks.

"'Kay, I gotta see if it's the measles," he says, wedging the tip of the hammer beneath the elastic waistline and snapping it against her skin. "Take this off, too."

"*Owww*," she exaggerates, whining a bit too loudly. "*Stoo000p.*"

As she moistens the marker's tip with her tongue and adds another coat to the doll's hair, Zeke tries again. "You can be the doctor next, 'kay?"

"I don't wanna," she mumbles, noticing the brown streaks she's gotten on her fingers. "Uh-oh."

"Well then, you might die soon and maybe go to hell."

Faith's head jerks to him, searching Zeke's eyes, as worry spreads across her face. "No, I'm not, Zeet," she whispers, bobbling to her feet. Still holding her doll, she slides down her briefs. "I'm not going to hell."

Zeke stands with his back to the door, studying her body. "Turn around in a circle," he says.

It's mostly the same as his, except that her private part is missing. As she completes the turn, he drops his shorts to his knees, beginning his own rotation, but his briefs trip him up, hurling him forward. He stops a few feet from his sister.

"Okay," he says, regaining his balance. "Now, it's your turn." He kicks the stethoscope to her and puffs out his belly. "Check if I have the measles."

The fort's wooden door rips open.

The children squeal as blinding midday sunlight floods into the playhouse. Faith staggers backward, dropping her doll. Zeke pivots to face the door.

His mother's grimace is peering in at them. "What are you doing in there?"

A dangerous silence lingers between the children, both too scared to answer. Zeke yanks up his shorts, shuffling backward. As he quickly leans over to snatch his wadded T-shirt from the ground, Faith's naked body is revealed, cowering against the back wall.

"You!" Snakelike eyes lock on the little girl. "You *filthy little whore*." Sylvia drops to her knees, blocking any escape. "Get out here," she snarls, clawing at her children. "You'll not have him, too!"

Terrified screams erupt in the fort. Zeke springs backward, colliding with Faith, his momentum pinning her bare back against a jagged splinter in the wall. She bucks off with a yelp, shoving her brother forward. He cannot stop himself in time. Sylvia's hand whips into the playhouse, latching on to his hair with the quickness of a striking rattler.

"I said, *get out here*," she hisses.

Zeke clings to his sister's tiny hand, pulling her along as he's dragged across the dirt floor. His body clears the opening, but before Faith makes it through, Sylvia slaps his wrist, breaking the children's bond.

She flings Zeke to the ground behind her, spinning back to his sister. As Faith clambers to her feet, her mother's open palm smashes into her face, driving the girl back across the playhouse in a tumble.

"No, not *you*, ya little bitch in heat," Sylvia bites. "You stay in there!"

Zeke scrambles to a stand, eyes trained on the back of his fuming mother. He's never seen her this angry, heaving and growling like an animal. Looking past Sylvia, he finds Faith on her knees, sobbing. The fear in his sister's watery eyes ignites a spark in his chest.

What have we done to make her so mad? What did Faith *do?*

Sylvia slams the wooden door.

Zeke charges. "Don't hurt her."

His clumsy approach gives Sylvia plenty of warning. She whirls around, catching him before he's even taken his second step. Her foot lodges at the center of his chest, sending her son flying off his feet again.

"You shut your mouth, boy!"

Zeke hits the ground, a huff shooting up from his gut. He cannot breathe. He smacks the dirt at his sides, his mouth gulping at the air above his face. As the color begins draining from his lips, he flops to his side, clawing for his mother.

Suddenly, his diaphragm releases. Slurping up the air, he

continues over to his belly, lurching up onto his knees. A scraping hiss coming from behind Zeke drives him to his feet, still heaving. Checking over his shoulder, he scurries up the back porch stairs, confused by what he sees. He doesn't know why his mother is raking a cinder block through the dirt, but it scares him nonetheless.

Although Sylvia has one foot wedged against the playhouse door, it bucks open slightly, revealing half of his sister's face in the gap. She locks eyes with Zeke for a moment. His breath catches in his throat as he teeters on the edge of the top step, wanting to help but too petrified to move.

"Get in the house, boy!" Sylvia hollers.

As she hurls the cement block against the wooden slats, the playhouse door snaps shut. Faith's eyes are gone. And, with a pounding stomp to the huge brick, sinking it into the ground, so is any chance of her escape.

"Please don't," Zeke bleats.

A mound of rocky dirt whizzes by his head.

"I said, get. NOW!"

Zeke breaks into a heaving sob, bolting into the house. He trips on the doorframe's bottom ledge. As he crashes through the partially open back door, driving its knob through the wood-paneled wall behind it, he hears Sylvia begin to scream. He doesn't wait to learn why. Scampering through the kitchen, he rounds the corner and flies down the long hallway. He bursts into his room, flinging the door closed behind him so hard that it doesn't latch. And, as he dives onto the squeaky twin-size bed, bawling into a pillow, Sylvia's voice booms from outside the window.

The back door slams, rattling the walls of the house.

Zeke bolts upright, eyeing the flimsy windowpanes. He listens for his mother's voice, but it's gone. There's only the distant squalling from his little sister.

The only thing more frightening than knowing Sylvia is close by is *not* knowing where she is at all.

Minding the whiny springs of the same mattress his mother slept on as a child, he slowly eases off the bed. As he tiptoes to the window, he notices the floor trembling under his feet.

Where is she?

Zeke freezes, realizing Sylvia is raging up the hallway toward his room. Her furious panting grows louder with each shudder of the floorboards. He spins to the bedroom door that is standing wide open. Panic hurls him toward it, but just as his hand touches the knob, he stills. It's too late; she's seen him. Zeke clings to the rickety handle, waiting for the blow.

But Sylvia rushes by him without stopping, a hissing blur of black fabric and frenzied hair escaping from its bun. Still clutching the knob, Zeke steps forward, peeking around the corner in amazement. As she disappears into his grandfather's old bedroom, slamming the door, he quickly ducks back inside. He checks that the latch catches this time and scurries across the room, wondering how it is possible he has just avoided the wrath of his mother.

FAITH!

Zeke can hear her through the window although her screaming has dissolved into a pulsing whimper. He pushes back a striped bedsheet that covers the glass, staring out at the small wooden shack in the backyard.

She's still locked inside there.

With his mother securely in her room, a flash of bravery takes over. Zeke presses his tiny hands against the bottom row of panes, lifting the window. It opens less than an inch before stopping. He eyes the sawed-off broom handle Sylvia placed in the top half of the frame for security. He considers sneaking out the door but is too afraid she might hear him on the creaky hallway floor.

As he watches helplessly through the glass, his mother's voice rises in the next room. "You ruined *one* already! Tempting that man until he favored only you and no longer wanted his *wife*. Succubus!"

Something heavy clunks to the floor.

Zeke jumps, dropping the sheet over the window. He focuses on a nail in the wall, paralyzed by a kind of rage in his mother's voice that he's never heard.

"You turned him away. *He* was too weak, and you turned his eye away from me!" Sylvia wails. *"Watch and pray that ye enter not into temptation. The spirit indeed is willing, but the flesh is weak!"*

As her voice trails off, Zeke hurries over, pressing his ear against the wall. *Is she crying?* He's never heard his mother so much as sniffle, let alone weep like this.

"But *I* am not too weak!"

Her bedroom door flies open.

Zeke spins around, backing against the wall as he inches away. Reaching the window, he slumps to the floor, eyeballing the door. He knew he hadn't escaped. Tears begin to blur his vision. His mother will be bursting into his room at any second now.

Sylvia's footsteps stomp past his door again. *"Put on the whole armor of God,"* she roars. *"That ye may be able to stand against the wiles of the devil!"*

As her voice echoes down the hallway, Zeke wipes his eyes.

He hears drawers being emptied in the kitchen, forks and spoons clattering across the floor. The windowpanes quiver as the back door opens and slams shut again. Zeke jumps to his feet, shoving the sheet aside, and peers into the yard. He cannot see his mother but knows she has to be out there somewhere. As Faith's sobbing rises again, he sees movement on the far side of the playhouse.

There she is.

Zeke spots the rippling black fabric first, and although he can't see the rest of her, he immediately recognizes Sylvia's dress. She's crouched at the far corner of the fort, peeking in through a space between the boards, watching her daughter. He presses his face against the window, smudging the glass with his wet cheeks, as he strains to see what she is doing.

Two cone-shaped horns rise from behind the playhouse.

Zeke jerks back from the window, unsure of what he is seeing. An angry face floats up from beneath the cones, but it's not a person's face.

It's . . . a mask.

The front of some kind of sack has been painted with stripes circling two gashes in the cloth to create a set of devilish eyes. A hole has been torn for a mouth, too.

Strands of his mother's dirty-blonde hair flicker at the base of the sackcloth, but he has never seen this person before. Zeke can't move. Clutching a handful of the striped sheet, he watches Sylvia round the little shack, panting as she goes. She reaches the far side again, and jerking to a stop, she slowly lifts her gaze.

The cloth's jagged mouth begins to move. *"The rod and reproof give wisdom: but a child left to itself bringeth its mother to shame."*

Sylvia heaves a large metal can from behind the playhouse. She swings it onto the boarded roof, ripping off its lid. "Whore! You'll not corrupt *another* man in this house with your wicked tempting," she bellows, eyeing her little girl through a crack. "You'll not have your brother, too!"

She shoves the container to its side, spilling gasoline across the top of the shack. As fuel streams down through the slats, Faith huddles in a corner, pressing her face into a tiny space between two boards. She spots Zeke at the bedroom window.

"ZEEEEET!"

He rushes forward, his heart pounding as he hears her muffled howl. In a sort of desperate tantrum, he yanks down his balled fist, ripping the sheet from the wall as his other hand slaps at the windowpane. "Don't hurt her!"

Sylvia notices the commotion at the window, whipping her head toward the house, as she sprinkles out the last of the gas. Zeke is unable to look away from the terrifying mask.

She tosses the tin can aside, and with a slow wag of her head, she addresses her son. *"The daughter,"* Sylvia snaps, fidgeting with something at her side, *"if she profane herself by playing the whore, she profaneth her father. And she shall be burnt with fire!"*

A tiny spark flashes. And, before Zeke realizes what she is doing, his mother flings a lit match through the air.

BOOM!

The playhouse explodes in an enormous fiery ball, shaking the house and hurling Sylvia to the ground behind it.

As she disappears, Zeke screams, pounding at the window, "Don't you do that to Faith!"

He hears his sister's frantic pleas burst into a coughing frenzy as thick black smoke floods in through the walls of the fort.

"Please don't hurt her!" He smacks the glass again, cracking it. A thin line of blood appears from the slice in his palm, but he doesn't notice. "Don't," he wails, slapping his bleeding hand against the pane. "DON'T KILL FAITH!"

Baring her teeth like a rabid coyote, Sylvia crawls around the side of the burning playhouse, gaze locked on him. Studying the savage face on the mask and the rage in the eyes behind it, Zeke's voice abandons him. His legs begin to quake, a warning of what he knows is coming. He clamps them together, but it's too late; the warmth is already trickling past his knees. He considers the fresh puddle forming at his feet but can't move.

When Zeke looks up again, scanning the murky yard, his mother is gone. Above the burning wood, he follows black plumes as they drift toward their neighbor's place a few miles down the road. He can see a dark cloud hovering at the back of the farm where Mr. Jordan is burning his trash. And, from a distant state of numb isolation, Zeke watches the separate ribbons of smoke from two very different fires dissolve into the blue sky.

———————

The Corolla's beeping horn startles Zeke back into the Buy-and-Save parking lot. He smacks his head against the trunk's lid, grumbling as he shoves the crumpled cash into his front pocket. He returns the rogue egg to its carton, gritting his teeth at the back of the customer's curly brown pixie cut.

The bodies stir in the neighboring car.

Cindy's glaring right at Zeke. Her eyes dart down to his hand, still buried in his pocket, and then over to her companion. As she whispers something in his ear, the guy cranes his neck around, spotting Zeke.

"You almost done back there, sir?" the perky customer asks.

Zeke doesn't respond. Distracted by the commotion in the next car, he slowly pulls his hand from his pocket. The driver's seat pops forward.

"Hey. Probably TMI"—the pregnant woman smirks—"but I'm gonna need to pee again soon, sir." She attempts to twist toward the rear of the car, but her belly catches on the steering wheel. "Hello?" she grunts, palming the rearview mirror instead.

"Yeah, I'm done," he mumbles, closing the trunk. "Have a nice day, ma'am."

Zeke snags the grocery cart and starts back toward the store as Cindy's friend flings his door open.

"Hey!" the guy barks, springing from his car. "I'm talking to you."

Continuing up the aisle, Zeke hears the Corolla's beeping horn and realizes it must have just missed hitting the guy.

"Watch where you're going," the woman scolds. "I almost ran right—"

"Yo, grandpa!" the guy yells.

He is closer now. Zeke strides through the parking lot, as though he didn't hear him, but the man is not backing off.

"Jim, don't," Cindy says as footsteps patter a little closer.

Zeke sees the guy approaching in the reflection of a car's rear window on his right. "What do you want?" he murmurs, spinning around.

A grimace spreads across Zeke's face as he takes in the guy, who is much bigger than he seemed to be when he was reclined in the car. He is at least six feet tall and more than two hundred pounds of what looks like steroid-built muscles.

Stunned by the quickness of Zeke's pivot, the red-faced block of a man stumbles backward, adjusting his cap. "The fuck you think you're doin'?"

"Just let him go," Cindy pleads, straightening her disheveled shirt. "He's harmless." She grabs Jim's arm, pulling him around to face her. "Please?"

"He's a fucking perv, is what he is. Just watching us with his hand down his pants." Jim jerks away, turning back to Zeke, who has already moved several cars away. "Hey!" he roars, stomping after him again. "I'm talkin' to you, motherfucker! I'm gonna—"

Zeke stops, peering back over his shoulder. *"For God hath not given us the spirit of fear,"* he mumbles, turning to his adversary, *"but of power."*

"Jim!" Cindy shrieks, snagging the back of the man's T-shirt. He stops but doesn't look back. "LET. IT. GO," she orders. "I still have twenty minutes, okay?"

"Fine," he concedes, still eyeing Zeke. "If I see your old ass again though—"

Cindy pulls his face around to hers. "We weren't done, right?" He starts to speak, but she presses her finger against his lips. "Shh. Come on. Forget about him, okay?" As she steers his giant head down into a kiss, Cindy covertly peeks past his shoulder.

Zeke starts to turn but pauses, locking eyes with her. *"Watch ye therefore,"* he mutters, *"for ye know not when the master of the house cometh."*

SEVENTEEN

DANI'S EYEBALLS TREMBLE beneath their dormant lids. Her left pinkie finger flinches, as though it weren't connected to the rest of her hand. She shifts to one side, trying to escape the pounding pressure at her temples that feels like she's dived too deeply into a pool. And, as her leg spasms, kicking out like a branded calf, she forces her eyes to open.

Blurry colors swirl together in front of her face. The room appears to be spinning. She inhales a labored breath, wincing at an excruciating pain raking across her chest. The coppery taste of blood lingers at the back of her mouth. She feels the sensation of being whirled around in a giant cotton candy machine, moaning as she squeezes her eyes shut again.

Bits of familiar moments flood her mind, flicking away before she can fully process them. She flattens her palms against the floor of the Plexiglas box, fighting back the urge to vomit as she concentrates.

A beautiful black man's smile. He's laughing over a plate of pasta, and there's wine. I like him. There are flowers, a hug. Is this a date?

FLASH.

A chubby old guy in a tight suit taps a picture frame on a wall. He undresses me with his shifty eyes. His name is . . . Frank? Yes, from the office. It's Frank. He's gross.

FLASH.

Biting into a chocolate ice cream cone. Nutty bits scatter. The stupid car won't start. What is that yellow Lego-looking thing? I'm reaching for the tiny block sitting on the dashboard.

FLASH.

THE GOAT HORNS!

Dani bolts up, smashing her forehead into the box's lid and the reality that she's not dreaming. Collapsing again, she wiggles her fingers around the container like a blind woman, her eyes watering. She grazes over her breast, rediscovering the gown. As she tugs it away from her body, a mound of bloodied gauze rips at her flesh. She winces with another deep groan. And, as she explores the wound, her mind begins to sober, recalling every savage detail of the hooded man.

A primal howl works its way up from Dani's belly, echoing so loudly in the box that she's not sure it belongs to her. She whacks at the lid in a wild tantrum of slapping and kicking. The cover shifts upward the same inch or so with each blow but falls right back into place.

There is a jangling sound as the lid drops again. She stops pounding, wiping away the breathy fog from the wall to her left.

Dani spots a wobbling pewter padlock. Claustrophobia invades the coffinlike container as she hammers at the lid, flailing like an unbridled shock-therapy patient. "Help me! Please, somebody," she heaves, "get me out! *PLEEAASE!*"

Her raspy screams trigger a reflex, and she bursts into a hacking frenzy. She braces herself against the lid, trying to steer her mind to just one thought—breathe. Her face contorts as she snaps her mouth shut, forcing herself to inhale through her nose. Eyes closed and lips clamped, Dani hovers at the cusp of unconsciousness.

Just breathe, she repeats in her head. *In, two, three. Out, two, three, four.*

With slow, deliberate inhales, she lies still, inching her way back to relative composure. *How can this be happening?*

The sour odor of what she thinks is puke opens Dani's eyes. The box is disgusting. An oily film coats the lid just inches above her face. As she squirms, her sweaty arms slip across a wet surface, leaving brownish streaks on the walls. Staring at the dark smudges, she realizes it isn't vomit she smells; it's rotting blood.

She commits herself to the fight, swallowing back a wave of panic. *I have to get out of here. I can get away if I just get out of this case.* She blinks through her welling tears, walking herself toward calmness. *Now, figure out how.* She presses her face against the dingy Plexiglas surface, scanning the shadows of the room for anything that might help her escape.

She notices a flickering light waving from beyond her feet and tries to lean toward it. The container is too tight for her body to fully bend in any direction.

Breathe, she reminds herself, feeling another meltdown bubbling in her mind.

Using her bare soles, she smears away the grime on the surface at her feet, spotting what looks like a wooden table sitting just outside. Rows of dancing flames cover its surface.

To the right, parallel to her, another table butts against a dark wall. This one is much longer, stacked with several glass containers of various sizes. The lighting is very dim, but she thinks there's movement in some of them.

Closing one eye, Dani tilts toward the wall. *What's in there?*

A popping sound shatters her focus.

She diagonally whips her head up toward the noise coming from behind her. As her vision filters through the filthy wall and shadows outside the box, Dani jumps. A set of glowing orange eyes floats between two gnarly horns. She quickly covers her mouth, stifling a scream.

She strains for a better view of the hood, trying to detect movement, but it is still. As she steadies her breathing again, it occurs to her that it could just be hanging from a hook, watching over her like some kind of demonic sentinel.

Several feet to the right of the hood, Dani notices a faint pulsing of light. She wipes at the Plexiglas, revealing a single clear bulb poking out from another wall. Glowing with the power level of a dying lightning bug, the bulb seems pointless in the cavelike darkness.

Is it a cave?

Her gaze continues past the light to what appears to be some kind of stairs. Three warped slats of wood lead up into blackness.

Dani's heart starts to race. *A way out!*

There's another cracking noise. She jerks her head back, discovering she was wrong about the hood.

Watching the terrifying eyes glide out of the shadows, tilting upward to uncover part of the man's creviced face, a tiny hum vibrates in her chest.

"Please don't hurt me," she whispers.

Zeke meanders by the box. *"Now the works of the flesh are manifest, which are these;"* he says, as though the weeping body trapped beside him were not there. *"Adultery, fornication, uncleanness, lasciviousness, idolatry, witchcraft, hatred, variance, emulations, wrath, strife, seditions, heresies, envyings, murders, drunkenness, revellings, and such like.*" Reaching the table at Dani's feet, he rattles a box of wooden matches. *"As I have also told you in time past, that they which do such things shall not inherit the kingdom of God."*

As a stick flares up, he lights some candles, mumbling something she can't make out.

I can't believe this is real. Until this very moment, she's been focused on getting out of the box, feeling, if she could just do that, then she would have a chance. As Dani watches the hood, listening to the strange words he is saying, doubts flood into her mind. *Even if I can break out of this container, I'll still have to face that lunatic.*

Zeke glances over his shoulder, shaking his head, as if warning her, as if he somehow heard Dani's thoughts. Dropping the matches on the table, he wanders back alongside her, drumming his fingers against the side of the box. *"When the Lord thy God shall bring thee into the land whither thou goest to possess it, and hath cast out many nations before thee . . ."*

"What——" Dani's throat tightens as she tries to speak, allowing the slightest whimper to escape.

Zeke notices her sound. As he pauses at her head, his eyes flit around her body, like a foraging rodent, finally landing on her chest. His tongue smashes between his serrated teeth as he grins at the soiled patch of gauze.

"Hittites!" he hisses, slapping the lid just above her face.

Dani's voice booms back into her as she roars toward the stairs. "Help me! Please, some—"

Zeke pounds the lid, silencing her. *"Neither shalt thou make marriages with them; thy daughter thou shalt not give unto his son, nor his daughter shalt thou take unto thy son. For they will turn away thy son from following me, that they may serve other gods: so will the anger of the Lord be kindled against you!"* he yells, dashing away. *"And destroy thee suddenly!"*

Dani jerks her body to her side, trying to follow where he's gone, but her shoulders catch. She has no idea what that crazy bastard just said to her or if he was even talking to her, but she definitely doesn't want him out of her sight.

Where is he?

She pushes herself harder against the lid, squeezing her arms inward as she turns. *Shit!*

Her body is jammed too tightly between the two surfaces. She can't move any more in either direction. Now stuck on her side, she faces the rickety staircase, a wave of hysteria surging through her. She kicks her legs back and forth, screaming and huffing, but the lid barely shifts.

PUSH! She lurches her torso forward, popping the cover up again.

As she folds her shoulders further into herself, her skin drags along the dirty lid, whining like a squeegee. With another push, momentum rotates her forward, flopping her into a facedown position. She peers into a rusty grate in the ground beneath her body as her breath fogs the acrylic surface.

"Somebody, please help—"

A piercing shriek cuts her off. She thinks the sound came from the direction Zeke went. As Dani directs her face up to the shadows, she makes out an opening or a doorway a few yards away. Old pipes moan into a series of staccato thumps from the darkness beyond.

Another room is back there. A laundry room or maybe a bathroom? She racks her brain for all the possible weapons she might find. *Or maybe there's a window. Even better.*

She holds her breath, listening for more clues.

Suddenly, a rising *whoosh* breaks Dani's concentration as a torrent of frigid water pounds against the back of her head. The force of the surge smashes her forehead into the floor of the box.

"Nooo," she groans, a prickling sting already spreading out

from her nose.

She lobs her hands against the opening halfway up the wall, but the pressure shoots her fingers backward, flinging her hands aside as the stream floods the box. Water moves into Dani's nostrils. She bucks up, jerking her head to the side. Guzzling a mouthful of air, she drops her body down into the water and attempts to flip back over. Her shoulders snag against the lid again, panic blasting through her mind. Caught on her side, she gulps for air like a river-banked salmon flopping about, trying to dislodge herself. She can't break free.

And, from the corner of her eye, Dani spots him standing above her head.

Zeke steps up to the top of the box, peering at the side of her upside-down face. *"He that believeth and is baptized shall be saved; but he that believeth not shall be damned."*

Dani throws her elbow against the lid, wishing so strongly it would shatter through and collide with Zeke's horrible face. "Let me outta here, you crazy fucker!"

"Every idle word that men shall speak, they shall give account thereof in the day of judgment!" Zeke barks, slapping the sides of the box.

As the waterline rises to the left side of her face, Dani's top leg begins to bob. She purses her lips, inadvertently slurping a splash of filthy water into her mouth. The side of her head crashes into the lid as she thrusts her face up out of the water, erupting with a spitting cough.

Zeke flattens his hands on the cover of the container. "I baptize you in the name of the Father, the Son," he bellows, "and the Holy Spirit!" His eyes roll back in his head as spit rockets above the box's lid. His tongue flutters outside his mouth.

And, while Dani thrashes like a hurricane inside the flooding box, Zeke's possessed words sputter across the—

Bing-bong!

The hollow gong of an old doorbell echoes from somewhere above them, snapping Zeke out of his trance. He throws the hood back, rushing to the base of the stairs.

Dani didn't hear the bell over the sloshing water, but she does notice Zeke storming off. She wipes at the Plexiglas, trying to follow him in the shadows. The box is too dirty; she can't see where he is.

Where'd he go? Stilling herself, she carefully scans the wall near the stairs. *There he is!*

Perched on the lowest step, Zeke stares up into the darkness as the metal bells collide again. *Bing-bong!*

He bolts from the stairs, muttering furiously as he flies into the second room. With a loud yelp, the gushing water stops.

Dani heard the sound this time. And, judging by Zeke's frantic reaction, the visitor upstairs is a surprise.

"Help me!" Dani pleads, pounding against the side of the box. "I'm here—"

"QUIET!" Zeke bites, slapping the lid. "Quiet, quiet, quiet!" Rushing to the table at her feet, he extinguishes the candles.

Bing-bong! Bing-bong! Bing-bong! Bing-bong!

As Zeke races up the creaky staircase, Dani braces herself on a raised elbow, smashing her mouth toward an airhole at the top of the box. And, under the echoing doorbell, she wails with all the voice she's got left, "HE'S GONNA KILL ME!"

EIGHTEEN

THE HEAVY DOOR flies open, rattling windowpanes throughout the entire house. Zeke stomps out on the porch, startling a keg of Brewer's blackbirds into flight in the neighboring field. He locks eyes with a bearded man in a worn pair of tan camouflage coveralls.

"Oh, shit!" the guy yelps, taking in Zeke's angry face. He shuffles backward, latching on to the banister to keep from tumbling to the ground.

"What is it?" Zeke grumbles.

"Uh . . . well, I—"

Dani's muted scream seeps out through the front door.

The guy stares into the gap. "Uh, is everything okay in there?"

"It's the TV," Zeke answers, stepping into the man's eyeline. He tugs the knob, pulling the door almost completely closed, and moves back to the center of the porch. "Watching a movie."

"Oh, damn." He chuckles. "Sounds like a wild one."

"What do you want?"

The man relaxes his grip on the railing, easing into a lean, as he smiles through his embarrassment. "Oh, well . . . we, uh . . . my brother and me," he says, flipping his head out toward the front yard, "were wondering about your van." He extends his hand. "Name's Joe, and that's Wes."

Zeke's gaze whips to a second person he didn't notice. A bald man, wearing a bright orange camouflage hunter's bib, has his face pressed against the van's rear window.

Zeke sizes up the bearded guy again, slowly stepping toward him. "What about it?"

"Well, I'd have called you, but there's no number on the sign," Joe offers. "And I stopped by last week, but I guess you weren't home—"

"So, how much you want for it?" Wes shouts from the yard.

One of the back doors swings open, banging against the side of the van before the man can catch it.

"Shit. Sorry about that," he calls out over his shoulder. "Prolly need to tighten up this hinge a bit or maybe even replace it."

"Hey!" Zeke springs past Joe, skipping the last three steps as he charges across the yard.

Distracted by something inside the van, Wes doesn't see him coming. He cranes in a bit further, tugging at a tattered blanket folded beneath a toolbox. "These ropes hanging from all the corners back here in the cargo will be perfect," Wes says. "Ruthie's gonna need—"

"Don't!" Zeke yanks the open door, pulling it shut, as he rounds the back of the van.

Wes is gone.

Zeke peeks into the rear window, noting the swinging rope, and scoffs. *I'm not done with the one downstairs.* And, because these idiots interrupted him, he'll have to start the ceremony all over. He has to work the mid-afternoon shift at the store today, too. "I don't have time for this," he grumbles to himself, remembering the clock in the foyer showed it was already twenty of twelve.

"Hey, what year is it?" Wes has appeared through the windshield. He is stretching across the hood, attempting to raise it.

Zeke swings around the opposite side of the van, fuming. "It's not for sale anymore."

As he reaches the front, Zeke finds that Joe has joined them and is discussing what a good offer might be.

"Listen, my wife's doing this cookie-company type thing," Wes drawls, brushing a hand over his stubbly scalp. "You know, like baking up cookies and brownies and stuff—"

"She does these little key lime bites," Joe interjects as he pulls out a Skoal tin and takes a dip. "I'm telling you what . . . them things are outta this world."

"Yeah, those are *real* good," Wes continues, hooking his thumbs under his bib's elastic suspenders. "Anyway, this van would be perfect for her to do her deliveries and whatnot. Now, what'd you say you wanted for it?"

"I didn't," Zeke snaps, maneuvering his body between the men and his house. "Somebody already bought it. This morning."

Wes checks in with his brother, disappointment registering on both their faces. "Really?" He pops his suspenders in frustration. "Well, damn the bad luck."

"No shit?" Joe huffs. "I knew we shoulda come by last night."

An awkward silence hangs in the air as they all stare at the van, waiting for someone to speak.

They have to go. Now.

"Well, uh . . . all right then," Joe says with a shrug. "Thanks anyway, I guess."

"Hey, they pay you yet?" Wes asks. "'Cause I got cash I could give you right now."

Zeke slowly shakes his head as both an answer and a warning. "I said, it's not for sale."

"All right, man." Wes gives up. "Well, listen, let me know if you change your mind," he says, tapping the hood. "'Cause she's perfect for what I need. We're only down the road, five miles or so, by the way. You know where Herm's Feed Store—"

"Help me!" Dani's scream reaches out to the front yard. It's much clearer this time.

As Wes and Joe quickly check in with each other, Zeke whirls around to face the house. The front door is now fully open. Two young boys race out across the porch, screeching as they jump the banister and tumble down into the side yard.

"Hey, you boys get back in the truck!" Wes shouts. "We're leaving."

Zeke shoots up the stairs, yanking the house's door closed. He spins back around and lumbers to the edge of the porch, scowling, as the kids shuffle into the backseat of a beat-up Chevrolet Suburban.

"*Bye-byyye!*" one of the brats shouts, bursting into a shrill giggle.

Wes meanders behind Joe, still considering Zeke's van, as they both make their way back across the yard.

"There's that station wagon," Joe mentions as they reach their vehicle. "The wood-paneled one in the Donadio's Pizza parking lot. You wanna drive over and check it out?"

"Yeah, I guess we ought to." With a final snap of his suspenders, Wes slides in behind the wheel. "And I gotta get these boys some food, too."

Zeke steps back into the house, closing the front door, and then he gently slides the wicker shade away from the window. The Suburban's engine fires up. The bearded guy pulls down a newspaper from behind his visor and then dials a number on his cell phone. With a quick thumbs-up from Joe, they circle past the van and drive off. Dirt kicks up on the long, bumpy driveway as the truck twists out to the main road.

The wicker shade slides back into place, lining up perfectly with its dusty outline on the wall. Zeke steps away from the window, noticing the door to the foyer closet is slightly open.

"Brats!" he scoffs, stomping over and slapping it shut.

As he starts back down the hallway to the cellar, he quickly glances at the clock again. He freezes.

The arms still point to eleven forty.

Zeke spots the second hand trembling in place like a dying insect. "*What?*"

He hurls himself down a second hall, passing the kitchen entryway. Behind the slamming bathroom door, the old farmhouse's water pipes groan as a showerhead hisses to life.

THE CHEVROLET SPEEDS down the curvy blacktop toward the interstate as Joe circles another ad in his newspaper. He spits a brown glob into a McDonald's cup, glancing over the seat at his snickering nephews. "What's with you, little monkeys?" He grins. "You guys have straight sugar for breakfast?"

"No," a little voice squeals.

"Come on now, boys. Settle down," their dad says, switching lanes. "We're just gonna check out one more, and then we'll get something to eat."

"Actually, this minivan is only half a mile past Donadio's," Joe says. "Maybe we ought to see it, too?"

"Yeah, might as well, I guess. Damn, that van was perfect."

"It was, wasn't it?" He chuckles, folding up his paper.

"Hey, you boys want Burger King or Wendy's?" Wes asks,

merging onto I-80.

"We like both," a boy says.

"Yeah," another voice joins in, chuckling. "We like *both*."

"Well," their dad scoffs, eyeing Joe, "we're not going to both. You guys gotta agree on one or the other."

"Actually, I think it's a Sonic now anyway," Joe offers. "The Burger King across from Donadio's closed down."

"Me and Jason want Wendy's, Dad."

"Okay. And, Jackson, what about you, bud?"

"Hmm," a garbled, cartoony voice replies. "Um, I want Wendy's, too."

The boys burst into an unruly fit of cackling.

Their father adjusts the rearview mirror to see the whole backseat. "Hey. What are you guys doin' back there?"

His boys dive behind the driver's seat, attempting to hide.

Wes nods to his brother. "What are they doing?"

Joe tosses the newspaper on the dashboard. As he cranes his head around, peeking into the backseat, the boys' laughter grows.

"Hey, you guys," he asks, leaning back further to scan the rear bench, "where's Jackson?"

"What?" Wes checks the rearview again.

"Wes, he ain't back there."

"What do you mean, ain't back there?"

"Boys, where is your brother?" Joe asks them again, more urgently. "This ain't funny!"

The Suburban swerves across three lanes, ignoring the assault of angry horns as it slides onto the shoulder. Lurching to a stop, the two men hop out. Wes yanks open the passenger door behind his seat, fracturing the boys' laughter into tiny whimpers as they huddle together.

Joe's head pokes in through the opening rear door. "Not back here, Wes!"

"Where's Jackson?" Wes grabs his oldest son by the arm, wrenching him out of the backseat. "Jason, where is your brother?"

Joe rounds the truck, watching Wes's wild eyes.

And, as the little boy explodes into tears, everyone panics.

Jason chokes out his words, "He was hiding!"

NINETEEN

THE CHIPPED PORCELAIN knob jiggles on the closet door. Jackson can hear it moving, but it's stuck. He knows it was a mistake to hide in here. He can't hear Jason counting anymore, and Justin hasn't squealed either, which is what his brother always does when he gets found.

At first, Jackson felt lucky. He never picks good hiding spots. So, although it was weird that his brother didn't check the closet before shutting the door—*or maybe he did peek in, and I was camouflaged too well behind all the coats*—he is proud of himself. But, now, he can't get out of here.

He listens for voices through the wood panel as he tries the tiny latch again. It slips away, snapping back into place. His fingers are too sweaty to get a good grip. He even tried wiping them on the ribbed wristband of a winter puffer at the other end of the rack. Didn't help.

If Jackson had realized there wasn't an actual knob on this side of the door, he would've picked a different place. He saw two halls leading further into the house, so there must be other rooms he could have hidden in before Jason got to his twentieth Mississippi.

Maybe Justin is nearby. And maybe he can let me out of here without Jason catching us.

He gently taps the closet door. "Justin?"

No response.

Staring at the strip of light beneath the door is making Jackson more nervous by the second, reminding him that he can't get out of this crowded, scary place.

And it stinks like feet in here.

Getting a new idea, he begins rubbing his fingers on his leg as fast as he can. As the friction burn from his jeans becomes too painful, he smashes his thumb against the latch again, grunting.

Open.

OPEN.

Pop!

The closet door shoots open, smacking against the wall.

Jackson tentatively steps out. Flipping his unruly dark hair out of his face, he taps his thick glasses back into place at the top of his nose. Huge brown eyes carefully scan the foyer. His brothers aren't here.

Home base is just outside, he thinks, tiptoeing to the front door, as he imagines himself slapping the bumper of their Suburban. *I might actually win this!*

He snatches the brass knob, giving it a tug, but it doesn't budge. *It's locked?*

Jackson slowly turns around, considering the hallways. If he can't get out, then neither can his brothers. *That means, they're hiding somewhere in here, too.*

Easing back to the center of the entryway, he weighs his three choices. To his left, a long, shadowy hallway leads to a door. Beside the closet on his right, there's a shorter hallway lined with several closed doors. And, in the middle, an archway opens up into a kitchen, he thinks, judging by the tiled countertop and cabinets. He hears a TV from in there somewhere but not his brothers.

"Justin?" he whispers.

No one answers.

Jackson's shaggy head bobs between the options, but he's unable to decide which way to go. The pride he felt just a few moments ago is gone. He planned to go find the boys, claiming his victory, but now, he's getting scared.

Where are they?

He fights the urge to cry, his mind flashing to his brothers and how they called him a chicken for not wanting to follow them into the house.

I am not.

He steps to the shorter hallway, staring at the light at the base of the last door. *I bet they're waiting in one of those rooms, ready to jump out and scare me.*

Remembering that his dad and uncle Joe are not far away brings his confidence back. *I'll show them,* he thinks, starting down the hall. *I'm not a chicken!*

Something moves from behind the first door. There's snorting, sniffing, and toenails tapping across a wood floor.

Jackson stops, trained on the shadow dancing under the door. *A puppy!*

His dad promised the boys a new dog after Brownie died, but they still haven't gotten one. She was a cocker spaniel mix of some kind and was more black than brown, but that was the name the shelter had given her, so it stayed.

"What's your name, doggy?"

As he reaches toward the puffing nose probing along the floor, the dog growls. It claws at the door, snarling a deep grumbled warning. Jackson hears what sounds like an animal much larger than Brownie pacing with excitement.

Did I pick the wrong hall?

Suddenly, a distant wave of applause rises from the kitchen area. He jumps back from the door, spinning to face the foyer. Unsure of what to do next, Jackson moves toward the entryway again, the floor popping beneath his feet. Before he takes his second step, heavy paws pound against the door. He springs forward, rounding the corner, as barking booms from the hallway behind him.

Stopping between an old stove and a row of cabinets, Jackson peers at an open door across the kitchen. The clapping sounds coming from in there are getting louder, making him nervous, but they're definitely not scarier than the dog.

He inches closer to the doorway, stretching his spectacled face into the parlor. His eyes sweep across the messy room, crowded with heaps of clothes and stacks of magazines. Sheets of newspaper scattered over the floor cover most of a shabby carpet.

On the far wall, Jackson discovers the source of the applause. *It's only a show*, he comforts himself, spotting the screen of an old TV where a crowd is furiously cheering for a preacher hollering from behind his podium.

Jackson slinks into the room, whispering for either of his brothers now. "Jason? Justin?"

A door slams from the hallway outside the kitchen.

Jackson whirls toward the noise, inadvertently whipping his glasses from his face at the same time. He fumbles to catch them, but it's too late. As they soar through the air, he darts behind a large upholstered BarcaLounger to his left, panicking. He hates his glasses because the kids at school make fun of how thick the lenses are, but the truth is, he can't see without them. Gazing out across the blurry room, he sinks down beside a couple of magazines, worried about the spanking he's gonna get for losing another pair.

As the quiet outside the kitchen returns, a single thought repeats in his mind, *Find those glasses.*

The TV's applause begins to dissipate, giving Jackson the courage to crawl from behind the chair. Sweeping his hands across the cluttered floor, he anxiously pokes through the clusters of paper. He thought he felt the glasses fly toward the center of the room when he turned, but they could be right in front of him, and he might not even know—

Ooh!

A familiar shape on the floor catches his eye. Even though it's farther away than he expected, he can make out the shape of what he's sure is a pair of black frames. He lunges. Disappointment swells in his belly as his fingers claw at the black-and-white image of a Pearle Vision newspaper ad.

A faint voice calls out from the other side of the room.

Startled, Jackson flops back onto his heels, focusing on the muffled cry. It's not coming from the television. Following the sound, his head slowly turns toward a large, black opening on the other side of the parlor. He hears it again.

Someone's crying. Justin!

He springs up from the floor, starting toward the fuzzy darkness, mumbling his brother's name. As he weaves in between the piles of magazines, his foot slips on shifting paper, pulling him into a stumble across the room.

Crunch!

Jackson's shock is audible. He knows what's happened, even without clear vision. As a whimper grows in his throat, he pulls the broken frames from beneath his foot and slides them onto his face. He can definitely still see through one of the cracked lenses although the view is fractured. A tiny twinge of relief sets in.

Maybe nobody will notice.

A more desperate plea comes from outside the parlor.

Jackson shuffles across the slippery floor toward the sound. Stepping out of the room, he realizes he is now in the longer of the two hallways. The moaning is coming from behind a single door to his right.

"Please help me."

"Justin?" he whispers, inching closer. "Jason, are you guys in there?"

Jackson notices there is not a knob or a handle on the door. Instead, closer to the top of the wooden frame, there's an iron slide. Pressing his ear against the door, he hears the crying more clearly now although it sounds too far away to tell whose voice it is.

What if there's no doorknob inside this closet either?

Stretching up onto his tiptoes, he barely reaches the tiny arm. As he taps the bar through its metal brace, the door pops, opening less than an inch. Jackson peers into the crack, but it's too dark to see anything. The crying has stopped, too.

"Hello?" he asks again.

A door slams from the other side of the house.

Jackson gasps, huddling back against the cellar door. His heart races as he hears the heavy footsteps clod up the hallway outside the kitchen. But what scares him even more is the sound of a jangling collar that seems to be coming with them. Considering the snarls and excited pitter-patter moving into the foyer, something tells Jackson he shouldn't be standing here. He darts toward the parlor as the massive black head of a rottweiler appears from around the corner at the other end of the hall. It's seen him. A thunderous bark explodes from the entryway as Jackson dives out of sight.

"Quiet," Zeke snaps. "Come on."

Dog feet claw across the wood floor as the front door swings open.

"I said, come on!" he shouts, shuffling out of the house.

COMPARED TO THE dull lighting inside the house, the afternoon brightness is blinding. Tossing his backpack and keys onto a large wooden rocking chair on the porch, Zeke closes the front door. He uses one hand to shield his eyes, still latched on to the resistant dog's nape with the other.

"What's wrong with you?" he scolds, dragging it down the stairs and across the front yard. As they pass the cargo van, Zeke attaches a heavy chain to the dog's collar, continuing around the side of the house.

Now completely focused on the sound of food pellets clinking into a metal dish, the rottweiler dances with restless anticipation.

Zeke returns, carrying a plastic tub of water along with a bowl of food. "Here," he mutters, setting down the two dishes. "Crazy—"

HOOONK! HONK-HONK-HONK! HOOONK!

Zeke's eyes rip across the wall of trees in front of his house, locking on the Suburban barreling up the driveway. As he shoots to his feet, the food bowl drops the last inch, spilling a pile of kibble into the patchy grass. He rushes across the front yard, staring at the men through the approaching windshield.

What do they want now?

A dusty cloud puffs up as the vehicle jerks to a stop. Wes flies out.

Zeke glares back at the bald man from the bottom porch step. "I'm late. I don't have time to—"

"Where's my son?" Wes barks, scanning the tree line surrounding the house.

Where's your son? A bewildered look spreads over Zeke's face as he stares at the two young boys peeking out from the backseat window. "What are you talking—"

"My other boy," he interrupts. "They were playing hide-and-seek." He cups his hands around his mouth. "Jackson! Where are you, son?"

Zeke follows the man's eyes to the trees. "I don't know what you're talking about, mister, but you gotta get outta—"

There is a ruckus from the back of the porch.

As Zeke spots the wobbling rocking chair, a mop-headed little boy scurries behind him, springing down the stairs.

There are three of them.

"Daddy!" Immediately bursting into a wailing fit, Jackson clings to his father's legs, slurring something about his glasses. "It was an accident," he snivels.

"What have I told you about wandering off?" Wes snatches up the boy, carting him back to the Suburban. "And what the heck happened to your glasses?" He doesn't wait for an answer as he shoves his son into the backseat and slams the door. "I'm gonna bust your little butt when we get home." Jumping in behind the wheel, Wes says to Zeke, "I'm really sorry about this."

Zeke ignores him, already snatching up his keys. He grabs his backpack and locks the front door. Behind him, the SUV speeds off, the dad's angry voice booming through the windows.

As he fires up his van's engine, Zeke snags the For Sale sign from the dashboard, crumpling it into a ball. He considers the front porch, wondering how he missed the boy hiding behind the chair. His gaze darts to the retreating vehicle in his rearview mirror. *"For in very deed, as the Lord God of Israel liveth, which hath kept me back from hurting thee,"* he says.

Checking the dashboard clock, Zeke shifts the engine into gear and races down the driveway, tossing the paper out his window.

TWENTY

DANI RELEASES HER hold on the airholes in the acrylic walls, sinking down. Her throbbing arms can't take any more.

I have to rest for a second, she thinks, trying to wiggle some blood flow back into her numb fingers.

A tiny wave surprises her, crashing against the side of her face. She clamps her lips shut. Bracing her forearms on the bottom of the box, she juts her chin out of the filthy water, like a turtle in some kid's forgotten bedroom aquarium.

She gazes through the foggy glass at the dim bulb by the stairs. Although it seems like forever ago that she heard a dog barking, Dani has no actual concept of time. She screamed and pounded on the walls for what felt like hours after he left, but she can't be sure.

And there's no telling when he'll be back.

Blowing out her exhaustion, she shakes her head, refocusing.

"You have to get out of this thing, Dani," she coaches herself aloud. "You just HAVE to."

Her eyes water—not from the fiery throbbing in her throat, but because she doesn't recognize her own voice. Her vocal cords have swelled from the wailing she's been doing since she heard the doorbell. The hoarse result is almost inaudible.

She swallows, trying again. "If you're still in here when he comes back . . ." Her voice dissolves into a toneless whisper, and she cracks.

Clawing her fingers back through the airholes, she collapses against a wall, silently crying into her elbow. *I can't.*

Ever since she was eight, she'd talk herself through tough situations. It was something her dad first taught her how to do at a YMCA pool.

She'd begged and pleaded all summer to go off the adult diving board. Finally, one Saturday, her dad said yes. Dani climbed up, tiptoed out to the end of the board, and froze. She was too terrified to jump. It took fifteen minutes to get the other children who'd climbed up behind her safely to the side, so she could come back down. They were all mad—her friends, the lifeguards, even the other parents.

"Such a bratty thing to do," she heard Mrs. Carmichael mumble. "So selfish."

It felt like everyone hated her. Except her dad, who met her at the bottom of the ladder and whisked her away from all the annoyed faces, saying it was perfectly normal to be nervous.

"Here's what I do when I get scared," he whispered, like he was sharing the biggest secret in the universe.

At the time, it amazed Dani that anything scared her dad, but she still hung on his every word.

"I talk to myself," he said. "I call my name out loud, okay? So, I know I have my attention. And then I say, 'Hank, you're amazing, and you can do absolutely anything you put your mind to.' And then, baby girl"—he smiled—"I put my mind to it."

By the end of that summer, the mantra had become an invaluable tool for her, and on the last weekend, she got back up onto the diving board. She talked to herself all the way up the ladder, out across that wobbly plank, and off into the deep end of the pool. She also peed a little bit on the way down, but that would stay between her and her new best friend, *Dani*.

Droplets from her soaked hair tinkle down into the dirty water as she squeezes her burning eyes closed. "Dani," she wheezes, "you're amazing, and you . . . can do . . . ." She eases back onto her forearms, teetering on the brittle surface between her will to fight and a complete mental breakdown.

Can I do it? Can I actually drown myself? The thought is oddly appealing. *I'd rather be dead than endure whatever that sick fuck's gonna do to me.*

Something brushes her jaw, latching on to her bottom lip.

Dani jerks her head to the side, raking her hands across her face. Her eyes spring open, trained on a tangled knot of blonde hair and snakeskin dangling from her fingers.

"Whoa!" she rasps, whipping the sopping clump against the sidewall near her knees.

She squeals through clenched lips, angrily pounding at the lid again–she's going to fight.

As she thrashes about, the foamy water swings back and forth between the Plexiglas sides, spurting through the airholes. A new plan comes to her as she hears the splattering on the cellar floor below. Cupping her palms together, Dani ladles handfuls of water to the quarter-sized opening above her hip. Most of it leaks through her fingers though, running down her arms before she can get it to the opening.

Fuck! She kicks the lid, watching the taunting padlock jiggle outside the box.

Inching her face up to one of the holes, she tries her voice again. "Please . . . somebody . . . help me."

She thought she'd heard another voice a while ago, but she can't be sure she didn't imagine it. As the sloshing settles, she presses her ear as close to the opening as possible, listening for any kind of response. All she can hear is the residual trickle in the grated drain beneath her container. There's nothing coming from upstairs.

Her own hot breath drifts into her face, igniting a flash of claustrophobia. She has to drop back.

Lying half-submerged in the murky water, Dani starts to feel light-headed. *You can breathe*, she reminds herself, staring at the airhole closest to her face. With a slow inhale through her nose, she closes her eyes and pictures the kundalini yoga class she took a few weeks ago. "Just relax."

A tiny brown-skinned man stood at the front of a moist, dark room, his voice almost hypnotic in its monotone drone. "The first chakra, the root chakra, represents our foundation," Metok said. "And it's all about feeling grounded and secure. So, let's all ease into a bridge pose, and with a deep inhale, begin Breath of Fire."

Inside the container, Dani's knees slowly lift out of the water. She concentrates on her rapid, staccato breaths, reenergizing her body. As she mentally works her way up the seven chakras, a sense of sharpened focus clears her mind.

The instructor's kind face pops back into her head.

"You all might be surprised at just how strong you are in this position," he said, guiding the room of yogis into child's pose. "Although balasana is a simple relaxation position, it can also be very active through breath. Incredibly powerful."

Dani's eyes fly open, grateful for that day with Metok and re-charged by the memory. She centers herself with another huge inhale and exhale. As the waves calm down again, she collapses her shoulders inward and rotates her body. This time, with just a slight nudge, her arm squeaks past the lid. She's facing the bottom of the box again, her head just above the waterline.

A splash of the filthy brine smacks against the floor outside, sending a volt of panic through her. She snaps her face toward the staircase, blinking dirty drops from her eyes.

What was that? Is he back? She searches for any movement, but her breath has fogged the walls again. *Is he out there, just watching me?*

She frantically wipes away some of the cloudiness from the side of the box, half-expecting his horrible face to be staring back at her.

He's not there.

Dani tilts her head toward a hole, listening for footsteps or a door or a creaking stair. Hearing nothing but her own labored breathing, she recommits to her plan.

Okay, now . . . just breathe.

Bracing her forearms against the walls for leverage, she slowly drags her knees under her chest. Her body starts to bob with short, explosive puffs as she reaches a panting state.

Focus. Sucking in a huge gulp of air, Dani drops her hands and dunks her head underwater.

She flattens her palms on the bottom of the box as she thrusts her back against the lid. It shifts slightly, rattling the metal padlock.

Again. Harder, she tells herself, falling back into position.

Dani visualizes crashing through the Plexiglas like a battering ram as she explodes up. Again. Again. And again.

The container's top jostles upward a tiny bit with each impact but doesn't open.

She yanks her head up, slurping for air. "Please," she moans through her sobbing gasps. *"Please!"* Her voice trails off as she snaps into a fit of hysteria, whipping her head about, and then a guttural howl vibrates up her throat.

Possessed by her desperation, Dani feels no pain. She plunges back under the water, and with a more violent heave, she plows herself into the lid again.

POP!

The screws securing the leaf of a hinge hasp to the top of the box fly across the room. She hears something smack against the sidewall but isn't sure what happened. Wiping water from her face, Dani peers back over her shoulder. The padlock is still fastened to the lower leaf of the hasp.

"Why?" she drivels, dropping her head in devastation. "Why is this happening to—"

WAIT! Her eyes dart back to the swinging lock. *The hinge has broken away from the top of the Plexiglas cover. I'M OUT!*

Adrenaline pumps through Dani's veins as she drives her back into the container again. Her body follows the swinging lid upward, and miraculously, she is up on her knees. As she clambers to her feet, the box's cover continues around, smacking into the adjacent table. She spins toward the ruckus just as the flimsy leg buckles, shifting several aquariums to the floor. She shields her face as shattering glass shoots across the room. A new terror suddenly grabs ahold of her when she hears the rattles of countless snakes escaping from their shattered terrariums.

What the fuck? Dani springs into a fighting stance, her fists balled.

She tries to steady her rubbery legs as she stares at the floor outside the box. Serpents of all sizes are fleeing the fallen heap of soiled newspaper shreds and broken glass. Incensed hisses rise over the room, like a pressure cooker ready to blow.

Holy shit.

For a second, Dani thinks she might faint. She's free of the box she was in, but her situation seems to have gotten decidedly worse. Something brushes against her leg, and she spastically kicks out, shrieking, before she can stop herself. The saturated bandage that was taped to her chest soars through the air, spraying tiny specks of her water-diluted blood. It thumps onto a drifting current of snakes, sparking a flopping knot of irate bodies.

"Oh my God," she whispers, wading to the head of the box. "How do I—"

Turbulent flapping from beneath the broken table catches her eye, and she pauses, inspecting the rubble. A crushed aquarium has pinned a thin copper-colored snake to the ground. Its open mouth whacks against the case's metal frame as a small pool of blood spreads out from its tail.

Dani scans the room, which is darker and much larger than she thought. She considers the stairs next to the dim bulb, wondering if she could possibly get to them without getting bitten. *No way.*

The entire floor appears to be moving. Although there is a large slab of concrete with a grated drain beneath the Plexiglas box, the rest of the room looks to be covered by a dirt floor. She scours the shadowy walls for a door or window, some escape or a place to hide.

The other room! He went somewhere back there. She peers at the path to the dark hallway across the room, which seems to be solid ground rather than a squirming blanket of reptiles. *Maybe there's something I can use—a broom, a hammer.*

Inching a bit closer, she checks the floor again. *Those aren't piles of clothes outside the doorway,* she realizes as a thick tail slides into a coiled mound. *Shit!*

She turns back to the only other option she can think of—the staircase.

Dani has never been particularly afraid of bugs or spiders or even the occasional copperhead. When she was growing up in southwest Texas, they were everywhere. But the thought of getting through a roomful of agitated rattlesnakes is almost immobilizing.

She wonders if a better option might be to wait for him to return, hoping he gets tagged before he can get over to her.

Unless he brings a gun.

Gazing at the dirt walls flanking the steps of warped boards, a panicked thought bursts into Dani's brain. *How long has he been gone? How long ago did that doorbell ring?* She places her pruned foot on the edge of the box, impulsively drawn toward the stairs. *I have to get out of here now! He could come back down here at any mo—*

WHACK!

A fat, flat head raps against the box wall just below her foot, sending her stomping back into the water with a raspy squeal. She considers her route to the staircase, noticing that, while most of the snakes have moved to the other side of the room, a few are still blocking her path. She eyes the largest one, a four-foot-long black monster, as it draws its scaled body under the bottom step, poised to strike.

"Oh . . . my God," she mutters. "How in the hell am I—"

Something moves in her peripheral.

Dani spins to find another reptile creeping up the center area of the lid. "Jesus!" she blurts, rushing to the foot of the box.

As she passes, the snake's wide diamond-shaped head flinches, its flickering tongue tasting the air in her direction. While tracking the progress of the climbing snake, she also peeks over her shoulder at the makeshift table that was at her feet.

Half-burned candles, seated in small wooden candlesticks, cover the entire surface of a large sheet of plywood. Two rickety sawhorses support the board from below. Dani squints through the darkness at a small, rectangular object at the back of the table.

It's a box of matches. Oh! Snakes hate fire!

Her fingers flutter with anticipation as she sizes up her distance from the cardboard box. Deciding that she has to reach it, no matter what, she checks the floor between her container and the sawhorses.

It is moving.

"Are you fucking kidding me?"

Dani glances behind herself again. The snake has made it further up the lid and is now stretching out over the water-filled box.

Do those things swim? She flips her ankle, shooing it back with pelting droplets to its head.

She turns back, taking a steeling deep breath. *I gotta get those matches now!*

Carefully placing her foot along the edge of the container, parallel to the table, she eyes the slithering floor again. The snakes don't appear to have noticed her. Bracing one hand on her thigh for balance, she stretches across the gap, snagging the base of a candlestick. She slowly pulls it in, passing it to her other hand, and preps herself for a second reach.

"All right," she huffs, pushing against her leg again for leverage. Her forefinger extends past several candles, brushing the corner of the box. *Almost there.* She leans further across the surface, inching a little closer. "Slow and steady, Dani. Slow and—"

The tabletop tips forward.

"Shit!" she screams, flailing to regain her balance.

The toppling candles slide toward her as the plywood swings up and crashes to the floor. In what seems like slow motion, the small box soars off the table. Dani flings her hand up with a desperate grunt, snatching the matches from the air. She stumbles back into the water, shooting a frothy wave up the Plexiglas wall. The splash crashes over the side, sending the approaching rattler sliding down the lid again.

"Okay," Dani coaches herself, amazed she actually caught the box. "Let's go, let's go!"

She clumsily slides off the matchbox cover and lights the candle's wick. The flame wavers as she raises the light above her head, scanning the room. "Holy shit," she mutters, wishing she weren't seeing this. As the glow expands to the far wall, chills prickle over her body. "There are so many of them." Too petrified to move, she stares at the mounds of reptiles, trying to quiet the mewl growing in her throat.

A trickle of melted wax hits her forearm, startling her into motion. As she wipes off the hot drops, Dani gets an idea. She quickly empties the remaining matchsticks to the floor, and using the lit candle, she ignites the cardboard box. As it flares up, she waves her hand, growing the flame into a little fiery ball. She targets a group of snakes near the base of the staircase, takes a focusing breath, and flings the blaze toward them. The matchbox hits the ground a few feet from the stairs, driving several snakes toward the dark hallway across the room.

Yes!

Dani cranes her head forward, peering at the staircase. She's not sure how many of them scattered away, and she can't see under the bottom step.

Is that huge one still under there?

Time is running out. The flaming box is almost gone. She decides to go for it, stepping one foot onto the cool dirt floor. The space just outside the container is clear, but she can't be sure about the shadows under the stairs.

KERPLUNK!

A splash hits the back of her leg. Dani spins around just as the fat rattlesnake resurfaces in the water, bobbing toward her. With a gurgled shriek, she lunges backward, tumbling to the ground. She flops over to her knees, still screaming, as she springs up from the floor and freezes. A thick, scaly head is extended out from beneath the bottom step, fluttering its ribbonlike black tongue, tracking her.

Tightening her fists, Dani realizes she still has the candlestick clenched in her hand. Focused on the darkness under the bottom plank of wood, she wriggles the wax free from its holder and tosses it across the room.

"Damn it!" she scoffs as it falls short, bouncing away from the stairs. "Come on, Dani."

Squaring her body up, she lobs the wooden candlestick at the snake's head. A lightning-fast strike hits the wood midair, knocking it to the floor, and the rattler darts to the far end of the step.

SHIT, SHIT, SHIT!

As the snake coils itself again, she inches closer. *Keep going!*

Now a few feet away from the bottom step, Dani can see up the staircase. There's a strip of dull light under a door at the top. She feels her chest tighten as she envisions her freedom.

"Move, you fucker!" she hisses, taking another step forward.

The tiny tongue flicks out at her from the edge of the step, like a taunting dare. She can't tell if the rising rattle is coming from the snake under the stair or another one she hasn't seen. Remembering how fast the candlestick was struck from the air, she's certain this is a crazy idea, but she sees no other options.

Trembling, Dani glances back up at the door and commits. She bounds forward, vaulting up from the floor and yanking her knees to her chest as the black body rockets out from the darkness, striking at her feet. Barely clearing the snake's head, she collides with the lip of the third step. She slaps her palms outward, bracing herself between the walls, and she scampers up the stairs without looking back.

On the top step, she pauses to choke back the wailing in her mind. As she steadies her breath, she presses an ear to the wood. There's a low rumbling of what sounds like voices, but it's hard to hear over the pounding in her ears. She can't make out any specific words. She feels as if her racing heart is going to explode through her chest.

I have to move.

Drawing a deep breath in through her nose, Dani gently pushes the door open. Its old hinges squeal like a baby bear whose mother is just out of sight.

Oh God!

As she balls her shaky fists, she shudders—not at the squeaky door, but at the man clearing his throat from the other side.

TWENTY-ONE

ZEKE LOOPS THE long cotton cords several times, pulling them into a tight bowknot. Tossing his neatly wrapped apron into a small wire basket, he steps into the checkout lane for customers with ten items or less. The crowded store swarms with early evening shoppers, registers chirping as cash drawers spring open like baby chicks begging to be fed.

A sickly woman standing in front of Zeke taps on her iPhone, advancing to the next level in her Candy Crush Saga game.

As her groceries slide up to the register, she drags a wrist across her runny nose. "I'm waiting for somebody," she mumbles without looking up.

Shane, the acne-faced cashier, scans the woman's box of honey buns and a two-liter bottle of cola. "Okay," he replies, shutting off the conveyer belt and sneaking out his own cell phone.

Zeke sets his basket on the floor, glaring at the preoccupied woman. His eyes volley between her over-permed hair and the zinging video game. *I need to get back to my work at home.* Glancing over the candy rack, he notices that the checkout line to his right is now empty. As he bends down to grab his groceries, he inadvertently backs into another customer.

"Hey," a lifelong smoker's voice barks.

Zeke spins around to a severe-looking old woman. Her sagging, spray-tanned face droops into a frown. As she gives her head a quick flip, the long bangs of her shiny blonde wig shift to the side.

"Watch it, fella," she mutters, slowly raising a newspaper. "Don't get fresh with me."

As her copy of the *New Jersey Herald* rises between them, Zeke spots the bold headline letters of an article.

RATTLESNAKE KILLER.

There's a photomontage of police crews huddled around tarp-covered bodies in a grassy field, in a shallow creek bed, and on a muddy riverbank. Alongside the column of details, a line of black-and-white photos reveals three women cited as victims—Elisha Cooke, Ann Haut, Jaimee Dilks. His eyes linger on the last two pictures, labeled *Missing*—Kristen Byrne and Dani Caraway.

You won't find them so easy.

"They don't have any more potpies, Mom," a squeaky-voiced teenager says. "Can we just get KFC instead?" The boy brushes past Zeke, almost knocking him into a rack of tabloid magazines. "Sorry," he says flippantly as he joins his mother, who's still locked on her game. "*Mah-ahm.*"

"I heard you," the mother whines as the video game trills, signaling the end of a level. She shoves the phone into her front pocket. "Okay," she huffs to Shane. "That's it then."

Zeke slowly turns back around to the article, but the newspaper is gone.

The older woman has moved up closer and is impatiently

smacking her chewing gum at him. She blows a quick puff of minty breath, shimmying her bangs from her eyes. "May I help you?"

As his gaze sinks to the newspaper tucked under her fleshy arm, she follows his eyeline. "Ugh! Excuse you," the woman snaps, shielding her bosom.

The conveyer belt jerks to life, breaking the tension, and Zeke sets his groceries on the drifting rubber. As the basket floats off toward the cashier behind him, he slowly spins back around to the register.

"Oh, hey," Shane mumbles nervously.

Zeke doesn't respond.

With an awkward nod, Shane scans the items, carefully avoiding eye contact. Zeke pulls a handful of crumpled tip money from his pocket. One at a time, he stretches the bills along the register counter's edge, flattening them into shape.

As the groceries move toward the end of the conveyer belt, a lanky guy with dark curls draped diagonally across his face steps up, still talking to his previous customer. "Whatever," Tyler scoffs. "He's the best QB in the league, man." He drags the rack of plastic bags closer to himself, blindly reaching for an approaching bag of corn chips.

"I'll do it," Zeke mumbles, pulling the chips off to the side. He goes back to straightening his singles.

Preoccupied with his other conversation, Tyler doesn't hear him. "Manning's the man!" he shouts over his shoulder as he snags a jar of spaghetti sauce. "Go Giants."

"I SAID, I'LL DO IT."

Tyler whips his head around to find Zeke's blank face staring back at him. "Oh, shit!" he gulps, releasing the jar of sauce. "What's up, Zeke? I, uh . . . I guess you've got this." He swaggers backward a couple of steps.

Zeke silently moves to the end of the sacking station. Tugging a paper bag from a stack, he begins packing his groceries.

"Oh, okay. No sweat." Tyler continues drifting back toward the sliding front doors. "Hey, Shane, I'm gonna run outside for a minute, in case anybody's looking for me."

Shane watches as Tyler pauses at the entrance, letting a group of shoppers pass into the store.

So fuckin' weird, the sacker mouths.

"I know," Shane whispers with a nod.

The register's scanner pangs, drawing Shane's attention down, where he rakes a dented can of Hormel Chili across the bar-code sensor again. This time, it beeps a successful scan.

Sending it down toward the other groceries, he slowly raises his head again, twirling his index finger at his temple, as he silently pleads to his buddy, *Help me!*

Zeke's eyes pop up to Shane. Caught, his gesticulation shifts to scratching his temple with an awkward grin.

"Busted!" Tyler cackles. "I'm gonna go gather carts," he says, crossing through the sliding doors. "That shit was classic."

Jerking his face down to the register, Shane taps a series of buttons, like an SOS call of Morse code. "Nineteen fifty-eight," he says, not looking up.

Zeke stares at the young checker, extending a wrinkled bill.

"Out of twenty," Shane chirps, snatching the money as he pecks away at the keyboard. The cash drawer springs open, and the nervous guy fumbles in the coin compartments.

"Zeke!" a man's voice shouts from across the store.

Ron is standing just outside his office, holding the door open.

Cindy steps out. "Thanks again," she flirts, popping a stick of chewing gum into her mouth. "See you tomorrow." As she heads toward the store entrance, she spots Zeke. Her smile fades, and dropping her head, she hurries out to the parking lot.

"Forty-two cents is your change," Shane says, offering the coins.

"I need to speak with you," the manager calls out, gesturing to his office.

Zeke skipped his break to make up for being twenty minutes late today, so he can't imagine what else Ron could want. He doesn't care either. *She's waiting at home.* "I'm off the clock already," he answers curtly, taking his change. "And I have to go."

Shoving the coins in his pocket, he snatches up his two grocery bags. As he whirls around toward the sliding doors, the bottom of one of his paper sacks splits open. The jar of spaghetti sauce crashes to the floor. A chain reaction of startled shrieks ripples across the checkout lines.

"Now, Zeke! In my office!"

A hush spreads across the front of the store as Zeke considers the chunky red sauce splattered up his pant legs. Dropping the ripped bag onto the pile of groceries, he steps out of the puddle in a huff, crumpling his remaining sack in his fist. Zeke strides toward the manager, his clenched jaw pulsing like the flashing signal at a railroad crossing.

"Shane!" Ron yells, eyeing Zeke. "Call somebody to clean that mess up." And, as an uncomfortable chatter starts up among the customers, the manager steps into the office, yanking the door closed.

TWENTY-TWO

THE TIPS OF Dani's fingers ease through the crack, like a mouse tentatively emerging from its hole. It's been several minutes now since she heard the man's voice, and she isn't going to wait for it to return. She grips the door, trying to minimize the noise as it slowly yawns open. Noticing the droplets from her soggy gown forming a ring at her feet, she considers her next move.

If I can just get outside the house, I know I can make it.

Squinting, she strains to see into the shadows. About ten feet away to her left is a large break in the wall that seems to lead to an adjacent room. The windowless wall on her right extends all the way down the dark hallway, opening up into another room. As her eyes adjust a little more, Dani makes out a line of light from the far side of that room, peeking out from behind a curtain or window shade. And next to it—

THERE'S A DOOR!

Eyes locked on the distant glow, Dani steps out of the cellar.

Pop!

The floorboards snap under her feet, and she jerks to a stop.

Oh, Jesus! She stands, petrified, a lump swelling in her throat.

As a light flutters from the adjacent room, new tears start to well up. She cocks her head toward the only thing between her and that front door, biting down on her lip to keep from screaming.

There are voices coming from inside.

Her head whips back to the foyer, her eyes locking on the door at the end of the hall. *Just keep going, Dani.* She holds her breath and inches forward, the old floor crackling with her every step. Her legs feel so numb, like they could give out at any moment. Finally reaching the edge of the opening to her left, she hikes up her soaked gown and takes a big centering inhale.

Okay. This is it. You gotta run.

"Go get her!" a man shouts.

Dani flattens against the wall, a tiny yelp echoing down the hall at what feels like a sports arena sound level. *Fuck! It's too late!* She balls her fists, ready to strike as she waits for him to come through the opening.

"If she strays from the path, the divine path," the man continues, "the Lord wants you to *go. Get. Her!*"

"Hallelujah," a small voice cheers.

"Praise God," someone else adds.

Wait, the other voices seem far away. Dani creeps closer, listening more carefully.

As a raucous but distant applause starts up, she slowly peeks around the corner. On the screen of an old television, a sweaty, flush-faced televangelist preaches to his lively congregation. He incites the groups on both sides of a long center aisle, flailing his arms about. As he jerks through his passionate message, pellets of his perspiration flick through the air, like a dog shaking off its bath.

That's the voice.

"You must drag her tortured soul back to the light of redemption," he continues.

The crowd's praises hiss from the TV's speakers, spilling out of the church and into the parlor. Dani releases her breath as she quickly scours the rest of the room that could easily be in an episode of *Hoarding: Buried Alive*.

Just inside, a massive heap of clothes that almost reaches the ceiling partially blocks the entrance to the hall. Beyond that pile, stacks and stacks of newspapers stretch across patches of stained carpet. Against the back wall of the parlor, the board of a wooden bookshelf sags under the weight of more newspapers. Next to the shelf, in the back right corner of the room, an open door reveals the cabinets and tile countertop of a kitchen.

Something flashes.

Dani's eyes whip to a flimsy TV tray in the middle of the room where light reflects off the handle of a metal spoon that is buried in a half-eaten bowl of oatmeal. Beside it, there is a large leather-bound book with gold lettering on its spine—*King James*.

As she considers the television, the cereal, and the Bible, terror grips Dani.

He's here somewhere. Get out! a voice screams in her mind. *GET OUT NOW!*

She spins back into the hallway again, wanting to run but unable to commit. *What if he's waiting for me down there?* She leans out to her right, trying to see around the corner at the end of the corridor. *He could be standing right there, just waiting to—*

Newspaper crackles in the parlor.

Dani's head snaps over to the enormous pile of clothes inside the room. There's a gusting wheeze of what sounds like a labored inhale coming from behind it. Her eyes dart to the floor, tracking movement. And, with a gasp she can't control, Dani spots the callous toes of a bare foot.

TWENTY-THREE

P AGES TACKED TO a crowded corkboard flutter at the slamming office door behind Zeke, but he is not fazed. He stands in the center of the room as Ron huffs by him, rounding a large metal desk. Slumping into a tattered old rolling chair, he crosses his arms, considering Zeke's emotionless face.

"Sit down," he orders, snuffing out the orange ashes of a discarded butt.

"I have to go," Zeke mumbles without moving.

"Hey, I'm trying to give you a chance here." Ron places both palms on a manila file folder spread open in the center of his desk. "So, grab that chair."

Zeke's gaze drops to the scattered paper, landing on the upside-down red ink at the top of a sheet.

Complaints.

Several dated entries are listed below it. As the manager's fingers drum his impatience, the page shifts, revealing the typed bold letters of a familiar name on the file folder's label.

CYNTHIA MALONE.

The second hand from a wall-mounted clock ticks over the tension hovering between the two men.

Ron breaks the silence, tapping at the folder on his desk. "Look, I don't want to get the authorities involved here, Zeke, but I will if I have to. So, is there anything you would like to tell me?"

Zeke drops the grocery bag. He retrieves a folding chair from behind the door, its metal legs whining as he drags it along the floor. Flipping it open in front of the desk, he slumps into the seat, folding his arms across his chest. "Like what?"

"Like *anything*," Ron prods, cocking his head to the side. "Because this is going to be your only chance."

Zeke glares into the eyes of the irrelevant man across from him. *What could he know?*

Silence.

Shifting his attention to a tear in his chair's upholstery, Ron switches tactics. "About an incident in the parking lot maybe?" he asks, ripping off a bit of yellowed foam stuffing and rolling it between his fingertips. "And Cindy?"

Cindy? "No," Zeke says flatly.

"Hmm. Well, okay, Zeke, have it your way." The old chair squeaks as Ron leans forward. "There's been a complaint that you behaved in an inappropriate manner yesterday." He flings the tiny foam piece into a garbage can by the wall. "Now, this obviously isn't the first time we've gotten complaints about you, Zeke," he continues. "And I have given you the opportunity to tell your side of it." Ron pulls a folder labeled *Personnel Disciplinary Action* from a drawer. "But you apparently have nothing to say. Is that right?"

Zeke slowly nods, considering the folder title.

"All right. Well, Cindy was too embarrassed to say what *exactly* you did," Ron explains, pursing his lips, as he flips through pages. "But she did say that you made a lewd gesture of some kind, and that type of behavior will simply not be tolerated here."

He scribbles Zeke's name at the top of an Employee Disciplinary Action form and signs and dates it. Scrolling down the page, Ron ticks off various violation boxes. "There was also a young man who witnessed whatever you did. He plans to file a complaint with corporate," he says, filling in the Employer Statement section. "And I understand you also left Cindy some angry voice mails. Now, Zeke, you've been given several notices about your attitude here, but this harassment situation is different. I am placing you on a thirty-day probation—"

"*Of the woman came the beginning of sin,*" Zeke grumbles.

Ron stops writing. "What . . . was that?" he asks, straightening up in his chair.

Zeke's head slowly lolls from side to side as he whispers, "*And through her, we all die!*"

"Okay," Ron says, gradually standing up. "I think it might actually be better if you didn't work here at all anymore, Zeke." He pulls the phone closer. "It's just not—"

Zeke springs to his feet, startling Ron into dropping the handset. Snatching up his grocery bag, he moves to the door. His gaze sweeps across the office floor, drifting up to the nervous manager. Zeke tracks the man's quivering hand as it inches back toward the phone.

"*Lying lips are an abomination to the Lord,*" he says, stepping out into the store.

THE CARGO VAN'S driver-side panel door jerks open, sliding on its track like a bowling ball speeding toward a strike. With rage bubbling on his lips, Zeke flings the paper bag against the back of his seat, sending a dented can of chili rolling to the floor.

"A proud look, a lying tongue, and hands that shed innocent blood," he scoffs, slamming the door.

As he climbs in behind the wheel, a flashing light in his rearview catches Zeke's attention. In the distance, he watches Ron hurry through the store's sliding doors just as a small white car pulls up to the entrance. A blue bulb on the vehicle's roof rotates sluggishly, like a lazy fanfare for its obese cargo. As the driver's door opens, an enormous rent-a-cop oozes out of the rocking car and lumbers up to Ron.

Zeke cranks the ignition and backs out of the parking space, slapping the dashboard with a growl as he speeds off into the evening's darkness.

TWENTY-FOUR

ZEKE'S WHITE-KNUCKLED FINGERS tighten around the steering wheel like a vise, pounding music rattling the van's windows as it plows through another Stop sign. He veers onto Polkville Road, drifting dangerously close to the rusty guardrail on a curve. He stomps the brake pedal, jerking his torso forward and snarls through the windshield at the Oldsmobile that chose not to go through the yellow light on Vail Road.

Simmering in the idling van, Zeke jabs the buttons on his stereo system. A man's raspy voice explodes from the speakers, raging through the lyrics of "Tempter" by Trouble. Zeke slumps back in the seat, joggling his head to the rhythm.

As he waits for the notoriously long light to change, he notices the glowing red low-fuel icon in the dashboard. He slaps the steering wheel, considering the boarded up gas station on the other side of the intersection.

Across from the failed business, a light flashes in the glass of a

Sonic Drive-In's opening door. Following the glare, Zeke zeroes in on the woman sauntering toward the cashier. She drapes herself across the counter to place her order.

"Harlots abound," he mutters, perusing the rest of the burger joint's dining room.

The woman appears to be alone. As she waits for her food, she meanders over to the window, pulling her thick red hair into a ponytail. Zeke's forehead taps his window, his eyes narrowed.

Cindy.

Her lone car is parked at a row of hedges that separates Sonic from the parking area of an abandoned electronics superstore. Zeke scours the darkness of the lot that's completely vacant other than an overfilled garbage dumpster that butts up against the bushes. It's obviously a local dumping spot with cardboard boxes and stuffed plastic bags spilling out onto a heap of broken furniture and other junk.

He turns back to his windshield, realizing the Oldsmobile is long gone. As the traffic light cycles to yellow, he gazes into the dark eyes in his rearview mirror. Bobbing his head to the music again, he ponders the empty road behind his van.

Peering at the Sonic parking lot again, he squeezes the steering wheel, his jaw pulsing.

"*A false witness shall not be unpunished,*" he mumbles. "*And he that speaketh lies shall perish.*"

With his jagged teeth gritted, Zeke blows through the red light, crossing the intersection. *A time for reckoning.*

CINDY STROLLS TO her car, fully aware that she's being watched. By the way the pimply young cashier refused to let her pay for her combo meal, she could tell that he was hooked. It's not even something she thinks about much anymore—being a flirt. It's just part of who she is. A free chicken sandwich and fries tonight, getting off with a warning instead of a speeding ticket last weekend—it definitely comes in handy.

She tugs her ponytail free, giving her hair a dramatic toss, as she smiles back at the burger guy.

Andrew? Alex? Whatever.

Shockingly, he's not ogling from behind the counter anymore. He must have gone back to the phone call she interrupted with her order.

Who cares? I got my food, she reassures herself, wedging a cell phone between her shoulder and jaw.

"Hey, it's me again. Sorry. I had to order," she says, rifling through the paper sack. "I'm starving."

Something rustles on the far side of the hedges parallel to Cindy. She slows, eyes panning across the deserted lot. A doorless refrigerator leaning against an overstuffed garbage dumpster appears to be wobbling.

Ew, it's probably a rat scrounging through the trash for dinner, she thinks, relaxing back into her normal stride.

"Uh, yeah, so Ron said he'd put him on probation," she continues, chomping on some fries. "But he'll probably end up getting fired." Just a few yards from her car, she pauses, wrestling a set of keys from her front pocket. "I feel kind of bad. I mean, he's so old. Where's he gonna get another job?"

"Hey, Cindy!" A couple of girls wave from the backseat of a black convertible Mustang as it speeds past the Sonic.

"Hey!" she shouts back, swinging her food bag. "I think that was Kerry and Michelle," she says into the phone. "Tony drives a Mustang, right?"

Rummaging for another bite, Cindy picks up where she left off.

"Anyway, I think he's just a weirdo, you know? And, for God's sake, he's, like, a hundred years old. I'm sure he's harmless." She snickers at the voice in her ear. "Well, yeah, and creepy! Jim was really pissed though," she garbles. "It was kinda hot. He said he would beat the shit outta him if I didn't—"

The cell phone slips off her shoulder.

"Whoa!" She drops her bag of food as her palm slaps the phone, pinning it against her thigh. While crouching to grab the upended bag, she pulls the phone back to her face. "Hey, I just dropped my food," she whines, staring at the loose foil wrapper and fries scattered across the pavement. "I'll call you back later, 'kay?" She ends the call.

Damn, the sandwich came open, too. Gross.

There's movement from near the dumpster again.

Cindy scans the bushes, getting to her feet. She's sure she heard a crackling that time. Her eyes drift along the base of the shrubbery, passing over discarded soda cups, Sonic bags, and other trash. She considers tossing her dropped food over to the dumpster but decides she'd rather not know what the disgusting little creature is. As she starts back toward her car, she does a double take at a strange object nestled among the roots in the dirt.

What?

It flinches.

That's a hand!

Cindy staggers backward as a large body shoots up from the other side of the hedges. "Oh my God!"

Shrieking, she whirls toward her car, accidentally flinging her cell phone through the air. As she runs, she hears jingling and realizes she's thrown her keys as well. They clunk against the rear bumper, dropping to the concrete below.

Without coming to a stop, Cindy sweeps up the keys, crashing against the trunk. Her eyes dart back over to the person floundering in the bushes where a painted hood has snagged in the tangle of branches. The person tears at the shrubs, snarling like a rabid animal, as tiny leaves and twigs spray across the pavement. The hood suddenly snaps free, revealing a man scrambling to his feet just a few yards away.

Rounding the car, Cindy yanks her door open. She dives in behind the wheel, almost breaking the key off in the ignition as she cranks the engine. In her peripheral, she sees the dark-clothed body burst through the hedges, barreling toward her.

"Help me!" she screams, slamming her door shut and tugging the gearshift into reverse.

The passenger door rips open.

"No!" Squeezing her face and body against her window, Cindy stomps the accelerator.

The car rockets backward, jerking the door from the man's hand. Her back wheels jump the curb bordering the parking lot as the car makes a huge semicircle and lurches to a stop.

The passenger door slams shut, but he's still coming.

As the man charges, Cindy throws the gearstick into drive and zips past him, now noticing the goat horns swaying from his hood. She careens out onto Vail Street, speeding through the red light without checking for traffic. With shaky hands, she angles her rearview mirror to the Sonic Drive-In lot.

It is empty.

TWENTY-FIVE

CLUTCHING THE PARLOR doorframe, Dani remembers her ninth grade field trip to Brazos Bend State Park where a teacher's aide accidentally wandered too close to a napping alligator. He spotted its moving claw and bolted away just seconds before the massive head came sweeping around.

"The scariest part," she heard the jumpy man tell their bus driver, "was that I didn't even notice the goddamn thing was there."

He is right.

Dani watches the scaly foot rise through the newspaper, its big toenail furiously grating at the opposite ankle. As tiny beads of blood pop up along the chalky lines of dried skin, icy panic ripples across her body.

He's right there!

She carefully backs away, swallowing the growing lump in her throat. Setting her sights on the front door, Dani creeps down the hallway. A floorboard pops, stopping her and she checks over her shoulder, panting like a nervous rabbit that is too scared to move.

He's sleeping now, she thinks, clenching the wet gown. *But for how long?*

With her eyes again trained on the metal knob at the end of the hall, a rush of courage rises in her gut. *Go,* she mouths to herself, coaxing her feet into motion. *You have to go now!*

Something clinks from the parlor behind her.

Dani spins back toward the sound. Her hands tremble at her sides as she stares at the entrance to the room, expecting Zeke to step out at any moment. She strains to identify the noise she heard, images flashing through her mind with the rhythm of her throbbing heartbeat.

The TV . . . the spoon . . . the bowl . . . the foot!

A door slams from another part of the house.

Dani jumps, shrieking before she has time to stop herself. She smashes both palms against her mouth, but as the ringing of her voice echoes off the walls, she's sure it's too late. Another television preacher bellows into the start of a new sermon, covering any sounds from the parlor.

Oh God, oh God!

Locked on the room's entrance, she continues shuffling backward, toward the front door. Her internal panic becomes a tiny, mumbling plea, *Please don't let him come out of—*

"Hey!" a raspy voice yells from right behind her.

Dani whips around with another hoarse yelp as an overhead bulb flicks on. Squinting in the new light, she spots a cadaverous old woman slouched in a wheelchair at the foyer end of the hall. "What the hell?"

Staggering backward, Dani's legs give out, and she crashes to the floor, still eyeing the skeletal creature.

The woman looks like a wax figure from some museum with

weathered skin sagging from her hollow face into a grooved, rootlike neck. Brittle arms poke out from an oversize, sleeveless housedress clinging to the chair's wheels. As the old woman maneuvers herself to block the front door, she tilts her head upward, scanning a wall.

Dani slowly climbs to her feet. *The door is RIGHT THERE!*

The old woman's head snaps down, her chapped lips pulling back, like an old dog brandishing its few remaining teeth.

As Dani flattens herself against the wall, the chair inches forward, and Sylvia calls out, "Zeke!"

"What? No!" Dani bucks off the wall, her mind shifting between wherever that hooded monster might be right now and the horrible sight rolling toward her.

Trembling, she drifts a few steps closer to the parlor, considering the space beside the woman. *You gotta get by her.*

"No," Sylvia hisses, as if she heard Dani's thoughts. "You're not going anywhere."

"Please, just let me go."

As the old woman creeps closer, Dani notices the bloody smears on her callous ankle. *That's the foot!*

Just as it hits her, Sylvia lunges forward, almost tipping out of her chair. "Whore!" she screams, clawing at the air.

Dani squeals as she whirls herself toward the parlor, balling her fists for whatever might be around the corner.

Behind her, the old woman's phlegmy scream rattles through the house, "You get back here!"

Rounding the corner into the sitting room, Dani crashes into the folding snack table, which has been moved into the doorway. The bowl clunks down onto a pile of newspaper, flicking cereal across the room, as she tumbles to the ground. Unable to gain her footing, she thrashes across the parlor floor like it's a sheet of ice. Floorboards pop in the hall, and Dani grabs on to a stack of magazines, using it to flop over onto her haunches.

Sylvia appears in the doorway, pausing at the edge of the laundry heap. Her mouth sags open with breathy pants as she gazes around the cluttered room. Ten feet away, Dani sits motionless. She didn't see the woman as clearly before, didn't notice her watery eyes or the large gray discs covering her pupils.

But, now, she realizes, *That thing can't see!*

"You cannot hide," Sylvia mutters, her head jerking around the corners of the room like a lizard tracking a fly.

Dani glances to the door she saw earlier that opened into the kitchen. It's closed now. *That must have been the slamming I heard.*

She considers the hallway behind the fidgety creature, wondering how close she could get without being detected. *Could I reach the pile of clothes? Maybe tip it over on top of her before bolting from the room?*

Deciding to give it a shot, Dani slowly draws in her feet, inadvertently crackling newspaper beneath her soles.

Sylvia's head snaps toward the sound. "There!" she barks, pushing her wheels through the debris. "There's the whore!"

Dani's legs slip out from under her as she launches herself backward, crab-crawling across the room. She topples through a pile of magazines, sending up a flurry of paper. Watching Sylvia claw at the fluttering sheets, Dani realizes she's underestimated the haggard old woman.

This is not some fragile old grandma in a wheelchair. This crazy bitch is trying to kill me!

With one hand anchoring her to the chair, Sylvia lurches forward, swiping another page from the air with a grunt. As the last piece of paper hits the floor, she slumps back in her seat, snarling from the side of her decaying mouth. "Ezekiel!"

Dani shoots to her feet, diving against the kitchen door. Her heart plummets. It's locked.

"Fuck!" she screams, desperately tugging the knob back and forth. *I gotta get out!*

As the wheelchair moves in closer behind her, Dani whips around, bracing her back on the door. *What can I use?* She scours the parlor. *I gotta find something to—*

Her eyes land on a second snack table, leaned against an easy chair to her left. *That!*

She springs to the table and lobs it across the room with as much force as she has.

"Zeke—"

It crashes into Sylvia's gut, knocking the wind out of her but not the fight. As she gasps, her gnarled hands lash at the air in a kind of violent windmill motion. She fumbles over the table's surface, latching on to an edge, and with a gurgling yowl, she hurls it back toward Dani. It hits the BarcaLounger's arm, bouncing to the floor.

"Devil," she barks.

Dani hurdles over another pile of paper, reaching the bookcase. As the chair crosses through the center of the parlor, she wedges her fingers into the tiny space where the shelves meet the wall, and with a quick rocking motion, she tips the huge piece forward. A new wave of dusty newspaper flaps across the room.

Shit, it missed her!

"You filthy bitch!" Sylvia screams, scratching at the air again.

Dani hurries back toward the kitchen door, determined to kick through the lock, but as she moves, she spots the old woman's head fidgeting, ticking to one side. It's as if she's trying to see around her cataracts. Her face jerks to the area next to the kitchen and stills.

Noticing the dark form floating on the wall to her side, Dani shudders. *She's tracking my shadow!*

A magazine thumps against the wall, just missing Dani's face. Shielding her head, she ducks down and drives her shoulder into the kitchen door. Another magazine slaps against her back.

"Come on," Dani begs, ramming into the wood again. "Please!"

"All the bright lights of heaven will I make dark over thee," Sylvia roars.

Her voice is too close. As Dani spins to the woman, something smacks into her face, lobbing her head to the side. She crumples to the ground, her nose exploding in a bloody gush. The throbbing pain is immediate; it's probably broken. As she wipes at her watering eyes, a savage groan rattles up Dani's throat. She gropes for the object, her hands finding the spine of what she discovers is the old Bible she saw earlier. Snatching it up, she shoots to her feet.

Dani wails, slinging the book.

The Bible collides with the side of Sylvia's head, knocking loose her bun of yellow-white hair. The sound of popping vertebrae crackles across the room. Dani thinks maybe she's broken the woman's neck.

"Please, just let me go," she whimpers, taking a tentative step away from the door.

Sylvia's head slowly cranes back around, bobbing unsteadily. She rakes up the hem of her housedress and pounds her fists against a set of naked sinewy thighs. Her jaw jerks through the air, like she's being slapped by some invisible demon. As her eyes clamp shut, the woman's body goes stiff. A fizzing glob of spit bubbles between her lips, trickling down her chin.

Dani hesitates. *Is she dying?*

The corners of the old woman's cracked mouth slowly peak upward into a hideous smirk. "Lord, I am your faithful servant," Sylvia says with the singsongy voice of a child. "And I hear you." She begins rocking her body from side to side in the wheelchair, raising her face to the ceiling. *"For they are the spirits of devils, working miracles,"* she titters. "And I am your warrior."

Dani flings herself back up against the door again, paralyzed by the performance.

"The Lord shall cause thine enemies that rise up against thee to be smitten before thy face," Sylvia spits, the childlike quality gone from her voice. She trains her cloudy eyes on the shadow above Dani's head. *"Yes, they shall come out against thee one way and flee before thee seven ways!"*

Sylvia stands up and steps away from the wheelchair.

What. The. Fuck?

Dani flops against the door, watching, as the old woman shuffles through the crackling mass of newspaper. As she waves her clawed hands, her head twitches back and forth, trying to pinpoint the exact position of her prey. Just feet from the kitchen door, Sylvia freezes. She drops her arms and lowers her head, as if her power cord has been unplugged.

Holy shit! Dani's eyes dart to the BarcaLounger. She's not going to wait around to see what this thing will do next. *If I can just get to that armrest, I'll jump to that pile of clothes and—*

Sylvia lunges.

"Oh my God!" Dani twists her body away just as the bony old woman smashes into the kitchen door.

She knows the woman is hurt, but she doesn't dare turn around to see how badly. Instead, she flies toward the hallway, springing over a fallen heap of magazines. As she lands, her front foot slips on a layer of paper, stretching her into a painful split. Dani latches her fingers on to one of the wheelchair's footrests, using its frame to pull herself up. As she starts across the parlor again, she hears scrambling behind her.

Before she can process what is actually happening, her head jolts forward. Spindly fingers scrape against her scalp as the old woman grips a handful of hair.

"*Ezekiel,*" she calls, reining Dani's face toward the ceiling.

"*Nooo!*" Slapping at Sylvia's hand, Dani staggers across the floor, toward the blasting TV. "Let go of me," she cries, dragging the woman's limp body.

Suddenly, in what feels like the kind of fast-forward speed you'd see in a movie, the creature is off the floor, shimmying up Dani's torso. She affixes herself like a giant tawny gecko, slapping a second leathery hand on Dani's shoulder while tugging the clutch of hair with her other. Sylvia hisses, slowly drawing her hands apart as she forces Dani's head to the side.

How is she so fucking strong?

"Get off me!" Dani screams, punching at the old woman's head. "Get the fuck—" Her voice breaks off.

Something has been pierced into the base of her neck. And, as her fingers scamper through a swelling glob of blood, Dani's mind swirls in a state of disbelief.

How can any of this possibly be happening? Why is this happening? Why—

Fiery pain zaps Dani back, reminding her that none of that matters now.

It IS actually happening. This thing is biting through my neck!

"*Nooo!*" A new wave of hysteria surges through Dani's veins as she rakes her fingernails across Sylvia's forehead, clawing for her eyes.

The women tussle to the floor, the old woman slamming against the carpet with a grunt. Although Dani lands wallop after wallop against Sylvia's head, she won't release her grip. Instead, burrowing her face deeper into the bloody gash, she tears at the flesh like a crazed fight dog.

Dani is no longer forming words, her screams having evolved into desperate growls. As she flounders on the floor, she manages to grab a patch of the old woman's hair. And, with a heaving yank, she rips the greasy clump from her scalp.

"Devil!" Sylvia snaps, finally releasing her frothy bite.

Dani flings the ratty strands aside, clapping her hand over the bloody punctures on her neck as she lurches up. But, she finds Sylvia is still with her. The woman's twiggy arm is now wedged at her throat. Dani wobbles up to her feet, ignoring the pressure tightening against her windpipe.

"We denounce you," Sylvia roars, "Satan's whore!"

Dani reels toward the hallway with the old woman clinging to her neck like a tattered cape of bones. She tugs at Sylvia's constricting elbow but cannot break the hold. Her head starts to spin a bit, and she notices a ringing beginning to rise in her ears.

Oh God! You cannot faint!

Her limbs are so weak; each step feels like she's dragging a huge concrete block through thick mud. As her eyelids slowly slide downward, Dani makes one more heft, bursting out of the parlor.

"We will destroy you!" Sylvia croaks as she works her legs up, locking them around Dani's waist like a scaly belt.

The women crash against the far wall, whirling down the hall like a tornado. As they teeter toward the front door, Sylvia readjusts herself, unlatching her ankles and loosening her elbow for a moment. Dani goes for a quick breath, but before she can inhale, the old woman stomps at the wall, sending them both up the hallway like a chaotic pinball.

The pressure at her neck lightens as they crash against the wall again, telling Dani exactly what her next move must be.

Squaring up her body, she hurls herself backward again. "Get the fuck off me!"

Sylvia huffs out another puff of rancid breath as Dani backs them into the wall. She feels the progress and seizes the moment.

Sucking in a huge breath, she totters toward the open cellar door. As she reaches the opening, she spins around, thrusting her unwanted cargo against the doorframe.

Something cracks in Sylvia's spine. With a low, agonizing groan, she finally releases her choke hold. But, while dropping her arms, she tears her gnarled fingers into the wound on Dani's chest.

Wailing at what feels like hot pokers ripping through her skin, Dani staggers forward. At the same time, she shoves the woman's arm up, biting into its crusty flesh. Her teeth easily break through the mottled skin, splitting it open like a sausage casing.

Sylvia cries out, but Dani doesn't hear her, now driven by an uncontrollable rage. She clamps down harder on the arm, oozing blood from the scabs with a final chomp as she grabs the cellar door for leverage. Spitting out the forearm, Dani flings her head back with as much force as she can muster, popping the cartilage in Sylvia's nose. In the same motion, she shrugs her shoulders, and like she's taking off a heavy coat, she spins herself out of the old woman's hold. She pivots around, coming face-to-face with her attacker, now dangling over the cellar stairs.

The battered creature clinging to the doorframe doesn't even look human anymore. Sweaty mats of hair streak across her face, leaving only one cloudy eye visible. Blood bubbles at the corners of her hissing mouth.

Just go, Dani thinks. *Just leave her and get the hell outta—*

"Burn in hell, you whore!" Sylvia growls, hawking up a bloody glob.

As the woman spits, something breaks in Dani's mind, and before she can stop herself, she charges. *"You first, bitch!"*

She stomps her foot squarely into Sylvia's bony chest, snapping her hands from the doorframe. The woman erupts in a retching cough as she flounders backward, grasping for anything to keep her from falling. She finds Dani's outstretched leg and rakes her jagged claws down the kicking calf. Unable to hold on, Sylvia slips into the darkness, igniting a frenzy of angry rattling.

"Ezekiel!"

Dani slams the cellar door, muffling Sylvia's final plea as she collapses to the floor. Tears stream down her cheeks, mixing with blood that she's not even sure is her own. Considering how close she just came to dying, Dani is suddenly overcome by the urge to vomit. She flops onto her hands and knees, succumbing to a series of violent dry heaves.

And, as thick pink drool puddles between her fingers, she hears her own garbled voice echoing in the hallway.

"Dani, you gotta run."

TWENTY-SIX

THE CARGO VAN careens down I-80, its windows rattling with another verse of "Tempter." As Zeke passes over the Delaware Water Gap into Pennsylvania, his head twitches to the song's beat. He chomps at the air, mouthing the lyrics to the disheveled Bald Knobber hoodie in his passenger seat, like it's some face-painted groupie.

Ding! The low-fuel icon sounds a reminder.

His eyes dart to the glowing symbol of a gas pump. With a furious scoff, Zeke yanks the steering wheel, speeding down the exit ramp. After a few hundred yards, he ignores a dented Stop sign at a T-intersection and makes a sharp right turn. He reaches for the horned hoodie sliding across the seat, but he cannot get to it in time.

"Damn," he fumes as it clunks onto the floorboard. Strangling the steering wheel again, he shoots down the dark side street toward a faint white glow in the distance.

As the song transitions into a lyricless section, Zeke fumbles with the stereo knob, shutting off the music. He finds the switch for the overhead lamp, slowly lowering his gaze to the rearview mirror. The tension that's been throbbing in his jaw since the Sonic parking lot quickens, and Zeke considers his reflection.

It's never happened before—one getting away like that.

"You were foolish," he snaps. "She was an impetuous quarry." His eyes narrow at the scolding he knows he deserves.

She might have recognized him, caught a glimpse of his face. He was too impulsive tonight.

"*He that hath no rule over his own spirit is like a city that is broken down and without walls!*"

As the eyes in the mirror tear up, Zeke's tone softens. "There isn't room for her now anyway," he consoles. "But soon."

He clicks off the light, still staring into his glossy, dilated pupils. "Yes," he whispers. "*Blessed are ye, when men shall revile you and persecute you and shall say all manner of evil against you falsely. Rejoice, and be exceeding glad: for great is your reward in heaven: for so persecuted they the prophets which were before you.*"

Zeke speeds down the road, pulling the van under the fluorescent canopy of a twenty-four-hour service station. A wiry old man sits in a glass booth at the far edge of the lot, thumbing through a newspaper. His thick-lensed glasses bob a greeting as Zeke drives past and stops at the furthest of four gas pumps.

"Ah, okay," the old man groans. Begrudgingly folding the newspaper, he tosses it to the counter. "Be right there." He spews a short jet of dark liquid into the crusted opening of a soda can.

Zeke sifts through a pool of coins in the ashtray. He begins to line up stacks of quarters along the dashboard, mouthing a count to himself. He notices the old-timer shuffling out of his booth. "Put in ten dollars' worth!" he shouts through the window.

"How much ya want?" the old man says, now halfway to the van.

Zeke cuts his eyes, impatience bubbling in his gut again. "I said put in—"

"I can't hear ya!" the attendant yells, waving his hand. "You gotta speak up, for crying out loud. Now, you want, I should fill 'er up or what?"

Zeke snarls. "TEN. DOLLARS'. WORTH."

A shrill ringing echoes from the tiny glass office, stopping the old man mid stride.

"Damn it," he says, circling back toward the booth. "Just hang on a minute. Believe I hear the phone."

A splash of tobacco hits the ground as he dodders back across the pavement, mumbling to himself, "What the hell does she want now?" Stepping inside the tiny room, he dusts off his hand on his filthy coveralls and yanks up the receiver. "I'm *working*, woman."

"Nine . . . ten." Zeke tosses the extra change back into the ashtray. Sliding the quarters off the dashboard and into an empty Styrofoam cup, he checks on the old man. He's still on the phone. "I gotta go," Zeke mutters, flinging open his door. He jumps out of the van, lifts the nozzle from its cradle, and flips up the gas pump's lever without noticing the pickup truck pulling in behind him.

"Still got your hands down your pants, perv?"

Zeke's head whips toward the voice as Cindy's boyfriend steps out from behind the van. The towering man slaps an aluminum baseball bat in his open palm, almost salivating.

"Huh?" Jim smirks. "You get a good show yesterday, you dirty old bastard?"

"Don't," Zeke grumbles, replacing the nozzle without shifting his eyes. "I'm warning you." He pushes his door closed, slowly moving toward the guy.

"Warning me?" Jim inches forward, tapping the bat against the van's back wheel. "So, you're a tough guy, huh?"

Suddenly, there are quick footsteps approaching from right behind Zeke. He starts to spin around, but it's too late. Another baseball bat slides down in front of his face, slapping against his throat. Struggling to breathe, he spots a second even larger guy in the reflection of his van window.

A puff of spit bursts from his lips as Zeke is hoisted off his feet, clawing at his neck. He kicks out, squirming against the man's grip, like an enormous hooked fish. With a series of gargling, retching grunts, the two men bobble between the gas pump and the van.

"What's wrong, grandpa?" the hulk grumbles at Zeke's ear. "Is it getting hard to breathe?"

"Hey, Slim, don't choke him out," Jim sneers. "I want him to feel this shit!"

Zeke slings a wild punch, but overshooting his target, his fist brushes past Slim's ear. His fingers grapple with the bat squeezing at his throat.

"Not so scary now, are you, tough guy?" Slim goads.

As Jim moves in, winding up for a home run, Zeke flings his legs out again. The swinging bat clips his toe, but he feels nothing. The moan vibrating in his chest is fury, not pain. His vengeance is coming. He knows it. Before he can draw his knees back up in defense, Jim lands another blow. The bat pounds into Zeke's gut, forcing a breathy huff from his reddened face.

"Huh, motherfucker?" Jim draws the bat back again. "Can't quite hear ya!"

"Hey," the station attendant barks out from his booth. "The hell's goin' on over there?" He adjusts his glasses, craning his twiggy neck toward the ruckus behind the gas pumps. "I don't want no kinda trouble around here!"

Jim swings again. The bat collides with Zeke's knee this time, ricocheting out of the man's hand before it clatters down under the rear of the van. Jim scrambles to the ground, grasping for the rolling weapon. Zeke notes the easing pressure at his neck. The giant is distracted.

Wrenching his fingers around the bat at his throat, he reminds himself, *David smote the Philistine in his forehead, and he fell upon his face to the earth.*

With a series of quick, pistonlike blows, Zeke smashes his head into Slim's face. As the man's nose snaps to the side, exploding with blood, he releases his hold. Zeke drops to the ground.

"Get the hell outta here!" the old man yells, shuffling toward the brawling men.

Flattened out on his belly, Zeke scours the area at the front of the van for the fallen bat. He spots it leaning against the inside of a tire, and checking that the big guy has staggered off somewhere, he shuffles up to his hands and knees. As a boot connects with his mouth, Zeke realizes his mistake. He lost track of Jim. The kick hefts his body up off the ground, spraying blood across the side of the van.

A shotgun discharges.

Everybody flinches, Zeke curling into a fetal position.

The old station attendant steps around the gas pumps. "I said, get the hell outta here, ya sons of bitches!" He volleys the gun between Jim and the bloody-faced mammoth, both now scrambling around the front of the van.

As their pickup truck's engine fires up, the old man cocks his gun. "Go on, get outta here!"

Zeke clutches the van's rear bumper, pulling himself up to his knees. As the truck screeches away, he wipes blood from his eyes and gazes up to the sky for direction. "What would you have me do?"

"I'd have you get the hell off my property," the attendant yaps, standing over Zeke, unaffected by the state of his battered face.

"And do it now."

Zeke hoists himself to his feet, staring into the side-by-side double barrels of a Mossberg Silver Reserve. He drags his sleeve across his nose, moving his gaze to the set of tiny, spectacled eyes.

"I ain't gonna say it again," the old man warns, the gun now wavering in his frail arms.

As his finger quivers toward the trigger, Zeke raises his palms, carefully backing up to his door. He climbs into the van, eyeing the bloodied face in his rearview mirror. His cheeks are already blackening from his broken nose, and his upper lip is twice its normal thickness.

The engine roars to life, his music vibrating through the walls again, as Zeke checks his side mirror. Finding the shotgun is trained at his reflection, he stomps on the accelerator, his mind already back in his farmhouse cellar.

There is much more work to be done.

TWENTY-SEVEN

"**C**OME ON," DANI begs herself. *"Get up."*

She hears the words and wants to move, but her body won't respond. Fiery tears blur her vision as the world around her reels. Her fingers claw at the floorboards, and with another series of convulsing heaves, she vomits. The warm fluid splatters across her hands, snapping her back into the present moment.

She flops back on her haunches, wiping thick, tinted spit from her mouth as her eyes drift down her body. Dani doesn't even recognize herself. Droplets from the bites on her neck speckle across the soaked bosom of someone else's filthy nightgown, now streaked with fresh puke. And bloody red stripes from the old woman's claws twist down her calf like a giant candy cane.

As she struggles to get to her feet, the fabric clinging to the wound on her chest peels loose. The pain sends a new wave of alarm surging through her veins, and Dani hears her own voice rise. "You gotta go now."

Bolting up from her knees, she hurls herself toward the foyer. "Run, Dani, run!" she croaks, eyes locked on the doorknob at the end of the hall.

As she flies past the parlor entryway, her foot hits a wet spot and she skids full speed into a wall. Grasping at the Sheetrock, she crumples to the floor again.

Applause rises from the parlor, as if the flustered televangelist and his congregation were watching everything, rooting for her defeat. The voiceless taunting enrages Dani.

"Get up," she snaps, launching back onto her rubbery legs. With fury rippling through her body, she wobbles down the hall, whispering encouragement to herself. "You can do this, Dani. You can do this."

Reaching the foyer, she stops, her heart pounding as she stares at the front door. Moonlight seeps through the wicker shade of a large adjacent window, reminding Dani how close she is to getting out of this house of horrors. Another crackling ovation erupts from behind her.

Make the choice, she tells herself, braced against the wall. *One. Two. Three.* Dani carefully peeks around the corner.

Zeke's not there.

Yet, she thinks, stepping into the entryway.

To her left, a second hall leads to the opposite side of the house. Halfway down it, a light shines out from the open door of another room.

A bedroom? Is he in there? Her knees shudder at the idea of that horned mask charging out of the room. *But, how could he not have heard everything? The old woman's screaming? The fight?*

As Dani inches toward the front door, a new thought hits her. She stares back down the long hallway she just came through. *Maybe he did hear it all. He could've doubled back into that TV room.*

Her focus volleys between the two corridors as she listens. Complete silence from the lit bedroom is on one side, and the distant chatter from the television minister is on the other. Shadows pulse from the parlor.

Now! a voice screams in her mind. *GO, GO, GO, GO!*

Dani spins back, scampering to the door. *Get outside, and just fucking run!*

Tears pour down her filthy, shattered face as she yanks the knob. She can almost feel the freedom of the night's air on her face.

What? WHY WON'T IT OPEN—

A key slides into the lock from the other side of the door.

Dani jerks her hand away, as if the knob scalded her. She stumbles across the foyer, panicked by the jangling metal coming from outside the house.

A closet.

As she rushes toward its open door, the dead bolt clicks behind her.

There's not enough time! Whirling back around, she dives through the kitchen archway just as the heavy front door huffs open.

A tile countertop and cabinets extend along the wall to the right. She recognizes the closed door across from her as the locked one she couldn't get through in the parlor.

She scans the empty kitchen. *There's nowhere to hide.*

As the front door slams shut, Dani hooks around an old avocado-colored refrigerator on her left, sinking to the floor. She listens for some sign of where the person might be but cannot hear past the Frigidaire's humming motor. Studying her surroundings, Dani draws her knees against her chest, trying not to breathe. She stares at the old stove across from her, racking her brain for how she might use it.

Start a fire? Gas explosion? There has to be some—

The floor creaks from just outside the kitchen.

It's him. Dani's throat tightens as she spots Zeke's blurred reflection in the metal teakettle across from her.

He staggers into the kitchen, slinging a grocery bag down onto the countertop. As it collides with the wall separating the kitchen from the parlor, he considers the closed door.

"I got your chips," he calls out, opening a cabinet.

That thing's not gonna answer him, and then what?

The only drawers in the kitchen, which might contain some kind of cutlery or other sharp utensils, are directly behind him.

I need a weapon! Dani eyes what appears to be a small broom closet to the left of the stove. *But, even if I could get to it before he gets to me, what if nothing is in there?*

The freezer door swings around, smacking off the wall above her head.

Dani clenches her teeth as ice crackles free from its tray and gets tossed into a glass on the counter. A single cube drops down and slides to the center of the room. She draws her knees even tighter against her chest, trained on the piece of ice.

With a frustrated scoff, Zeke slaps shut the freezer door. The seal on the refrigerator door gasps as it slowly glides open, stopping just short of Dani's huddled body. She flattens against the wall, preparing to kick him off-balance as his hand snatches up the ice cube. He tosses it into the sink, draping the fingers of his other hand over the top edge of the door.

Listening to him rifle through clinking jars, she's certain it's all over for her now. *He's gonna hear me,* she thinks, staring at his filthy, bloodied nails. *He's gonna—*

As the refrigerator closes, she finds herself facing Zeke's back. He fills a glass with fizzing cola, oblivious to the petrified reflection in the teakettle. Separated only by the strangling air between their bodies, Dani's terror rumbles up her throat, and she has to clamp down her lips to stifle a scream.

"Hey," he grunts. Draining the last of the soda into a glass, he tosses its container into the garbage bin next to the stove. "You hear me?" he asks before taking a drink. "I got you more chips." He slouches against the counter, eyes closed, as he presses a bag of frozen peas to the side of his face.

The TV blasts from the other room, but there's no response to his question. Zeke mumbles something to himself that Dani can't understand. Finishing his soda, he sets the glass down and moves to the parlor door. He tries the knob.

"Hey!" With a huff, he flips the tiny switch, pulls the door open, and steps into the room. "Why'd you lock the—"

ZEKE EASES INTO the parlor, taking in the disaster. "Sylvia?"

His eyes dart from the empty wheelchair to the overturned bookshelf. The floor is covered with even more trash than usual. He spots the broken cereal bowl, and across the room, he sees the heap of clothes spilled into the hall.

Why did she do all of this?

The kitchen door's latch clicks behind him.

Zeke whirls around, slapping it back open as he charges into the empty kitchen. Pausing at the stove, he listens for anything other than the blaring television.

"Sylvia?" He continues toward the foyer, not noticing the bloody smears on the floor and baseboard next to the Frigidaire.

Where is she?

Sirens whine from a commercial advertising a law firm that specializes in hit-and-run victims. Zeke storms back into the parlor, smashing the TV's power button with a growl. He scans the cluttered floor around him again, but she isn't here.

Following a trail of crinkled newspaper, speckled with what looks like blood, Zeke crosses into the hallway. "Sylvia!" he yells toward the front door. "Where are you?"

No answer.

As he turns toward the cellar door, a faint glimmer on the floor catches his eye. He leans down, sliding his finger through congealing droplets of blood. His head whips back up to the open slide bolt. The bag of frozen peas slaps against the hardwood floor as Zeke rips open the cellar door.

TWENTY-EIGHT

"**S**YLVIA!"

The bubbling rage in Zeke's voice has Dani paralyzed, flattened against the foyer wall just outside the kitchen. She stares at the doorknob across from her, knowing she has to get to it. But she's afraid he'll hear her.

"Sylvia?"

He's going down there, she realizes, noting his voice is further away.

Holding her breath, she peers around the corner. At the other end of the hall, Zeke is slowly descending the stairs. Dani can no longer stave off her panic as she imagines what's going to happen next.

He's gonna find that creature down there with the snakes, she thinks, her hands trembling at her sides. *And he's gonna see I got out!* She curls her fingers into shaky fists, beginning to lose control of herself, as his body disappears into the cellar. *And then he's gonna come after me.*

"Go," she snaps to herself. "Now!"

Dani catapults across the foyer, seizing the front door's knob. She twists and yanks, but the door doesn't budge.

Come on!

Her eyes shoot to a ring of keys tinkling in the dead bolt. Grabbing ahold of it, she quickly glances to the cellar door again while wrestling with the stubborn lock. The hallway is still empty.

It's too quiet. Hasn't he found her yet? Maybe he's been bitten—

Pop! The key snaps off in the dead bolt, sending the ring clanging to the floor.

What? Dani rakes her fingers across the jagged piece of metal poking out from the lock. There's not enough to grip. "Shit!"

Zeke's spine-tingling howl echoes up the hall behind her.

Dani whirls around, eyes locked on the cellar door.

"NO," she hears him growl as he stomps up the stairs.

Shrieking, Dani spins back, abandoning the door for the adjacent window. She dives behind the wicker shade and presses her hands against the wooden rail, shifting the glass upward slightly. She finds enough space to drive her fingers into the gap. The window's shade bounces against the back of her head, blocking her vision of the hall. She can't see him, but she knows he must be at the top of the steps by now.

OPEN!

With a pained squeak, the glass starts to move again, sliding several inches higher. Dani hears the cellar door smack against the wall at the other end of the hallway. At the same time, the window jerks to a stop. Its frame is caught on something.

"Oh God! Come on!" She throws all her weight into the effort, but it won't budge. "Please!"

"You did this," Zeke snarls, slapping the wall. "You, you, you!"

He's up the stairs! Dani flies into a series of chaotic convulsions, squealing like a banshee, as she heaves with all she's got. "OH,

PLEASE," she wails, hearing the floorboards pop under Zeke's charging feet.

The bottom edge of the window frame shoots up another couple of inches. Dani's not sure if there is enough room for her to get through, but she can't wait any longer. With another yelp of terror, she dives through the opening.

"You get back here!"

Her torso flops over the windowsill, arms stretching for the ground, but suddenly, she stops. Her butt is caught on the frame; she cannot fit through the opening. She wags her hips from side to side, thrusting forward at the same time.

He's right there!

"No, you don't!" Zeke barks.

Dani's fingernails rip away chips of old paint as she tears at the house's exterior wall. "PLEASE, GOD, PLEASE," she wails, frantically squirming in the jammed window. Clawing down the siding, she manages to latch her fingertips on to the edge of a plank of the wooden clapboard.

As she pulls herself a little further out the window, in her peripheral, she sees the wicker shade rip from the wall. Dani tries to wriggle free, but his hold on her thighs is too strong to break. He has her.

"Get back in here," Zeke growls. He yanks her thrashing legs, wrenching her body backward, like an alligator wrestler.

"LET ME GO!"

The window frame grates against her lower spine, sliding up a bit as she writhes. Feeling the shift, Dani bucks her body another couple of inches back outside the house. She focuses on the lowest siding board, extending her fingers toward it. If she can just get ahold of that—

Her body jerks upward, raking the window's edge further up her back. Zeke has wedged his foot against the sill, using the leverage to drag her in. Jagged splinters rip up from the windowsill, jabbing into her skin with every heave.

But Dani isn't thinking about the shavings of her skin that are caked to the window's bottom rail or the splotches of her blood smeared on the foyer wall. Her mind is consumed with one single thought. *If I fall back into this house, he will kill me.*

Zeke sways forward, preparing for another pull. Dani takes aim, and while peering over her shoulder at her target, she kicks back as hard as she can. Her bare heel connects with his jaw, snapping his head to the side. As strings of spit fling across the pane, his hold loosens just enough.

The tips of Dani's fingers reach the last board. She hooks on to its edge while throwing another wild kick. This time, she hits him directly in the mouth, even harder than before. He releases his bear hug, shuffling across the entryway.

Regaining his footing, he lunges at her again. "You're not going anywhere!"

It's too late. With another quick buck, Dani's legs slip through the gap. She's out of the house. Her body crashes to the ground in a squealing heap.

I got out! She quickly flips around to face the window in a state of stunned disbelief.

From inside the foyer, Zeke clutches the frame. He thumps his body against the window, hoisting upward, but it doesn't budge. He locks eyes with Dani, his breathy huffs beginning to fog the glass. In the full moon's light, his swollen, gashed face looks like a contorted Halloween mask.

"Beelzebub," he roars, slapping the hazy pane as he darts out of sight.

The pounding on the front door jars Dani back into motion.

Scrambling up to her feet, she spins away from the window and staggers back from the house. She shifts from foot to foot as her eyes adjust to the outside lighting. *Now what?* She scans the rocky land in front of the farmhouse.

A few feet from the porch, she spots Zeke's van. Its white paint, which appears to glow in the moonlight, and the sporadic clicks from its cooling motor make the vehicle seem like a living creature.

Maybe there's a spare key. Dani bolts across the front yard, yanking open the van's passenger-side front door. She has to squint to see past the bright overhead dome but realizes nothing is in the ignition.

"Please," she whispers, tugging down the visor. Zeke's Buy-and-Save name tag drops to the floorboard.

Dani gives the dashboard another quick sweep while running her hand along the steering shaft. As she checks the base of the turn-signal lever and flutters her fingertips over the lock cylinder, she gasps with an idea.

A few weeks ago, she caught a segment of *Dateline* where a wild-eyed convicted felon showed Chris Hansen how easy it was to steal a car by simply jamming a screwdriver into the ignition.

Dani pops open the glove box. *Please let there be a screwdriver in here!*

The compartment is completely empty.

Shit! A new panic bursts into her mind as she realizes how much time must have passed. *He'll be out here any second.*

She flops back out of the van, still searching for her next move. *Run or hide?* Her head snaps toward a small doorless barn across the yard, on the opposite side of the house. Inside, a huge tarp drapes across the body of a car, covering all but its wheels.

Hide, she decides, sprinting toward the barn. *I'll stay in there until he drives off, looking for me, and then—*

Dani stops dead in her tracks, noticing the stacks of glass

aquariums next to the car. *More snakes? No fucking way!*

As she turns away from the barn, she hears a jingling sound coming from alongside the house. She immediately begins to shuffle backward, identifying what she is all but certain is a chain. Before she can fully process the implications of the rattling links, the enormous black head of a snarling rottweiler emerges from the darkness. A throaty grumble erupts from its slobbery muzzle, and in a flash of brown and black, the dog leaps up toward her face.

Dani shrieks, vaulting backward.

The massive jaws snap shut just in front of her chin, sending her stumbling to the ground. Having reached the end of its chain, the animal rises up on its hind legs, jerking its body, as she scuffles away. The snarling growl explodes into a booming, frenetic bark.

At the same time, a light snaps on from the side of the house, and a screen door claps against its frame.

Gooo! Dani springs to her feet, hurling herself across the yard and into the woods.

As she scampers into the darkness, she glances back over her shoulder. A second large shadow has joined the rottweiler, still ferociously chomping at the air.

Dani slows, trying to move as quietly as possible between the trees, as she watches Zeke rush over to the van. *Get in, and drive off,* she thinks, remembering the second car.

The hollow woofing reminds her that she'd never be able to reach the barn anyway. And, as Zeke moves back across the yard, mumbling something to the dog, Dani carefully disappears into the dense woods.

TWENTY-NINE

"**T**HE EYES OF *the Lord are in every place,*" the Bald Knobber shouts, pulling his hood over his head, *"beholding the evil and the good!"*

As Zeke stares up into the cobalt sky, the rottweiler's barking dissolves into impatient whimpering. It sits down and follows its master's gaze, cocking its head in confusion.

"In there?" he whispers, his eyes shifting to the dilapidated barn.

A flashlight clicks on as he and the dog slowly cross the yard, staring at the tarp-covered car.

"Neither is there any creature that is not manifest in His sight," Zeke says, crouching to direct the light between the tires. Finding nothing, he starts into the barn, waving the beam toward the back wall. *"But all things are naked and opened unto the eyes of Him with whom we have to do."*

A gargled warning rumbles from behind him. Zeke stops. *Have I misunderstood?*

He considers the dog. Its ears are at attention as it gapes into the woods, anxiously licking its chops. Zeke glides the light through the tree line.

Yes. He starts across the yard, nodding.

"For the eyes of the LORD run to and fro throughout the whole earth, to show Himself strong in the behalf of them whose heart is perfect toward Him."

Zeke pauses at the edge of the woods, directing the flashlight's ray into the darkness. *"Herein thou hast done foolishly!"* he recites. *"Therefore—"*

A twig snaps from deep within the trees.

His head jerks toward the sound as he sweeps the light over a crowd of pine boles. Another branch pops from somewhere behind them, even further away.

"Therefore," he says again, his voice building, *"from henceforth, thou shalt have wars!"*

DANI BARRELS THROUGH the trees as his words echo from behind her.

Although her arms are ablaze from the stinging lashes of the branches, the same thought repeats in her head, *Don't stop, no matter what!*

As she moves further into the woods, the moonlight fades above the canopy. She has to strain to see, even a few feet in front of herself. Dani yanks a hand up, shielding her face, as she checks back toward the farmhouse. Zeke's body is out of sight, but she spots the flashlight waving through the trees. The beam pauses on a group of saplings a few yards to her right and then continues sweeping in her direction.

A sagging limb whips across her knuckles, startling her back around, just as her hips collide with an enormous fallen tree. "Ugh!" she grunts, flopping across the thick trunk.

In her peripheral, the ray of light begins moving again. She has to get out of sight. In a fluster, Dani latches on to the bark and hurls herself over the top of the tree.

A bolt of what feels like fiery lightning shoots up her leg as her bare arch plunges down on a spiky rock poking up through the underbrush. She collapses to the ground, choking back a scream. Shoving the heel of her hand into her mouth, she clamps down in agony, pretty sure the rock has sliced through the muscle. Above her, the strip of light passes over the fallen tree, continuing its surveillance. She drags her injured foot closer to her body. It's too dark to see, but considering the amount of blood oozing between her fingers, she knows the gash is really bad.

Oh God. I can't run anymore!

Dani pulls her knees to her chest, dropping her head, as tears trickle down her face. And, unable to hold back any longer, her tiny, broken voice concedes. "I'm gonna die."

The relief is immediate. No longer scared or in pain, her mind begins swirling through rapid clips of her life, each one briefly appearing on the backs of her eyelids. It's as if she were watching a collection of performances where she was playing the lead character. Only it's not on TV or in a movie. It feels closer somehow, like a play. As her thoughts flicker through a cloudy collage, one image slowly emerges more clearly than the others—her father's eyes.

———————

Her old man never cries, but his eyes are definitely glossy right now. Dani just told her parents she would be moving up north, but the conversation hadn't gone the way she planned. When the time was right, she'd intended to cook them a fancy steak dinner and open a good bottle of wine even though her dad was usually more of a beer guy. And then, as they all worked their way toward a batch of her famous Kahlua brownies, she was gonna spill the beans.

Instead, while smearing black-cherry jam on her husband's toast this morning, her mother once again addressed the elephant that had been following Dani into every room for weeks. "Have you, um . . . heard anything from Michael, honey?"

"I just don't want to talk about any of it right now," Dani said. "I need some time to process everything."

She had told her parents they broke up but not disclosed any details. Frankly, it still felt too embarrassing to discuss.

Apparently, a month is the statute of limitations for not talking about it.

Before Dani knew it, she had told them about Mike's cheating, her friend's vacation house in Pennsylvania, and finally, her plans to move. Their surprise grew into concern with each new detail she'd shared until, eventually, they all stood quiet.

Then, when her mother could no longer stare at the kitchen linoleum, she poured herself a fresh cup of coffee and reignited the discussion. "That's a bit dramatic, Dani," her mom said. "Don't you think?"

"Can't you *find* yourself on the other side of town?" her dad asked. "Or, hell, move to Dallas or Austin. Texas is a big damn state, baby girl."

Now, hours later, they're all standing in the front hallway, and the silence is unbearable. The debate is over, but this is not how Dani wants to leave things.

What else can I say?

Her dad is leaning against the spindly banister that leads upstairs, gazing back at her with his glassy brown eyes. She has never seen him like this.

He looks destroyed—

He wiggles his bushy, salt-and-pepper mustache.

Dani's heart explodes. For her entire life, she's been able to gauge her dad's mood by the specific movement of that facial hair, and at this exact moment, when she needs his support most, it's telling her he loves her.

She charges toward the burly man for a hug, smiling like a little girl whose daddy has just given her a puppy.

"By the way, how's writing a *brag* gonna pay the bills?" he asks in his typical display of corny humor.

"It's a blog, Dad," she replies, grinning at her mother. "I have a little savings, and I'll get a part-time job to cover—"

"Honey, we will always support you and whatever you choose to do," her mom interjects. "We'd just like it better if you weren't moving so far away." She smiles at her worried husband. "I mean, don't people blog down here?"

"If anything happens to you up there, Dani," her father jumps in, "I couldn't—"

"Dad, nothing's gonna happen to me."

————

FLASH.

Jess stares into the paper cup, scraping at the last bit of her DQ Blizzard. She's been trying to hide her tears, but Dani's already noticed.

"So, this isn't, like, a vacation or something? You're *moving* there?"

"Yeah, I think so," Dani answers, chomping on a French fry. "For a while. Probably a year at least."

"A *year*?" Jess slaps her empty cup on the wooden picnic table. "Where am I supposed to find a substitute workout partner for a *year?"*

"Hey, I cannot be responsible for your diet challenges any longer."

"Ugh!" Jess palms her chest, feigning devastation, as she strolls to a large garbage bin. "You're a horrible person," she huffs. "You let me get a *large* Oreo Blizzard, and then you just dropped *that* bombshell on me?"

"So selfish, I know."

"Look, not being around for me so that I can whine about my moderately attentive husband several times a week is one thing, but wanting me to get fat is just vile!"

"Want some fries to forget the pain?"

Jess chuckles, flinging a wadded napkin at her lifelong best friend. Her eyes tear up again as she slumps down next to Dani. "This sucks."

"I know. I'm scared shitless, but I gotta do it." A somber expression spreads down her face as she stares at the passing traffic. "I mean, I'm thirty-two years old, and I've never really been on my own. I've always lived with my parents or roommates or a boyfriend. I think I need to prove that I can do it by myself, you know?"

"Prove it to *who?*"

"Me, Jess. To myself. Prove to myself that I'm a smart, strong woman, who can survive on my own in the big, bad world."

"Is this just because of my brother?"

"Oh, *nooo.*" Dani smirks, oozing sarcasm.

"'Cause Mike's an asshole."

"Oh, *I know*," she scoffs, "believe me."

"Fuck him!" Jess shouts, grabbing the attention of the family waiting in the drive-through line. "And fuck that Mandy, too!"

FLASH.

"It's not Mandy's fault," Mike says, stepping over the puddle of cola and ice cubes as it spreads across their kitchen floor. He rips a dish towel off the cabinet and blots his split bottom lip. "She didn't even know about you, okay?"

"No, it's not okay!"

Dani slouches onto a barstool, staring at a shard of the shattered tumbler she threw. Somehow, it landed in the living room of the apartment she couldn't really afford to move into in the first place. The splashes of soda will probably stain the expensive plush carpet.

Who fucking cares? she thinks, trying to wrap her mind around the messier of the situations. *I hate him so much. I think I could actually stab him with that chunk of glass.* A twinge of humiliation swirls in her gut as another thought takes over. *I don't want to lose him. It's so pathetic, but I don't.*

The conflicting emotions of being repelled by the sight of his face while at the same time needing him to choose her more than she's ever needed anything in her whole life is debilitating.

Dani closes her eyes, waiting for her heart to literally explode from the incredible pressure swelling in her chest. *How could he do this to me?*

A crackling from the freezer breaks the silence as the automatic ice maker spits out a new batch of cubes. She glances up and finds Mike gazing back at her. His expression has softened. His eyes seem so sad now.

Has he realized that it's me he really wants? A flare of hope ripples through her body. *Even if he has, am I capable of ever getting past this?*

She combs her fingers through her hair, taking a deep breath. "How long?"

"What? That doesn't matter—"

"It fucking matters to me!" she screams, slapping the countertop.

Oh my God. He's not choosing me.

As Mike squirms, Dani can see potential responses fluttering by in his eyes, like a human slot machine of lies. She expects that whatever bullshit he says next could quite possibly push her over to the darker realm where she would stab him with that chunk of glass.

She leans in, clutching the side of the bar. "Well?"

"About a year."

Wow. Humiliation wraps its tendrils around Dani's neck, strangling her voice away. *I believe that is actually the truth. And it hurts worse than any lie he could have told me.*

Her head slowly sways from side to side, and for the first time since this all started, tears well up in her eyes. "How could you do this?" she whispers. "Mike, how could you do this to me?"

"Oh, *come on*, Dani," he snaps. "Gimme a break." He flings the blood-spotted towel into the sink. "You know you've been unhappy for a long time now. Like, a *really* long time. 'I'm a loser. I hate my job, but I need the money. What am I doing with my life?' It gets fuckin' old, okay?" He dabs his lip and checks his finger for blood. "You used to be fun, you know?"

"You are a piece of dog shit."

"Oh, that's really mature. Whatever. Now, you get to crawl back to your parents again and tell them how yet another person dicked you over. 'Cause, you know, nothing's ever *your* fault, Dani—"

"*Fuck you!*" She springs up from the stool. "How exactly is you screwing Mandy for the past year *my* fault?"

"Dani, I am not fighting with you anymore, okay? I'm done." Mike grabs his car keys off the counter and heads toward the front door, kicking the broken hunk of glass out of his path. Wrenching the doorknob, he turns back over his shoulder. "You know, I'm sure you don't see it like this right now, but this will probably help you out actually. Now, you can go figure out what else makes you happy." He steps through the door, shaking his head. "Besides always choosing to be a fucking victim."

"Go to hell, Mike," she bawls. The lidless two-liter bottle of Dr. Pepper crashes against the slamming door, spraying brown fizz across the living room carpet. "I'm not choosing to be a fucking victim."

———————

Several twigs pop from somewhere in the woods, forcing Dani back into the present moment.

Huddled against the fallen tree, she wipes tears out of her stinging eyes, still listening to the words echoing in her mind. *I'm not choosing to be a fucking victim! I'm not choosing to be a fucking VICTIM!*

An angry current floods through her veins as she claws at the dirt, mumbling a new version of the phrase, "I'm choosing NOT to be a fucking victim!"

Dani flops over to her knees. Peeking over the collapsed trunk, she can't tell how far away the wagging flashlight beam is, but as Zeke's voice booms again, she knows he's close.

Sinking her fingertips into the bark, she hoists herself to her feet. "And fuck *you*," she mumbles, hobbling deeper into the woods. "I'm not gonna be *your* fucking victim either."

THIRTY

THE GOAT HORNS sag at Zeke's back, clacking together, as he moves through the woods. Stepping over the protruding roots of a huge white oak, he approaches the edge of a cliff. He locks one hand on the thinner trunk of a neighboring tree, peering down at a brook running parallel to him, thirty feet below. He shines the light along the muddy banks, pausing at a large clump of shrubs.

It's not her.

Several hundred yards farther to the right, the shallow stream ends in a stagnant pool. The flashlight hovers at the opening of a large drainage pipe above the water.

"Submit yourself therefore to God," he bellows out across the drop. *"Resist the devil!"*

A big gust hisses through the treetops, shifting Zeke's attention to the other end of the ravine. As the wind blows, he sweeps the beam further upstream, tilting his head to the side and sniffing at the breeze like an air-scenting cadaver dog trailing its subject.

Something crackles off to the right.

Whipping the light over, he quickly sidles through the trees. A set of glowing yellow eyes pops up from behind another cluster of thick bushes. Zeke stomps toward them. As he approaches, a pair of white-tailed deer bolts up from the thicket, vaulting away. Their fluffy tails signal an alarm, prompting the rest of the herd to scamper off into the rustling blackness.

"The young lions roar after their prey," he calls out, *"and seek their meat from God."*

A branch snaps from the area he just came from and he waves the light through the densely packed trees, pausing on a large bunch of shuddering leaves. He clicks off the flashlight. His feet crackle over the dead leaves as he carefully moves along the edge of the bluff toward the white oak.

"Can any hide himself in secret places that I shall not see him? saith the Lord," Zeke recites, arriving at the large tree. *"Do not I fill heaven and earth? saith the Lord."*

Click.

A bright streak of white light splits the blackness, spotlighting Dani's bloody leg trembling from ten feet above him. A grin works itself across Zeke's bruised face as he raises the beam to her panicked, bloodshot eyes.

"Help!" she hoarsely squawks to the sky. "Please, somebody, help me!" Gripping rubbery twigs on both sides of herself, Dani teeters out onto the thick bough of the tree, trying to keep as much distance between them as possible.

Zeke drops the light to the ground, darting behind the giant trunk.

DANI'S EYES VOLLEY to each side of the tree, as she expects

him to spring out at any second. She thinks she can make out his hunched torso skulking behind the base of another tree.

What the hell is he doing? She cranes her head but can't quite see beyond the hazy perimeter of light.

As he bobs back and forth, jerking at something on the ground, the loud crack of splitting wood echoes through the trees.

Startled, Dani almost loses her footing. She tightens her grip on the branches she's balanced between, her pulse drumming in her ears. Staring down at the trunk of her tree, she hears her own broken voice trickle out in a string of tiny, whimpering pleas. "I need help . . . somebody has to help—"

The Bald Knobber emerges from behind the tree, hood pulled up again. His distorted silhouette spreads out across the ground as he approaches the flashlight.

Spotting the glowing orange eyes below sends a new jolt of terror through Dani. "Oh, please," she mutters inadvertently. "Please don't."

His fiendish gaze slowly rises, tipping upward, until the painted eyes are out of sight. In their place, Zeke's haggard, shadowy face peers up at her. *"Humble yourself therefore under the mighty hand of God!"* he shouts. *"That He may exalt you in due time."*

He springs toward her.

The flashlight whirls into a flurry of waving beams, creating a strobe-light effect through the trees. She scrambles to avert her eyes but isn't fast enough. And a burst of bright light hits her with glaring rings expanding past a series of black splotches. Dani tightens her hold on a wiry limb, shuffling backward, as she aims her face to the sky, trying to recover from the flash blindness.

WHACK!

The branch trembles beneath her feet. Dani yelps, clawing through leaves to maintain her balance. As another wood-cracking thump sends vibrations wobbling up her legs, her sight returns. Now, she realizes exactly what Zeke was doing behind the tree. *He's got a stick.* She hops over a swinging baseball-bat-sized branch headed for her ankle.

"No," she squeals, narrowly avoiding the blow. "Just leave me alone!"

Zeke shifts to reposition himself directly underneath her, winding up again. *"The Lord is nigh unto all them that call upon Him,"* he growls, flailing his branch upward. *"To all that call upon Him in TRUTH!"* The stick smacks against the bough, breaking in half. He snarls, flings it aside, and aims the light up at her eyes again.

Dani avoids the beam this time. As she inches further out on the branch, she hears a thud on the ground. The flashlight is no longer waving up at her. Steadying herself with a fistful of a tree limb, she peers down into the darkness. Zeke's gone, but she spots a small yellow orb glowing on the opposite side of the trunk. An alarm blares in her head.

Why would he drop his light?

Dani's branch shudders, swaying much deeper than before. One of her feet slips off. "Shit!"

She tears through a dangling clump of leaves, snagging a sturdier limb just in time. As she scurries back up, a fluttery movement at the center of the tree catches her attention. *Are those fingers?* She hears Zeke's labored grunt, and it hits her. *He dropped his flashlight because he needed his hands free. HE'S CLIMBING UP HERE!*

"Why are you doing this to me?" Her raspy scream dissolves into wheezing breaths as she lobs her body up and down, trying to break his grip. "Why?"

Stomp his fingers, she thinks, realizing his hold is too secure on the bouncing branch. *Gotta knock him out of this fucking tree.*

Eyeing his interlaced knuckles, Dani starts toward him, but it's too late. She jerks to a stop as Zeke pulls himself up onto her branch.

"Trust in the Lord with all thine heart," he pants, slouching back against the trunk. As he fishes his Taser from the hoodie's front pocket, his full voice slowly returns. *"And lean not unto thine own understanding."*

A spark of blue-and-white claps in the darkness, lighting up the front of his face. And, with another throaty grunt, Zeke lunges for her.

"Nooo!" Dani croaks, springing backward. She quickly shifts into a sidestepping motion, sliding further out on the narrowing branch. As she continues past the edge of the cliff, the limb bows under her weight, bobbing her over the vast black space below. "Help me—"

CRACK!

The branch breaks, catapulting Dani's stomach into her chest. She erupts into a torrent of thrashing arms and legs, unable to scream. Pinballing downward, she slashes through huge clusters of leaves and snapping twigs, unable to latch on to anything. As she crashes through the foliage, a raucous hiss swells around her, like the tree is fighting to fling her off itself. She plows through the lowest tangle of limbs, and with a final *thwack*, sinks into complete darkness.

Time seems suspended somehow. In fact, the air is so black that, if it wasn't for the wind fluttering her hair up around her cheeks, she might not even know she was falling. It's as if she were breathlessly plunging downward on some horrible amusement park ride in the middle of outer space. Her mind whirls in the strangling, never-ending nothingness.

Suddenly, a tremendous force explodes against her back, punching the last bit of air from her lungs as she hits the ground. Sludge oozes up around her, creating a suctioned mold of her body. Dani can feel the cold earth beneath her and see the tiny specks she knows are stars, but she cannot move.

Am I still alive?

As she is wedged in the doughy levee, her lips begin to quiver, supping at the air like a fish out of water.

I am alive, but I CAN'T BREATHE!

Above her, a glowing orb appears at the edge of the cliff. Her body fell straight down without drifting very far from the face of the bluff. She tracks the bright beam as it stretches down to the creek. It moves across the wet bank in wild sweeps, spotlighting various bushes along the edge of the water. Her heartbeat hammers against her chest as the light pauses at a ripped garbage bag caught on a rock a few yards to her left.

Something shifts inside Dani—an enveloping calmness. Although she still cannot breathe, the fight to do so is leaving her. The driving internal voice is so far away now that she can't even remember what it was saying. In its place, a soft, limpid message rises from somewhere much closer, granting her permission.

You can go to sleep now, Dani, it whispers. *Everything's going to be okay. You've done all you can. It will all be over soon.*

Her heavy eyelids submit to the drowsiness, easing downward, as she tiptoes toward unconsciousness.

No!

Dani's diaphragm jolts back into motion, and she explodes into gasping convulsions, slapping the ground. She scrapes deep gashes in the soil as she gulps for air, like a clogged vacuum hose. Her feet kick out in spasms, flinging mucky splatters across her body.

Trying to harness her breathing, she squeezes her eyes shut. *In, two, three. Out, two, three. In, two, three—*

A light hovers above her face. *He's found me!* But, as loose branches shatter against the ground at the base of the bluff, she realizes the light is further away than she thought. Still heaving, she cracks her eyes, following the beam up to the top of the cliff. *He's still up there.*

A bolt of desperation surges through her. *I gotta move!* She reaches across her body, sinking her fingers into the dirt, and drags herself over to her belly with a huff.

Above her, the light appears to be bobbing away, moving along the rim of the bluff. She hauls herself up to her hands and knees, trying to identify the clacking sound between her wheezes.

The horns! Oh God, he's climbing down here.

Thrusting herself to her feet, Dani pivots around, scouring the area for an escape. Her eyes have adjusted to the light of the night sky, so she can make out that she's standing in a kind of giant horseshoe-shaped gorge. The vertical embankment on the other side of the water is at least a hundred feet high and extends around to the right, connecting with the bluff behind her.

I gotta get up there somehow, she thinks, searching for any possible footholds. *There has to be a way.* She starts toward the brook, studying the rocky clay wall.

"Ahh," Zeke cries out.

Dani spins toward the sound, tracking the flashlight as it jounces down the escarpment. He's dropped the light.

Shit! She has no idea where he is now.

Considering the steep climb again, she doubts herself. *I'll never make it all the way up there in time.*

She glances back over to the flashlight, wondering if she can try to run past him. If she hugs the wall, she can maybe slip out of the gorge before he makes it to the bottom.

Another angry shout rings out as Zeke loses his footing. He shuffles down the last few feet of the slope, tumbling into the opening of the horseshoe in a groaning heap.

There's nowhere to go. Dani staggers in a frantic circle as Zeke scrambles toward his flashlight.

Scanning the length of the creek again, she gasps. There's a drainage pipe fifty feet to the right. Hurling herself into a clumsy gallop, she hobbles off to the large metal tube. She checks back over her shoulder as she runs. The light is rising from the ground again, moving further into the horseshoe.

She whirls back just as she arrives at the pipe. The opening looks to be about three feet in diameter, which Dani's sure she can fit through. It's the water she's worried about. *There's gotta be snakes in here,* she thinks, reluctantly eyeing a stagnant pool beneath the pipe.

She considers the distance from the edge of the water, wondering if she could jump. *No way,* the pulsing gash in her foot reminds her. *And, if I fall, the splash will bring him right to me.*

Zeke is getting closer, his light bouncing between the bluff and the edge of the water. *"Enter into the rock, and hide thee in the dust,"* he roars. *"For fear of the Lord, and for the glory of His majesty."*

Gooo!

Sucking in a fortifying breath, Dani steps into the water. The doughy bed squishes up between her toes, and she immediately feels a stinging sensation in her wounded sole. As she wades further in, something skims past her ankle, daring her to wail.

Keep going, she commands, stifling the scream. *He's so close.*

Submerged to her waist now, she reaches the opening of the tube. It's too dark to see past the first few feet inside the shaft, but a quick glance at the probing flashlight behind her is all the motivation she needs.

Whatever's in there is better than what's out here.

As quietly as possible, Dani grips on to the drainage pipe's lip. She draws her body inside, positioning herself so that she's facing out over the creek.

Zeke moves along the stream bank, mumbling to himself, as he waves the flashlight. Discovering a large pile of branches at the base of the cliff, he stops, then rushes to the heap, his light aimed at the space just behind it.

Please, just let him turn around. Let him think I made it out before he got down here.

The light sweeps back toward the water as he resumes his search. Continuing toward her, he pauses at an area in the middle of the valley. The spotlight lingers over an indention in the ground. Dani's throat tightens. He's found the cast her body made when it plunged into the squashy levee.

As Zeke begins to move again, more swiftly now, she realizes her huge mistake. *My footprints.*

The beam slowly glides across the bank, following the desperate trail she left in the mud.

"Oh my God," she whispers, jerking her head back into the shadows. *He's gonna*—

A blinding flash lights up the drainage pipe, highlighting Dani's face.

"*Ask, and it will be given to you!*" Zeke shouts, breaking into a sprint. "*Seek, and you will find.*"

"No!" Dani propels her body backward.

Flopping over onto all fours, she dives deeper into the dark tunnel, squishing over small heaps of rotting leaves. As she frantically squirms through puddles of foul water, she hears a large *kerplunk*. He's made it into the pool.

Rays of light shoot past her body, projecting her floundering silhouette along the walls and giving her a glimpse of what is up ahead. In another twenty feet, the pipe seems to rise, curving off to the left. Making a mental note of the path, Dani squeezes her eyes shut and wriggles through another splash of putrid water, trying to only breathe through her nose.

"*Knock,*" Zeke sneers, tapping the side of the pipe, "*and it will be opened to you.*"

The flashlight clicks off.

THIRTY-ONE

WHAT THE HELL *was that?*

Dani lurches to a stop, staring into the darkness, trying to hear over the echoes of her breathing. She's pretty sure there was a sound, a gurgling or growling from up ahead. It's been pitch-black since she rounded the curve in the tunnel several minutes ago, but she couldn't chance slowing down.

He could be right behind me. I can't stop. She checks the pipe at her back. *Is he gone?*

Not willing to risk being wrong, she starts forward again, dismissing the sound.

An angry hiss breaks into what sounds like a series of spitting coughs.

Dani freezes again, certain she heard something.

Having no idea what the creature is or how close she might be to it, her mind flips through images of terrifying varmints that could have made this place home. *It's too tight in here for a bear, right?*

Maybe a skunk? Or a—

Dani gasps as a memory from back home pops into her head. *A possum!*

She once saw a patchy, rabid-looking one tear up a dog that got too close.

"Oh God," she begs, shielding her face, "please don't be a possum."

A frenzied commotion puffs air across her cheek. She flinches backward, unable to stop a squeal, as she flips a filthy wave toward the ruckus. Reacting to the water, another raspy hiss gusts into her face, telling her the creature is much closer than she realized. Reared up, Dani braces herself for the attack, but nothing happens. For a split second, she wonders if she imagined the whole thing.

A whining yowl fills the tunnel. At the same time, claws feverishly scratch against the metal floor. As they move, Dani sees not only are *two* animals barreling away from her, but they're also running toward a soft glowing light. And, in a flurry of stripes, a pair of fat raccoons dives out of sight.

The end of the drainage pipe!

With her heart still racing, Dani considers her next move. She has no idea how long she's been in here or where she is now. *But he probably does. Could he be out there?* She's paralyzed by the thought of him crouching outside the pipe, waiting to pounce.

She peers back into the darkness. *Or is he behind me?* She thinks she hears a huffing behind her. *Is that wind, or is it him?* Her hands begin to shake. She can't decide what to do. *Where is he?*

Suddenly, a humming rumble swells from outside the pipe. She jerks her face to the light, focusing on the sound. As the murmuring tapers off, it hits her. *That's a motor. There's a road!*

The idea that she could flag down someone for help flashes into her mind. *I'm almost there. Help is just outside!* Fighting back the impulse to dissolve into a hysterical mess, Dani springs forward, sloshing to the end of the tunnel.

A roll of rust-colored water gushes from the drainage pipe as she scrambles out into a dank roadside ditch. Throwing herself up into a fighting stance, she pivots in a circle, fists balled, as she scans the area like a cornered dog. The muddy trench is flanked by the steep fifty-foot slope of a mountain and a much more shallow climb to a two-lane blacktop highway. Other than a slight breeze and a sporadic bullfrog bellow, the night is eerily quiet.

He's not here.

Quickly crawling up to the road, she watches a pair of glowing taillights zigzagging down the curvy asphalt to her left. *They're so far away.* She doubts the driver would see her if she ran out to try to flag it down.

A shock shoots through her foot. *I don't even think I can run now,* she worries, as the small bulbs disappear around the side of the mountain.

Dani eyes the dense woods across from her, realizing it's the area she tunneled under. *Did he follow me in?* She glances down at the drainage pipe. Considering the time that's passed and the lack of noise, she discounts that idea, returning her attention to the tree line. The sheer silence sends another option fluttering into her mind. *What if he's gone already? Maybe he decided it would be better to just get the hell away from here while he still could.*

Something rustles from deep in the trees.

No way. He'd never let me go. Reviewing the twists and turns she made, Dani pinpoints the general direction she believes Zeke would be coming from.

Was that his flashlight? She gasps, almost positive she just saw a light flicker in the trees. *He's heading right toward me.*

Headlights rise from over a hill to the right.

"Oh, thank God," she blurts, scrambling up to her feet.

As she moves into the road, Dani flings up her sludge-caked arms, waving at the oncoming car. "Help me! Please help!"

A light-colored station wagon swerves past her, blaring its horn. It crackles onto the rocky shoulder, scattering dusty pebbles across the pavement.

"Stop," Dani pleads with all the sound her grated voice will allow. "Please stop!" Staggering after the speeding car, a stabbing pain rips through the gouge in her sole, forcing her to the ground. *"Please* help me."

From behind Dani, a bright white light spreads across the glimmering asphalt. As she spins around, a deep, moaning foghorn sound startles her up to her feet. Several smaller lights outline the front of a huge vehicle, and as the roaring diesel motor downshifts, she realizes it's a tractor-trailer.

"Hey!" She rushes toward the slowing truck in a gimpy hobble, flailing her arms. "Please stop!" she yells from the middle of the road. "PLEASE!"

Air brake blasts off, slowing the eighteen-wheeler to a whiny halt. Dani bolts to the driver-side door where an old bearded trucker leans his pudgy cheek against the window, examining her. He scrolls down her body as she wrenches herself up onto the rig's step tank and bangs on his door. Smears of blood and dirt coat her limbs, and the sagging neckline of the gown reveals the festering wound on her chest. Muddy clumps of hair cling to the side of her head, stretching down to the gory bite marks on her neck. As their eyes meet, Dani registers his alarm. She must look worse than she imagined.

"Please, sir," she begs, tears streaming down her grimy face. "Please help me! There's a—"

Branches crackle from the woods on the other side of the eighteen-wheeler.

Dani shrieks, craning toward the noise. "Oh God," she whimpers, slapping the window. "He's coming!"

The man jumps in his seat and whips his head to the side of the road, scanning the tree line.

"*Please!*" Dani wails, nodding to the woods. "He's right over there!"

"Step down," the man says through the glass.

Dani shuffles off the rig, moving far enough away for the door to open. *Come on, COME ON!*

Her eyes volley between the front and back of the truck, terrified Zeke will pop out. The trucker appears in the window again. His stoic expression agitates her.

Why isn't he opening the fucking door?

Sorry, he mouths, shaking his fat head. And, with an almost remorseful shrug, he releases the puffing brake.

Dani's heart drops through her stomach. "*What? No!*"

Charging back toward the door, she lands one pounding fist, but the truck is already crawling by her. As it growls up the highway, she lumbers after it, pleading with the taillights, "Wait, don't leave me!"

Beep-beep!

Dani spins around, flinging her body at the approaching lights. "STOP!" As she reels toward this new vehicle, it pulls off to the side of the road a few yards in front of her. "You have to help me!"

The headlights flick to a blinding set of high beams. Shielding her eyes, she continues toward the sound of the rumbling motor. "Please help me," she calls out to the driver. "He's gonna—"

"*Rejoice with me,*" Zeke responds through the driver's window of his van. "*I have found my sheep which was lost.*"

"NOOO!"

Her fractured howl screeches up into the night as Dani registers his voice. She recoils, hurling herself back toward the mountainside.

Adrenaline surges through her body, numbing her ripped up foot, and she bounds across the concrete with absolutely no pain. Flopping into the ditch, she sloshes through the muddy leaves. As she clambers up the steep, rocky face, she hears the van door slam shut.

Zeke moves into her peripheral, charging across the blacktop to the base of the mountain, his horns clacking. With a grunt, he jumps up to a protruding tree root. *"I said therefore unto you, that ye shall die in your sin,"* he barks, pulling himself several feet up the slope. *"For if ye believe not that I am He, ye shall—"*

His foot slips on a loose patch of dirt. Grappling at branches, he shoots down the crumbly incline, finally latching on to the wispy trunk of a tree. His feet dangle in a dusty cloud above the ditch as he growls up at her, finishing his verse, *"Ye shall die in your sins!"*

Dani hears the scuffling commotion move closer behind her but won't look back. Assuming he's only inches away from grabbing her ankle, she changes course. Springing to her right, she locks her hands around a new branch. As she draws herself up another few feet, she spots the brow of the cliff.

You're almost there, Dani. MOVE IT!

Kicking off the side, she sends down a shower of rubble. Zeke blusters, spitting out the powdery dirt. His throat-rattling snarl tells her she hit her mark.

"Get away from me!" she screams, stomping at another large hunk of clay. As it plunges down, Dani hoists herself over the crest.

Heaving to catch her breath, she collapses back onto her heels, scanning her dark surroundings. A new current of panic ripples through her as she sees a solid wall of earth shooting straight up into the sky. *This isn't the top?* Dani jolts up to her knees, taking in the ten-foot squared ledge of rock she's perched on. *Oh God! There's nowhere to go. I'm trapped up here!*

Another grunt from below spurs her back into action. Flattening to the ground, she slides over to the edge of the cliff and carefully peeks over. The outline of Zeke's gnarled horns slowly rises through the drifting cloud.

He's still coming!

Dani shoves herself back from the lip, raking her hands through patchy clumps of weeds. *I gotta find something to fight with*, she thinks, flipping through a pile of leaves. *But there's nothing here.*

A stiff wind gusts through, blowing her stringy hair across her face. She braces herself against the ground again, reviewing her lack of options. As the trees sway from the brink of the mountain another fifty feet above, Dani notes a rattling sound coming from right behind her. She springs to her feet, prepared to kill whatever it is. Squinting into the darkness at the rear of the ledge, she spots the source of the noise lying against the base of the stony wall. A small bunch of leaves shimmy from the end of a large stick.

Diving over to it, she seizes the fallen limb and ducks into a shadow. Clutching the wood like a Louisville Slugger, she rises into position. A wave of confidence floods over Dani, warming her entire body, as flashes of the countless extra hitting drills her father forced on her click through her mind.

As a child, she hated all the boring practices. She really only stuck with softball because she loved spending so much time with her dad, the coach. When she got to high school though, she swapped out the senior division softball practices for a spot on the Odyssey of the Mind team, never looking back. She was relieved at how quickly her dad had adjusted, shifting his pride for his national home-run champion to his OMER award winner. So, every once in a while, she'd throw the old man a bone and hit some balls with him, always swinging at the top of the ball like he'd taught her.

"I'm gonna take your fuckin' head off," Dani grumbles, trained on the edge of the cliff.

Honk-hooonk!

She listens for Zeke but cannot hear anything from below other than a car's horn. There is no grunting or cracking of twigs anymore, and she hasn't heard any of his crazy Bible talk for several minutes now.

Her confidence wavers a bit. *Where the hell did he go?*

Hooonk-honk-honk-honk!

An irate motor swells as tires screech on the blacktop highway. Dani creeps toward the brink again.

Did he speed off?

Crouching to one knee, she peeks down the slope. Zeke's white van is still idling on the side of the road, its bright headlights shooting into the woods. She checks the rocky wall below. He's not there.

What?

Her eyes dart to the red taillights down the highway, wishing she were in that honking car.

The swift shuffling from the darkness to her right reminds Dani that she is not.

Somehow, Zeke has climbed up to the far side of the ledge without her noticing him. Dani shuffles back from the edge just in time to find the glowing orange eyes barreling toward her. Unable to get the stick into position or to even move out of the way, she flops onto her back, drawing her knees up.

Zeke plows into her, hissing, as he jabs his Taser at her neck. With snapping blue flickers just inches from her face, Dani kicks out. She connects with his gut, flinging him into the steep wall. He crashes to the ground in a snarling heap, the Taser flying from his hand, careening off the bluff.

Dani vaults up to her feet, seizing the makeshift Slugger. Brandishing the limb in front of herself, she slides closer to the wall, tears of fury now sparkling in her eyes.

Zeke rises, huffing out into the center of the area like an angry bull. As he squares up with her, she notes labored wheezes rattling from his bloodied mouth. He glances over to the edge of the cliff, now parallel to them, and flexes his fingers. The sound of popping knuckles ripples in the air between them as the Bald Knobber slowly swings his face back to Dani.

Her stance doesn't falter. *Watch your target,* she reminds herself. *Be patient.* With a laser-focused glare, Dani lowers her body, drawing the stick up behind her head. *Keep breathing.*

Zeke eases into his own fighting stance. His chapped mouth slides into a grimace. *"I can do all things through Him who strengthens me."*

"Yeah, me, too, motherfucker," Dani growls back. "So, come on!"

Zeke lunges.

As he bounds toward her, Dani stands her ground. *Wait for it,* she tells herself, choking up on the stick. *Just wait.*

She pushes every horrific second of her time in that farmhouse out of her mind, solely concentrating on this exact moment. Anxious butterflies flit around her gut, like she's back on her dad's softball team again, listening for his cue.

Wait for it.

Chills scamper up her spine as Zeke crosses an invisible line, and from a distant dugout in her mind, Dani hears her coach.

Now!

She steps through, smashing into the man's jaw with a grand-slam swing. Zeke sways backward to the ground like a felled pine tree, his head hitting the dirt in a teeth-clacking thump. Blood spurts up through his lips as the hood gathers beside his ears. Other than the rising and sinking of his chest, his body is still.

Dani moves back into position, drawing the branch up for

another hit. *He's faking it. He's gonna jump up and come at me again.*

Scanning Zeke's mutilated face, she notices a change in his breathing. The gagging is gone and there is no longer any heaving. She cranes her neck for a clearer look, but his head has lolled toward the mountain wall.

A horn wails from down below from another frustrated driver.

"Get outta the way, asshole," some man bellows.

Dani gasps, remembering the van. She eases over to the edge of the cliff. *It's still running!* Just as a spark of hope ignites, she considers the sharp slope down to the blacktop. Suddenly nauseous, she glances to Zeke's static body, eyeing one of the hood's twisted goat horns. *He's either dying or regrouping. And I'm not waiting around to find out which.*

Resigning herself to the potentially deadly descent, Dani flings the stick out toward the road.

"You can do this," she whispers, carefully moving down the face. "You're almost—"

Her foot slips off a skinny tree trunk, and before she can grab on to a protruding rock, Dani is plummeting down. She flails her arms, grasping at passing limbs, but she cannot stop her fall. Hoarse, whistling screams follow her sinking body. As she scrapes by a tree that has grown out almost parallel to the road, she drives her forearm around its thick bough. Her body jerks to a stop, clinging to the branch by one arm. With her heart racing, she checks over her shoulder. The ditch is now only ten feet or so away.

You're so close—

Zeke moans from above her.

Whipping her head back up, Dani sees the Bald Knobber hood glaring down from the ledge.

He is alive!

Keeping her eyes locked on the mask, she swings her legs out, finding a foothold. Her toes catch on the lip of some kind of root, allowing her to haul her body toward the mountainside again. As she works down the slope, sandy bits begin to sift down from above, pelting her head.

He's coming! Move it!

"Pour out thy wrath upon the heathen that have not known thee," Zeke groans with a croaky, demonlike voice. *"And upon the kingdoms that have not called upon thy name!"*

Gritting her teeth, Dani pushes off the wall and plunges into the ditch, sloshing into a clump of soggy leaves. As she scrambles across the road toward the van, she checks Zeke's position above.

"Nooo!" He steps off the ledge.

With an explosion of snapping twigs and shuffling rocks, his floundering body hurtles down the hillside, ricocheting between trees. Before he can shield his face, a jagged branch rakes up his cheek, tearing through the corner of his eyelid, as he shoots to the ground.

Racing across the blacktop as fast as her broken frame will allow, Dani reaches the van. She hurls herself up behind the wheel and yanks the door shut, pounding down the lock. Scouring the side of the road for any activity, she grabs on to a handle and begins frantically rolling up the window.

Something moves in the side-view mirror.

Yelping, Dani cranks the ignition of the already running motor. An ear-splitting squeal grinds from under the hood. She jerks back, releasing the starter, as if she were zapped by a high-voltage shock. "Fuck!"

As she reaches for the gearstick, Zeke slams into the driver-side door. "Open," he barks, smacking his horn-framed face against the glass.

Dani spins to the glowing eyes gazing in at her, wailing in a series of piercing screeches, as Zeke's teeth sink into his bottom lip.

"Open this door!" he shouts, walloping on the window.

The engine grunts as Dani jerks the van into gear, but before she can accelerate, the side-panel door behind her seat unlatches.

Zeke's bloody hand darts in, grabbing a fistful of hair, snapping her head back. *"For Thou hast girded me with strength unto the battle,"* he growls over her hysterical shrieking. *"Thou hast subdued under me those that rose up against—"*

Dani stomps the accelerator. "Get off me!"

They are suddenly careening down the highway, Zeke's body thumping against the outside of the van, his fist still clinging to her hair. As the burning pressure spreads across her scalp, she realizes he's using her to pull himself into the cargo area.

"No," she howls, yanking down on the steering wheel. "Let go!"

The van reels from side to side, slamming Zeke against the door, loosening his grip with each impact. Dani gives the wheel another violent tug, and as the tires squeal across the asphalt, his body finally catapults off to the side of the road.

THIRTY-TWO

THE VAN FISHTAILS down the blacktop road several hundred yards with Dani's eyes locked on the driver-side mirror. Although she just watched Zeke soar into the ditch, she's convinced he's not gone somehow. As wind flaps into the cargo area behind her, she imagines Zeke's tattered body diving in through the open panel door again.

But if I don't stop, he can't get in.

As the van gradually climbs a low-grade hill, hooking around the steep mountain to the left, it begins to slow.

"Come on," Dani begs, stomping the pedal to the floor. "GO, GO, GO!" She subconsciously leans toward the dashboard, willing the van to speed up.

Ding, ding, ding, ding!

The steering wheel jerks from her hands, shuddering wildly, as though she were rattling across a long stretch of railroad tracks.

What the hell?

She clutches it, straining to keep the van on the curving pavement, but with a short clicking sound, the power steering gives out, locking up the wheels.

What is happening? She slaps the dashboard, searching the control panel for an answer to the pinging alert.

She finds the glowing low-fuel icon.

"No way," she mumbles. "Please no." Her gravelly voice breaks off, whistling into a hoot, as she kicks open her door and hops out.

She stares back at the shadows at the edge of the mountain, listening to the night. Other than an orchestra of crickets chirping from the wooded drop-off behind her and the light breeze floating past the van's clicking engine, there is silence.

He could stagger around that corner at any second, she thinks, checking the cargo area for some kind of weapon. *There's gotta be something in here.*

Dani spots a small black-and-red chest resting against the rear door. Leaning further inside, she makes out the word *Craftsman* on its scuffed up side. *A toolbox!*

Just as she's about to dart around to the back doors, a waft of gasoline hits her. Following the scent to the opposite back corner, she finds a dented metal gas can. *Oh my God!* She dives into the van, grabs the can's handle, and drags it back out with her.

When she hits the pavement, fuel sloshes up against the side of the jug, dousing Dani's hopes. It's almost empty.

Hoping the gas will at least get her a few miles away from here, she hobbles to the fuel door on the side of the van. She pops it open, double-checking the curve in the road again. The metal gas cap swivels from her hands, clanking down to the ground.

Fuck it, she thinks as it bounces under the van.

The low hum of a motor startles her. She drops the tin can, spinning toward the road. *Where's that coming from?*

With her back to the van, she stands petrified. She can tell that the vehicle is getting closer but still cannot identify what direction it's coming from. Terror claws its way up her chest where her heart is attempting to pound out through her ribs and escape on its own. As Dani forces herself to draw in a breath, a set of golden headlights appears down the road to her right.

"Oh, thank God," she wheezes, rushing toward the glow.

As the lights move closer, she hears blasting music and somebody wailing along to a familiar song. Afraid the driver won't hear her, Dani shuffles out into the path of the oncoming vehicle, straddling the lane-dividing line.

She thrashes her hands above her head, yelling as loudly as her inflamed vocal cords will allow. "Please stop!"

Grating rubber screeches across the asphalt, creating billows of gray smoke behind the tires, as a vehicle skids across the road. Skewing away from the mountain, a light-colored Jeep Wrangler swings around, jerking to a stop. The van's headlights point into the doorless front seat, shining in on a woman's terrified face.

"Please help me," Dani croaks, bolting toward her.

The driver is a small-framed woman of about forty. The name *Alaine* is embroidered on the breast of her light-blue waitress uniform.

"Are you okay?" the lady shouts, trying to see past the headlights.

With almost no sound coming from Dani, Alaine can't hear her. "Do you need some help or something?" she continues.

Dani appears at the passenger door, and Alaine can't help but jump. "Oh my Lord! What—"

"Please," Dani bays with the guttural tone of an injured animal. She lunges into the passenger seat, curling her feet under herself, grabbing the woman with another agonized moan. "Help me."

"What happened?" Alaine exclaims, recoiling at Dani's bloodied, lacerated body.

"He's coming," she rasps, spiraling into hysteria. Shaking the woman's arm, Dani points toward the edge of the mountain, wheezing. "He's gonna kill us!"

"What? Who's gonna—"

Dani pounds the dashboard with both fists, roaring with the last bit of sound she can muster. "JUST FUCKING GO!"

Terror flashes in Alaine's eyes. Now shaking herself, she stomps the clutch and grinds the motor into gear. The Jeep lurches forward, veering back into its lane, as it shoots past Zeke's van.

"No!" Dani grabs for the wheel. "Don't go this way!"

Alaine throws her arm up, blocking Dani's reach. "This is the fastest way to get help, honey," she snaps, shoving her back in the seat. "Just hold on."

But he's gonna try to grab me and pull me out, Dani howls in her mind, yanking up her knees.

Shifting into a higher gear, the women fly around the blacktop curve, almost tipping up to two wheels as they speed down the road. Dani clutches the bottom of her seat, scouring the gravelly shoulder, expecting to find Zeke's crumpled body, but there's nothing.

"Where is he?" Craning forward, she searches the shadowy ditch. Still nothing.

Maybe we already passed him somehow, she thinks, squinting into the darkness behind the Jeep.

"Look," Alaine blurts. "You see that?"

"What?" Dani whirls back around in her seat. "Don't slow down!"

She follows the woman's pointing arm to a small heap on the side of the road up ahead. As they approach, the yellow headlights sweep across what could be the bony antlers of a deer. Dani's blood goes cold.

Recognizing the gnarled goat horns and one of the hood's

terrifying orange eyes, she slaps her seat. "That's him!"

As the Jeep zips past, both women scowl down at Zeke's slumped body.

"Well, he doesn't seem to be moving now," Alaine mutters. "What hap—"

"Please, just get us outta here," Dani begs, staring at the comatose image in her side mirror.

"Okay, honey. Here," Alaine says, gently tapping a cell phone on Dani's arm. "We should be able to get service once we get over this next hill." She snags a camouflage sweatshirt from the backseat and passes it over. "And put this on. You must be freezing."

Finally looking away from the ditch behind them, Dani takes the sweatshirt. As she pulls it on, she notices the bloody wounds on her arms and legs. Snapshots of the snakes in that cellar and the creature in the wheelchair flash through her mind, like some macabre slide show she can't switch off.

I don't even know what day it is.

Stretching the bottom elastic down over her knees, she clenches the phone, gazing out at the road ahead.

Is it really over?

And, as the wind whips in across her tear-flooded face, she hears a tiny voice answer from somewhere deep inside her head, *It is, Dani. You made it.*

"As soon as we pass that barn up there," Alaine offers, "we should be able to get a good connection."

Dani nods, noticing the woman's face for the first time. She's pretty with a tight black ponytail pulled back over small doll-like features. The corners of her mouth tip upward with the slightest beginnings of a smile.

She's like a little fairy, Dani thinks, taking out the cell phone, *a little fairy angel.*

As the Jeep drifts down the hill, she centers herself and tries to speak. "Thank you," Dani squeaks out. "You saved my—" Her voice breaks off again.

"It's gonna be okay, sweetie," Alaine whispers, patting Dani's arm before she takes back the phone. "I'll do the talking."

THIRTY-THREE

THE BURBLING OF a chambered muffler breaks through the silence at the base of the mountain, scattering a flock of ruffed grouses from the ditch. As they flutter up through the trees, the two headlights of a Dodge Challenger rise over the hill, poking through the wee-hour darkness.

A young man in his early twenties uses his thigh to steer while he dusts cookie crumbs off his New York Jets jersey. Bobbing his head to his radio's techno beat, Neil reaches for a sip of coffee. He's driven this patch of road tons of times, but the series of curves coming up always makes him nervous. Back in high school, his friend Cory lost his truck to the hundred-foot Blue Mountain drop. Tossing back his last Double Stuf Oreo, Neil grabs the wheel again.

As he rounds the first bend, a couple of his pre-med textbooks slide off the front seat, clunking to the floorboard.

"Damn it," he mutters, discovering that some of his Post-it note bookmarks have fluttered into the gap beside the door. He decides reaching for them now would be suicide, so straightening out the car, he returns his attention to the music's relentless drum kicks.

He notices a vehicle pulled off to the side of the road up ahead, its hazard lights flashing. *Dude, that was close,* he thinks, eyeing the short space between the van's front tires and the wooded drop-off.

As he continues toward it, his mother's syrupy voice drifts into his head. *"You'd better see if they need help, Neil."*

"Ugh," he scoffs to himself, checking his watch. Between working an early morning shift at the Wawa, his classes, and a study group of mostly slackers, he's been up for almost two days now. *And I've gotta be back at the store in four hours!* He grabs a swig of cold coffee, easing off the accelerator, debating on what to do.

Neil hears his mom again, as if she were sitting right next to him, shaking her head in judgment. *"I know I'd want someone to stop for you if you needed help."*

Growing up with a nurse for a mom, he's gotten used to stopping to offer assistance.

He's watched her help out countless stranded travelers throughout the years, always reminding him, "Things happen for a reason, son," and, "Thank goodness it was us who came along."

Pondering her logic, he'd sometimes wonder if, by always swooping in to the rescue, they were perhaps robbing the next mom-and-son team. *Maybe other people would appreciate an opportunity to be heroes.*

This discussion almost always led to the mildly passive-aggressive statement that Neil was obviously going to be a lawyer, given how much he liked to argue.

Okay, Mom, he thinks, conceding to the guilt, *you win.*

Neil taps the brakes, clicks off the high beams, and pulls off the blacktop. As the Challenger hums to a stop a few yards behind the van, he checks his rearview mirror. He didn't see anybody in the front seat as he passed. There doesn't seem to be anyone around back either.

Maybe they started walking toward town. And maybe somebody already picked them up.

He glances at the inky darkness ahead. The closest place he can think of to get gas is the old Gulf station, which is probably eight or nine miles down the road. And it's definitely closed right now.

Then again, what if they're just in the backseat, hurt maybe, and I'm the only person who has come by for hours?

He taps his chunky high school ring against the steering wheel, his conscience winning out as he kills the engine.

"You need some help?" He swings his door shut, locked on the van's rear windows. He clears his throat before trying again. "Hello? Is somebody there?"

Still no response.

It occurs to Neil that the driver might have needed an emergency bathroom stop. He's definitely been known to pull off to the side of the road from time to time after his buckets of study coffee kicked in.

Probably just taking a piss out there, he thinks, continuing alongside the van.

Neil pauses at a strip of light he didn't notice when he drove past. *Was this open?* he wonders, eyeing the cracked side-panel door.

As he leans past the gap for a peek, movement in the front seat catches his attention.

With another step, he sees the overhead dome lamp reflecting off a set of swinging keys in the ignition. Now peering directly through the front window, his gaze drifts down to what appears to be blood smeared across the seats.

Whoa. Somebody's definitely hurt.

As he steps back over, sliding the panel door fully open, Neil notices the van rocking from side to side. "Hey, are you okay?" he asks, craning his head into the van. "Do you need help?"

There is nobody inside.

What's going on?

Other than a small toolbox, the cargo area is empty. Neil finds more blood smudged across the back floor. His arm hair stands up in alarm as he follows a large rusty streak to the open toolbox and realizes its handle is swinging. The trail continues to the rear of the van, as though something were dragged out the back door . . . which is now open.

Someone was just back here.

"What the hell?" Jerking out of the cargo area, he starts toward the Challenger. *This shit just got too weird.*

Zeke steps out from behind the van. His fractured face is caked in bloody mud and pieces of underbrush. A tangle of mossy grass dangles under his jaw, like a patchy, unkempt beard.

"Whoa!" Neil shouts, jolting backward. "Holy shit!"

Without a word, Zeke charges the young man.

Neil defensively draws his hands up to shield his face, but it doesn't matter. As Zeke latches on to the Jets jersey, the head of a small sledgehammer connects. It clinks against his senior ring, driving the metal band straight into his finger bone, which pops Neil's hand back, shattering the bridge of his nose. Blood sprays down his chest as his knees buckle.

Ignoring the young man's moaning gags, Zeke sinks another blow into the bloody gash between his eyes. Neil flops backward to the ground, his legs bucking in wild, unconscious spasms. And, with a final pulsing gurgle, he is gone.

SLUMPING THE STUDENT'S lifeless body into the trunk of his

own car, Zeke looks to the stars. Panic is swelling. *"Examine me, O Lord, and prove me!"* he shouts to the stars. *"Try my reins and my heart."*

As a pair of headlights rises over the distant hill, Zeke abandons his van. He slides into the Challenger, and firing its grumbling motor to life, he speeds off down the infamously dangerous road.

THIRTY-FOUR

T HE THICK-BODIED ROTTWEILER heaves against its chain, reared up on hind legs like Anubis protecting his sacred graves. With a hollow, deep bark, it warns the set of approaching headlights. The Dodge Challenger skids to a stop in the front yard, sending the dog into a berserk fit. Thick slobber flings from its massive head as it lunges, chomping at a rising dust cloud.

"Quiet," Zeke snaps, startling the animal to the ground, as he leaps from the car.

With the horned hoodie sagging down his back, he charges to the house's front porch. "Sylvia," he cries, pounding at the locked door, refusing to believe she is truly gone. "Sylvia!"

The slats beneath his feet creak with each pummeling blow, but the door doesn't budge. And his mother doesn't respond. As Zeke throws one final jab at the door, he slouches against the house, whining like a baby wolf that's lost its pack. *She can't be gone!*

Weeping desperate, heaving gasps, he crawls to the edge of

the porch.

"My God, my God," he wails. *"Why hast Thou forsaken me?"*

He latches on to the railing, pulling himself to his feet as he plods down the stairs. *"Why art Thou so far from helping me,"* he implores the speckled sky, *"and from the words of my roaring?"*

Zeke continues across the yard, dragging his feet like a petulant child. *"Our fathers trusted in Thee: they trusted and Thou didst deliver them."* He begins raging to himself, the fury in his belly growing like a fire. *"They cried unto Thee and were delivered: they trusted in Thee and were not confounded."*

Suddenly, he stops. Swinging his body around, Zeke squares up with the Challenger. "Why?"

With a gargling snarl, he lunges to the car. He pounds his fists down onto the trunk, exploding into a flailing tantrum. "Why?" he demands, tears streaming down his filthy, deformed face. *"Why, why, WHY?"*

Whimpers start up behind him, pulling his attention. Zeke whirls around to face the anxious rottweiler.

"But I am a worm, and no man; a reproach of men," he snivels to the dog. *"And despised of the people."*

He stumbles about in a series of sloppy circles, slashing at the air, alternating between sobbing gibberish and a deep-rooted moan. *"He hath fenced up my way that I cannot pass,"* he shrieks, frantically pointing up to the stars. *"And He hath set darkness in my paths!"*

Finally sinking to his knees, he collapses forward. As he hits the ground, the dog scrambles to the end of the chain, cocking its enormous head in concern.

Drool streams into a tiny pool beneath Zeke's gaping mouth as he lies in a quivering heap. His glossy eyes glide past the dog, bouncing from object to object inside the barn. They settle on a pair of tires peeking out from beneath an old tarp, and releasing a husky groan, he lowers his eyelids.

The rottweiler nervously paces across from its master's frozen body. As its snorts evolve into grumbling barks, a fluttering breeze drops down through the treetops, ruffling across the farm. Reaching Zeke, the wind suddenly shifts from a gentle sigh to a lashing howl, spraying sandy bits of dirt against his slack face. The dog's ears perk up in attention as the gust becomes something that sounds like a haunting, faraway voice.

"Yooouuu," the air seems to whisper.

Zeke's eyes spring open. "I hear you," he mutters, staring into the barn again as he claws himself up to his knees. "Yes, I hear you!"

Trained on the tires, Zeke gets to his feet and starts across the yard. "There hath no temptation taken you but such as is common to man," he reminds himself, reaching the covered car. And as he lifts off the tarp, a crooked smile spreads across his face. He pulls up his hood, ignoring the pain as it grazes his lacerated face. "But God is faithful, who will not suffer you to be tempted above that ye are able," he whispers to the Bald Knobber reflection in the windshield glass. "But will with the temptation also make a way to escape, that ye may be able to bear it."

Rummaging through a wooden crate along the sidewall, he grabs a screwdriver and returns to the front of the old sedan. With a few quick twists, he removes its plates. He replaces the tarp, pulling it down low enough to cover the bumper.

"A gift is as a precious stone in the eyes of him that hath it," he recites, rushing back across the yard. "Whithersoever it turneth, it prospereth."

Zeke swaps out the license plates on the Challenger, exchanging the blue and yellow shades of Pennsylvania for the old maroon tint of Missouri. As he tightens the last screw, his eyes drift over to the final letter in the sequence. He hears a familiar little boy's voice.

———

A tiny, dirty fingernail traces along the bright white Z that seems to glow against the dark background of the license plate. The finger starts to move back to the beginning of the series but quickly returns to this letter—*his* letter.

"Z, like Zeke," he tells himself. "And that's me. So, the letter Z is for me—"

"What are you doin', boy?"

Zeke yanks his hand back from the plate, like it's a snapping dog, and spins to face his mother. She's standing on the front porch, way across a huge, weedy field from him, but when she yells, the hairs on his neck always bristle, as if she were right behind him. Before he can decide the safest way to respond, the rickety screen door slaps shut. Sylvia's gone.

"Better not be horsin' around out there," she warns from somewhere inside his grandfather's house.

Elder Paul died not long after Zeke was born, so he doesn't remember him at all. Sylvia never talks about her father—or any of her family for that matter. In fact, he only learned his grandfather's name a few years ago, and that was because he overheard his parents arguing.

"Well, this ain't Elder Paul's house no more," his father barked as he stepped out of Faith's bedroom one night, "and I'll do as I please in it. And with whoever I please!"

Zeke pushes in the little silver button on the trunk. Its lid springs open, releasing a strong scent of gasoline. He used to love that smell. For a while, he even kept an old work rag he'd found, stashing it under his mattress, to sniff when he was alone. Then, he learned that gas makes fire, and fire is the scariest thing in the world.

Zeke's head whips toward the sounds of glass shattering from inside the kitchen. *Or at least the second scariest thing.*

He's the smallest seven-year-old in his class, even shorter than

some of the girls, so getting the big metal cans over to the house
will be hard.

I gotta get it done though, he thinks, clambering up onto the
bumper. *Who knows what she'll do if I don't?*

Normally, his mother's rages are like bad storms that make a
lot of noise and break lots of stuff, but eventually, they drift away.
Today is different. That man from the school came by again this
afternoon, yelling through the front door. Sylvia has been on a
rampage ever since.

This time, the man told her that he was an officer of the county
although he wasn't wearing a uniform and that he was coming
about Faith for the last time.

"Truancy is illegal!" he shouted. "And this is your final warning,
ma'am. If your child isn't in school tomorrow, it'll be Sheriff Mead
you're talking to."

"She's not here anymore," Sylvia snapped back. "She's with her
father now—"

"I think you're lying, ma'am," the man said, cutting her off, as
he huffed back to his car. "But you can discuss that with the sheriff
now. I'm through fooling with you."

But it's the truth, Zeke thought, assuming that, since he'd not
seen his father around for several years, he must be dead, too.

The tornado began the moment that tan sedan drove off. Sylvia
fumed through the house, throwing dishes, breaking furniture,
and grumbling to herself. She overturned her dresser, stuffing its
drawers of clothing into trash bags. In the kitchen, she packed all
the pots and canned goods into old pillowcases. And, finally, with
their old Plymouth jam-packed and the sun almost completely
gone, his mother sent him out for the gas cans.

It takes both hands to lift the first heavy container, and even
then, it's a struggle. Getting it safely to the ground, he hops back

into the trunk for the second can. It must be only half-full because it's much lighter, easier to manage. Resting it against the trunk's edge, Zeke attempts to reposition his hand, but the handle slips away. With a dull, tinny *clunk*, the can hits the dirt. Fuel starts to trickle from the loosely capped lid.

Panicked, he checks for Sylvia on the porch. She's not there.

Phew! The flash of relief quickly vanishes as he realizes she could be watching from a window, just waiting to grab him by the hair and drag him off to be punished again.

Scrambling to the ground, he uprights the leaking can, his heart pounding.

Like a mule pulling a plow, Zeke hauls the load toward the house, the heavier can leaving a gashed trail in the ground behind him.

Sylvia stomps through the door as he reaches the front steps. She snatches the full container away from him, carting it back inside. "Leave that other one there, and go get in the car!" she shouts. *"And get the lead out, boy!"*

Racing across the field without looking back, Zeke leaps through the Plymouth's front passenger door. He shoves a large wadded roll of linens to the side and plunges into the cramped backseat. As he sits wedged between a pair of black plastic bags, listening to his own breathing, he notices a shadowy movement from above. A wiry mosquito hawk is repeatedly thrashing itself against the glowing dome light. Zeke stares up at the confused insect, entertained by its chaos.

You can get out so easily, he thinks, glancing at an open window, *if you just ignore the light and fly away.*

"Stupid bug," he whispers, reaching up and smashing its body against the ceiling.

As the tiny winged carcass flutters to the floorboard, he hunches forward to retrieve it. He discovers a lidless cardboard box filled with pages from old newspapers. His eyes are immediately drawn to a group of strange faces in the black-and-white photo of the top clipping. Forgetting about the dead bug, Zeke lifts the sheet of paper up for a closer look. In the photo, a small gang huddles against a split-rail fence, arms proudly crossed. Each of their heads is covered by a horned mask with a furious painted-on face.

The screen door claps against its frame, and Zeke gasps, whirling toward the window. Sylvia lumbers along, sloshing gasoline across the front of the house.

As the splashes hit the windows and shutters, her grumbling rises to a full voice. *"Be strong and of a good courage, fear not, nor be afraid of them: for the LORD thy God, He it is that doth go with thee,"* she roars, disappearing around the side of the house. *"He will not fail thee, NOT FORSAKE THEE!"*

Unable to help himself, Zeke returns to the clippings where another picture catches his attention. Five people, linked by the shackles at their feet, stand outside a big brick building. They are surrounded by a large crowd, and although the page is too smudged to make out the faces, each man is holding one of those scary masks in his hand. Below the photo, there's a caption.

CHARLIE GRAHAM CONFESSES. BRINGS DOWN BALD KNOBBERS OF CHRISTIAN COUNTY.

Zeke sounds out a few sentences of the article that detail *the allegations against several confirmed members of the vigilante gang*, but he doesn't understand much. He skips to the list of names instead, which are more fun to pronounce, like Paul Adison.

Paul, like Sylvia's father, he guesses, dropping the clipping back into the box.

Zeke grabs another newspaper photo, so mesmerized by the masked men standing in front of a huge oak tree that he doesn't notice the lynched woman swinging from one of its branches.

The trunk lid slams shut, starling Zeke. He bolts back up in his seat, cowering between the bags for cover. Without time to get the clipping back in the box, he shoves it into his pocket, slapping his folded hands down onto his lap.

Sylvia's sweaty face appears at the window, panting. *"Every word of God is pure. He is a shield unto them that put their trust in Him."* Her eyes dart around the backseat, locking on Zeke, as she whispers, "You'd better not be diggin' through Elder Paul's box, boy."

She slides in behind the wheel, pulling her door shut, killing the overhead light. As darkness fills the car, the old motor groans to life, and Zeke notices the orange glow outside the window. He shuffles to his feet, pushing aside another roll of linen. He cranes his head closer to the rear window, watching as burning curtains drop to the floor and the old house's den bursts into flames.

"Good riddance," Sylvia mumbles under her breath at the blaze in the side-view mirror. "Turn around, and sit down," she hisses, clawing back at Zeke.

As they jostle down the dusty road, she drapes her palm across a Bible lying in the passenger seat. The car pauses at the end of the shale drive. Sylvia closes her eyes, bowing her head.

With a deep breath and the softest tone Zeke's ever heard from his mother, she recites from Jeremiah 26:14, *"As for me, behold, I am in your hand. Do with me as seemeth good and meet unto you."*

THIRTY-FIVE

HAZY WHITE CLOUDS stretch from the collapsed barn walls to what's left of an old farmhouse. Unfazed by the light breeze, the sooty billow hovers over the wreckage, like a ghostly spirit guarding its haunt. As first responders carefully move through the shambles, a loud splitting of wood echoes from the back of the house. Suddenly, the flooring above the cellar caves in, releasing a new puff of smoldering black smoke into the mid-morning sky.

A distracted young officer unrolls a Police Line: Do Not Cross banner, passing one end to an older officer. "Holy cow," the rookie mumbles.

"Yeah, I know." The older officer nods, dragging his end of the tape toward a tree. "It's unreal."

"No, look at that crazy shit!"

Glancing back at the smoky rubble, the second officer spots it. The banner flutters to the ground as he stares, mouth gaping. The foggy dark mass lingering over the back of the house has formed what looks like a face with three jagged breaks in the cloud that appear to be slanted, angry eyes and a grimacing mouth.

The rookie points to the image. "Do you see a face there? With, like—"

"I don't see shit," the older guy snaps, spinning away from the house. "Jesus, Mary, and Joseph," he mutters as he crosses himself and hurries after the slithering yellow police tape.

Blaring sirens draw the young cop's attention. He watches an approaching ambulance move up the drive and pull off into the grass. Two paramedics hop out, nodding to an officer leaning against his cruiser, and hurry around to the back of their truck.

The rookie glances back to the house just as the face above it dissolves into another murky cloud. Unrolling a second spool of police banner, he strides off in the opposite direction of his partner, marveling to himself. "Wow. That shit was wild."

CRIME SCENE INVESTIGATOR Al Snider is not happy about this shit at all. He was supposed to be off fishing today, but with several guys in the department down with the flu, his boss all but demanded that he cover the shift. Now, instead of relaxing on the lake, he gets to be the only one from his office to spend the next God knows how long combing through this messy disaster for some kind of evidence to process.

He climbs through the frame of what was the farmhouse's front door, stepping into several inches of turbid water. *Great. This is gonna be a blast.*

Noting the charred wood pieces floating across the foyer, he doubts the security of the floor and decides to work his way around the edge of the room. CSI Snider slips on his dust-proof face mask as he sloshes toward one of two passages, hauling his waterproof toolkit. He stops at a partially destroyed wall, separating him from the kitchen, which was the source of the fire, he was told. Through the hazy air, he spots a couple of firefighters prodding their roof hooks through wreckage in the next room.

"Hey, you guys think this floor is—"

"Watch it!" someone yells from another part of the house. "*Watch it!*"

A huge crash from down the hall gushes a wave of sooty water against Snider's ankles, continuing out into the foyer.

"Everybody all right?" a voice calls from outside the house.

"Yeah, I'm good," Snider replies.

"All good in here," one of the guys adds from the next room. "Think that was one of the last damn walls standing in this place."

"Over here, Snider," a new voice shouts from inside the kitchen.

The CSI carefully teeters into the room. There is almost no water on the floor, but he clings to the doorframe all the same. Beside the scorched shell of an old stove, a fireman crouches over the remains of a body. The clothing and much of its flesh have burned away, but by the size of the bones, it's clear the person was probably male.

Pulling a camera out of his toolkit, Snider squats down, examining the singed skeleton. "Okay, whaddaya got?"

"They found a wheelchair—or what's left of it—in the next room," the fireman reports. "So, I think this guy might've abandoned his chair, trying to get out on his own, and he just couldn't make it."

"Ah," Snider says, lifting the camera, snapping a shot.

"Also, somebody definitely helped get this one going."

"Yeah, it smells like it."

"Hey, did you see his head?" the fireman asks. "Looks like something bashed right through the front of his face. Maybe he fell or something," he offers, pointing to the jagged hole in the skull. "Although I don't see anything in here that would've done *that*."

"Jesus," Snider mutters, taking another picture as he circles the corpse. "Do me a favor," he says, noticing something near the hand. "Push that shit outta the way for me."

The fireman knocks a small pile of rubble off the wrist, revealing a dented class ring lodged in the man's finger bone.

As the camera flashes, a gravelly voice crackles from the CSI's walkie-talkie. "Snider, we got another DB over here by the cellar."

"Copy that," he responds, returning his camera to the toolbox. "On my way." He nods a thanks to the fireman and clambers back out to the foyer.

AS CSI SNIDER rounds the side of the porch, he sees a group of officers clumped together near the back of the house. The chattering men are staring down through a collapsed floor, several of them pointing at various spots in the cellar area.

"Somebody got another DB for me?" Snider asks, joining the clump.

"Down there," a squirrel-faced young officer points. "Looks like an old woman is wedged under those boards. Fire didn't really get down in there too much, doesn't look like."

The CSI scans the wreckage, agreeing that only the top few planks of the wooden staircase seem to have burned away. Halfway down, a series of steps leads under the splintered wood and debris from the fallen upper level.

Snider's eyes bounce around the circle of officers, amazed. "So, why hasn't she been pulled outta there yet? How do you know she's a DB?" He steps toward the edge, shaking his head at the laziness.

"Hey, you might wanna wait a few minutes," an officer cautions.

"Definitely," another jumps in. "Called AC already, so they should be here shortly."

"What?" Snider asks impatiently. "Why's AC coming out—"

"Snakes, man!"

Snider whips back to the cellar, gasping at how close he was to climbing down there. Now, he sees them. Several dark ribbons glide across shattered glass, stopping every few seconds to taste the air. Squinting, he counts at least ten heads bobbing up toward the sky, searching for an escape.

"Christ almighty."

"Yeah, we heard the rattles. No telling how many of them things are down there under all that mess."

"Oh, fuck!" a man yells from behind the house.

The crowd hurries around the corner and into the backyard. There are a few sections of green, but the area is mostly covered by yellowish crabgrass and dirt. Standing in the middle of the yard, twenty feet back from the house, a heavyset officer is waving his billy club at a spot on the ground.

"I thought the fucker was a stick," the thick man huffs, gesturing to a patch of grass where a small gray snake zigzags itself along. The lower third of its body drags behind it, having been scorched too badly to function anymore, but the tiny rattling from its slack tail is unmistakable.

"Did he get you?" the squirrel-faced officer asks.

"Nah, it struck but was really slow. Something's wrong with it. Think it must've been in the fire."

"Hold up," Snider interjects, pointing to a hole burned through the house's back wall. "Look right there!"

Three distinct snake heads dart out through the charred gash, sporadically probing the backyard air. A foot away, two more long brown bodies have already made it out of the wall and are winding their way toward the back tree line.

"Everybody, watch yourselves!"

All eyes hit the ground, scanning for any more reptile survivors.

"Heads-up," an officer barks, thinking he spots another one approaching the group.

As the men stagger backward, the heavyset cop trips over something in the grass. He tumbles down in a scoffing heap.

"You get tagged?" the young guy yells, rushing toward him.

Two officers lug the big guy to his feet while peering through the blotchy grass.

As they separate again, the embarrassed man points to a bare spot on the ground that's darker than the rest of the yard. "I tripped over that thing," he huffs, nodding to a two-inch piece of PVC pipe poking up through the dirt.

As he steps toward it, a small yellowish body darts out of a patch of crabgrass and slithers into the pipe's opening.

"Shit!" The big guy flinches, almost falling again. "The little bastards are everywhere!"

A chorus of static from several walkie-talkies startles the group with a crackled announcement. "AC is pulling up the drive. Where should they go?"

"Get them to the backyard ASAP!" Snider yells.

"Hey, quiet, you guys," an officer commands, crouching over the small pipe. "I hear something."

The men settle around him, focusing on a faint whistlelike sound coming from the opening. Confused expressions ripple across their frozen faces as another airy wheeze rises from below.

The young officer leans in toward the sound. "I think it's a per—"

"Help me!" a woman's broken voice suddenly shrieks up through the pipe. "I'm down here. Please help me!"

"Holy shit! Somebody's down there!"

The officers bolt into action, spreading out around the yard. Crouched over the opening, Snider jabs his pocketknife into the soil at the base of the pipe. "We hear you down there, and we're gonna get you out."

"PLEASE HURRY! PLEASE!"

"Just stay calm," Snider replies as he tries to shift the pipe. "This thing is buried really deep," he says over his shoulder. "It's not moving at all."

The heavy cop drags his billy club around the perimeter of a large square in the darker dirt. "Look at this."

All the other officers begin kicking at the ground within the etched outline.

The squirrel-faced young cop stabs his billy club at the soil, loosening it into large chunks. As he drives the stick into the same spot again, it sinks in a few inches and stops. "I got something!"

The rest of the men join in, stabbing and pushing away the dirt, slowly revealing the top of some kind of large plastic container. The underground screams get louder as they clear away the soil.

"We're almost there!" Snider shouts down the pipe.

"It's a door," an officer cries, kicking away a dusty clod to reveal a two-foot square hatch. "Oh, shit." He points to a corroded flat-key dead bolt. "There's a lock on it!"

"Shoot it!" the young cop yells.

"Wait! You might get her," the heavy officer blurts.

"A fucking snake just got down there with her. We gotta do something right now," Snider orders.

The CSI leans in, yelling down to the woman, "Ma'am, I need you to get as close to the pipe as possible, okay? But be careful." He considers his words for a moment and then commits. "I think there could be a snake in there with you—"

"It's rattling," she croaks. "GET ME THE FUCK OUTTA HERE!"

"Okay, we're gonna get you out right now. Are you by the pipe?"

"YES. HURRY UP!"

The bullet hits its target perfectly, splitting the lock. Half of it clunks down into the container. The heavyset cop dives forward, grabbing the latch handle, and heaves. The other officers surround him as dust shifts off the lifting door. A combination of hysterical sobs and the overpowering stench of human waste explodes up through the opening, sending a few men stumbling backward, covering their mouths.

"PLEASE!" the woman screams, clawing at the door's edge. "GET ME OUT!"

"You're safe now," Snider tells her, gripping the woman's wrists. "We got you."

A voluptuous woman wearing stained blue jeans and a ripped T-shirt slowly rises from the darkness. Straggly red hair clings to her filthy pale face as she shields her eyes from the daylight.

"We need paramedics back here!" the CSI shouts into his two-way. "Now!"

"What's your name, ma'am?" the heavyset officer asks.

Gripping the officer's uniform like a vise, she chokes out the words in delirious repetition, "Kristen Byrne. I'm Kristen Byrne. *I'm Kristen Byrne!*"

THIRTY-SIX

ALMA'S BRAIDED CLIP-IN bun tilts away from her head as she hunches over the hostess stand, scratching dried grape jelly off a menu. Lifting her gaze to greet a family of hungry travelers, she feels the slight tap of the bun tipping back down. She scoffs, remembering the hefty price tag of the drugstore Elegance in a Rush chignon.

More like Elegance in a FLUSH, she thinks, ushering the diners to a vinyl booth along the front window.

JD's 24-Hour Pancake House sits a couple of miles west of Interstate 81 in Virginia. As the last home-cooked option before crossing into Tennessee, it's always bustling with cross-country truckers and road-tripping families. Also a daily hub for local veterans and retirees, the diner is never short on war stories, political chatter, or its regionally famous banana-pecan flapjacks.

Leaving the family, Alma picks up menus from an elderly couple a few booths away. She heads to the long breakfast counter in the center of the room where she leans against an attached barstool. Taking a little weight off the fifty-year-old knee that's been bothering her lately, she scribbles out a quick order.

"Need two B-P short stacks, JD. Eggs, over easy!" she shouts through the kitchen window. "Side of bacon and side of links."

She snatches off the ticket and clamps it to a metal order wheel just inside the smoky kitchen. Shoving the pad into her apron pocket, she moves down the bar, topping off the coffee cups of a few regulars.

"You hear me, Jay?" Alma yells over her shoulder.

A barrel-chested man in his sixties with a high-and-tight crew cut emerges from the hazy breakfast cloud. He adjusts his disposable paper chef's hat, smirking with a face that's seen it all. "Oh, that lovely screeching?" Jay teases, grabbing the new ticket. "Who could miss it?"

As a regular chuckles, eyeing his buddy down the line, his coffee stream stops abruptly. He realizes Alma's staring him down, but before he can say anything, she leaves his mug half-filled. She moves to the next guy, who, having caught on, stifles his snicker.

"Old buzzard," she mutters.

At the family's booth, a little boy bounces in his seat, grazing his sister's leg under the table. As she whines to her oblivious parents, Alma unloads their beverages along with a handful of crayons.

Continuing her rounds, she drops off some orange juice and a bowl of fruity rings cereal to a man at a small table against the far wall. "Here you go, honey," she says, distracted by a squabble that's broken out over the crayons. "Uh, anything else for you, dear?"

The man adjusts his dark baseball cap, shaking his head as he digs into the cereal. Assuming that's a no, Alma tears off his check, sets it on the table, and heads toward a dinging bell in the window.

"Order up," JD calls.

The front door swings open, clanging against a metal trio of birds dangling from the ceiling. Their cheerful jingle announces another diner.

"Morning, Carl," Alma says from the counter.

A bristly old widower approaching seventy moves past the booths, heading straight to his regular stool at the breakfast bar. He takes off his American by Birth, Virginian by Choice hat, setting it aside, as he palms a white cowlick at the back of his head. "Morning," he mumbles to the room, overturning an empty coffee mug.

A wave of bobbing heads returns his greeting while Alma delivers breakfast to another table.

"Usual, honey?" she asks over her shoulder, already returning to the bar.

"Yep, that'd be fine." As black coffee streams into his mug, he nods to a mounted television next to the kitchen window. "Hear about that business up in Pennsylvania yet?"

Alma refills coffee in a few more mugs down the line before replacing the pot. "I heard a little something about it in the car this morning," she says, lobbing two heaps of steaming oatmeal into a bowl, topping it with a scoop of blueberries. "Said some folks got killed in a big fire up there?"

"Yeah, happened last night," a regular chimes in. "Say it's one of the worst fires in years."

"Oh, hang on," she says, delivering Carl's hot cereal. "Here it is again."

Dusting off her hands, she points a remote up to the TV. As the volume rises, an African American woman wearing a stiff suit jacket shifts in her seat, addressing the camera.

"Now, Bill," the anchor says, quickly adjusting her bubbly voice into a more somber tone, "you have a very disturbing story you've been working on this morning."

A large plastic-looking face topped with motionless yellow hair appears on the screen. He smiles sadly, revealing his remarkably perfect teeth that look like a row of bleached corn kernels. "Indeed, Laurie," he replies. "Authorities made a startling discovery while investigating one of the largest fires in Pennsylvania's history late last night. Now, uh, we're working with our affiliate at Channel Five News for the latest details . . ."

"They say the fire spread out into the woods around the property," Carl remarks, shaking his head. "Torched up a several miles of land around Scranton."

Aerial video of the burning farm replaces the reporter's face as he continues, "We've learned that the property was owned by an elderly woman who lived there with her son."

The screen switches to live coverage of the scene where emergency response teams are combing over the destroyed structures. A few firemen work at recoiling hoses on their trucks.

"Now, here's where the story gets really unimaginable," Bill continues. "Dani Caraway, the Pennsylvanian woman who had been missing since Wednesday evening, appeared at a state police department very early this morning, saying she had been held prisoner at that farm."

The video morphs into footage of a dark-haired woman wearing a light-blue waitress uniform, standing next to her Jeep. *Alaine—Good Samaritan* appears in the banner along the bottom of the screen.

"She said she was being kept in a dungeon or something before she escaped," Alaine tells the camera. "Said the guy was some kind of religious freak. Had horns and snakes and everything like that."

"Now, Laurie, we have also just learned that *another* missing woman was discovered on the property in an underground container," Bill says. "Her name hasn't been released yet, but a source from the police department has confirmed that this farm is now believed to have been a sort of lair, if you will, for the serial murderer known recently in the local media as the Rattlesnake Killer."

The picture flips back to the studio, revealing Laurie's horrified face, unaware she's live again.

"It seems that, after putting out the four-alarm blaze that destroyed most of the farm and spread into the woods just miles away from Lackawanna State Park," Bill continues, "investigators discovered close to a hundred rattlesnakes—many of them still alive—roaming freely in the basement area of the house."

"Oh my gosh," Laurie gasps, covering her mouth. "Um, do we know—"

"Though not identified yet, I'm told that there were two bodies found on the property, which police believe might be the mother and son who lived on the farm. That's all we know for now, but the investigation continues, and we'll give another update as soon as we can. Back to you, Laurie."

Regaining her composure, the anchor brushes her bangs off her forehead, acknowledging the camera again. "Thanks, Bill. Okay, well, we'll bring you more details on this incredible story as they develop." And, as if a studio engineer somewhere has flipped a switch, a saccharin perkiness replaces the grave tone in her voice. "Up next, we're going to be chatting with a woman who says she has the uncanny ability to communicate with fish. So, stay tuned!"

Alma lowers the volume, moving to the kitchen window, as the television picture shifts to a military recruitment commercial. She surveys the dining room. The annoyed expressions from the elderly couple by the window prompt her to check on their order. "Got those flapjacks yet, JD?"

"It's gettin' crazier every day, seems like," Carl says before downing a lumpy bite.

"Oh, yeah," Alma scoffs. "World's goin' to hell in a handbasket. I've been saying that for years." She heads toward the small table on the far wall again. "What kind of maniac does something like that?"

The man in the baseball hat stands as she arrives, craning his head toward a doorway in the wall.

"Yep, restroom's just through there, honey," she says, collecting his dishes. She snags the cash from his table. "You need change, sweetie?"

Without answering, he disappears through the doorway as JD calls for another pick up at the window.

"You know, it's gettin' so that you don't even wanna watch the news at all," Alma complains, sliding the dirty dishes into a tub under the counter. "Just too doggone depressing."

"You just can't tell who the crazy people are anymore," Carl adds.

Alma grabs the elderly couple's food, starting toward their table. "And then the—" She stops, spinning around, setting the plates back in the window. "Need links on one of these, JD." She gives a quick nod to the old couple. "Be right over there, folks." While waiting, she scans the various faces at the breakfast counter, finally landing on Carl. "And all those snakes? My God!"

Behind her, Jay swaps sausage links for bacon without her noticing. He pounds the bell, startling Alma. She shrieks, whipping her face to the window, and slaps the bell herself in retaliation.

"Hey, Alma," JD goads, already back to work at the sizzling griddle, "I like that fancy new bun you got."

"Buzzard!" she barks, huffing off.

"Well, would you look at that?" Carl says, staring at the television again.

The magnified driver's license photos of Zeke and Sylvia fill the screen. Somebody down the counter comments with a whistle.

Alma glances to the picture as she returns to the bar for the coffee pot. "Goodness," she mutters at the severe faces. "Mother and son, huh?"

"Wonder what the father looks like?" Carl asks his sniggering buddies.

The birds chime from the door again as a young couple stumbles in, laughing.

"Excuse me?" The guy starts toward the bar, trying to speak through his hooting, "Um—"

"Sit anywhere you like, folks," Alma calls out, snagging two laminated menus.

The youngsters burst into a new fit of cackling, prompting a few of the regulars to shift around on their stools for a better view of the scene. Alma pauses, considering what she thinks might be a couple of junkies blitzed out of their minds.

"Um, there's a car outside," the young guy composes himself, "with its window rolled pretty far down and—"

"Stop. It's not funny," his girlfriend whines. "That thing could kill somebody."

"And, when we walked by," the guy continues, "a huge dog's head lunged out at us. Scared the hell outta her!"

As he explodes with another outburst, the man wearing the dark baseball cap returns from the restroom. He moves toward the front door, eyes lowered to the floor.

"She jumped so far," the young guy wails. "*Oh my God, oh my God!*" As he staggers backward in a frantic reenactment, his flailing hand smacks the guy's baseball cap to the floor.

"Hey!" Zeke yells with a battered face that looks like some gruesome latex mask from the monster aisle of a costume shop. One eye is swollen shut, and the bloated bruising on his cheeks makes it impossible to determine the actual natural shape of his head. "Move!" He grabs his hat, pushing past the shocked expressions and out the door.

"Whoa, man. Take it easy." The young guy titters, stumbling back against an empty table. "What the *hell*?"

"Hey," the young girl blurts at the front window, "that's the car with the dog."

Alma slaps the menus onto the table, watching the light-blue Dodge Challenger peel out of the parking lot. "Hell in a goddamn handbasket," she mumbles with a sigh. "You two want coffee?"

THIRTY-SEVEN

S HEETS OF WHITE rain slide across the parking lot, like the closing curtain of a giant proscenium stage. Dani's forehead taps the glass of the front door as she stomachs how miserable this is about to be. The warm, dry nirvana of her Toyota Highlander awaits a mere thirty yards away, but considering the two landscaped islands and the river of fresh mulch flowing between them, she's pretty sure this is gonna suck.

The quivering ring from her desk reminds her that she hasn't forwarded the phones. She drops her purse at the door and slowly hobbles back, still not adjusted to the cumbersome boot. The unwieldy souvenir taunts her with each and every step. Apparently, the rock she landed on in the woods the night she escaped sliced through the muscles in the arch of her right foot. She learned that the recovery could take a year or more.

All the doctors told her how lucky she'd been as they reviewed her staggering list of injuries. The most serious was the staph infection from the removal of her tattoo. It had transitioned into sepsis, requiring emergency surgery, followed by more than six weeks in the hospital. During the stay, her three cracked ribs healed themselves, and the scabby bite on her neck faded into a light-pink scar.

The specialist examining her lacerated foot was the first one to actually say it. "It's a miracle. I can't believe you were able to walk on this, let alone *run*. You're pretty amazing."

Well, I did have a little motivation, she thought.

With the buckets of pain medication they piped into her IV, Dani didn't talk much. When she did manage to slur something, people just stared back with confused looks on their faces. She knew her words weren't making any sense. So, once again, she smiled and blinked her gratitude to the spectacled old man.

"God was watching over you, young lady," he said, heading to the door.

As his words hovered above her, Dani stared out the window. A tear rolled down her face.

The phone echoes from her desk again but stops halfway through its ringing cycle.

As Dani reaches it, she notices the glowing green light on the main line. *Shit*. Now, she'll have to wait for the call to finish.

A flash of lightning pulses in the darkness outside, and she decides lingering a while longer is probably a good idea anyway. She slumps down in her rolling chair, studying the beautiful arrangement in a vase. He has been sending flowers every single week since he learned she was in the hospital—always roses, always pink.

"Dani, you still here?" Larry yells from the other side of the building.

She clambers to her feet. "Yep. Just about to head out."

"Don't forget to—"

"Forward the phones," she interrupts. "Yep. Doing it now."

As she waits for the confirmation beep, she sniffs a rose, looking forward to Friday night. *I don't know how he can possibly be this perfect, but I'll take it. Hell, I've earned it!* She eyes the card again, smiling.

Dinner at my place? No pressure. Just your beautiful eyes and my beautiful teeth . . . and maybe a beautiful pizza?—Eric

Beep, beep, beep.

At the door again, Dani stares out at the relentless rain. *If I don't get outta here soon, it'll almost be time to come right back.* She glances at the stiff flower-patterned sofa, imagining sleeping there for the night. She pictures waking up to Frank the Lecher salivating over her reclined body like it's an all-you-can-eat buffet.

"Ick!" She snorts involuntarily. "Okay, night, Larry."

The pounding drops assault her from every angle as she steps out into the deluge. With the first huge gust, her umbrella betrays her, flipping inside out. At the same time, her long skirt flaps up her legs, making her immediately glad she went with the black wool tights today. Tucking her purse under her arm, she wrenches the snapping skirt fabric into a fist and leans into the wind. The umbrella's mutinous canopy snaps back into place, as if on cue, as Dani soldiers through the flooded lot.

She reaches her row as another whipping squall joins forces with the stream at her feet. Instinctively dropping the skirt, she latches on to the closest vehicle with a yelp, barely keeping her balance. Thankfully, the soaked material has lost the ability to fly, instead molding itself to her body. Next to her hand, upper taillights suddenly flash red. Dani jerks away, teetering onto the muddy landscaped median, unable to breathe.

A white cargo van.

As the vehicle backs out, she spots the local electric company's decal—PP&L, Co.—on its side. The surprised driver notices her and slams his brakes. He waves apologetically as he continues past her, crawling out of the parking lot.

Dani sloshes down the aisle, carrying what feels like several new pounds of water weight. When she clicks the keychain fob, her Toyota lights up, welcoming her back with a perky chirp. Something darts by in her peripheral. As she reaches her door, a flurry of wind yanks the umbrella from her hand, flipping it across several car hoods.

Piece of shit. Fumbling with the handle, she begins to open the door when she feels a strong constricting pressure.

Her eyes whip to the large gloved hand clutching her left ankle.

Before she can react, Dani's jerked off her feet. Her head smacks into the window of the neighboring car as she slides down its door. Her body flopping against the submerged concrete, she flails for something to grab, but another tug pulls her further under her vehicle. Finally, she's able to latch on to the Toyota's running board, but it's too late. She's going under.

The hissing storm muffles her screams as her writhing body shoots under the truck. She claws at the undercarriage, stomping at her attacker's hands. Flopping to her side, she spots the twisted goat horns and the painted orange eyes.

"Nooo!"

"Dani!" someone yells. "It's okay, baby. Dani, *it's okay!"*

Her eyes spring open, darting around the flower-filled hospital room. She realizes she's panting but can't stop it. A latex-covered hand dabs a tiny droplet of blood at her wrist where she ripped off the IV tape.

"Shh, shh, shh," she hears as someone caresses her other arm. "You're all right, baby."

Dani follows the soothing voice, finding her mother standing at the side of the bed. She notices the smudged eye makeup and crazy hair and realizes her mom's probably been here for a while. A blanket of calmness moves over her. She feels safe again.

"Well, good morning," her dad says in an unnaturally cheerful voice. "The doc says you're gettin' a special boot today, so I was just lookin' into some dance classes for us." He sets a couple of steaming Styrofoam cups on a side table and takes over for his wife.

"Looks like you'll be getting out of here pretty soon," her mom chirps, sipping her coffee.

Vaguely familiar memories whirl around Dani's mind, as though she were watching scenes from a friend's life. Thoughts appear, only to vanish seconds later, and although she can hear her own words, none of them make sense. She gives up on trying to understand any of it, allowing her eyelids to ease shut. And, as warm tears spill down her cheeks, Dani clings to her father's hand with all she's got.

THIRTY-EIGHT

A CRUMPLED FANTA can skids across two lanes of late-night traffic as Katie Perez wipes the residual soda from her top lip and continues along the Arkansas stretch of I-40. Unzipping her *The Twilight Saga: New Moon* backpack, she pulls out the last of her provisions—a king-size Butterfinger. She considers saving it since she's not really sure when she'll be able to get more food.

It's been two full days since she left Memphis. Her mother has probably lost her mind by now.

I bet she's really sorry for the fucked up stuff she said.

"He's a pothead and a loser, Katie," her mom yelled. "He only wants *one* thing from you, and once he's gotten that, he'll drop you. Trust me."

Well, I guess you were wrong, bitch, Katie thinks, scuffling down the shoulder, *because I left his ass!*

———————

Josh is basically the best thing that's ever happened in Katie's shitty life—like, ever. He is tall, really cute, and so smart that he got his GED and didn't even have to finish high school. But her favorite thing about him is that he *loves* her, like get-drunk-and-cry-about-how-he'll-die-without-her loves her. He has his own apartment, too, which is where they usually hang out since her mom is really strict and doesn't like Josh because he is a little older. Yeah, he just turned twenty-three, but that doesn't matter to Katie.

Age is just a number. In two more years, I'll be an adult, and nobody'll care anyway.

Getting cut early from her Starbucks shift tonight feels like a miracle, because it means she can surprise Josh with the amazing news in person. She pictures his scruffy face sliding into a proud smile and almost squeals.

As the bus huffs to a stop, Katie dashes off, partly from excitement, but mostly because she has to pee again. She makes it up the street and to Josh's apartment faster than ever before. Finding the knob is locked, she knocks several times, but there's no answer.

"Hello?" She hears Eminem blaring from the radio inside, so she knows he is home. *He must not have heard my knock.* She pounds on the door this time. "Hey, baby. It's me."

As the stereo volume lowers, a set of fingers shuffle through the mini blinds, but he still doesn't come out.

"Josh!" Katie shouts, getting annoyed at his game. "Yo, you don't hear me out here? What's up? I gotta pee."

The door flies open, revealing some bleach-blonde whore, standing in her underwear. "The fuck do you want?" the woman snaps, her eyes squinting through a reefer cloud. "Why you out here, blowin' all this noise?"

The color drains from Katie's face. She immediately feels like a little kid, like she's being scolded by some hag of a teacher for being somewhere she shouldn't. And the woman is so old.

Like, thirty at least. Who is she?

Katie peers past her into the smoky living room. "Where's Josh?"

"He's in the shower," the woman slurs. "Why? Who are you?"

"I'm his *girlfriend*! Who the hell are you?"

"Oh, that's so cute." The peroxide skank smirks, almost giggling. "But, not anymore, honey," she says, backing into the apartment and closing the door.

Before Katie can stop it, puke is coming up her throat and cascading over the second-floor railing.

This can't be happening. That bitch is lying!

Smearing away thick strands of spit, she stomps back toward the door, but laughter coming from behind the blinds stops her—*that's Josh's voice.*

"What'd you tell her?" he asks through his snickering. "Her mom's probably gonna be calling me any minute now."

A bomb explodes in Katie's gut as she scrambles down the concrete stairs, pausing at the bottom to vomit out another retching flood of humiliation. Continuing to the street, she ignores the red light and bolts through traffic, half-wishing a car will smash into her and end all this.

As the 42 Crosstown pulls up to the corner bus stop, she rushes on, crumpling into a seat in the very last row. With her work apron draped over her face, she leans against the window and tries not to imagine what is going on in Josh's apartment. *How can he do this to us?*

At home, her mother is comforting at first, saying she is so sorry, but that maybe it is better this way. Then, all of a sudden, something changes. She takes a big step back, her gaze moving down Katie's torso. As silence swells in the room, watery fear spreads into her eyes. "You're pregnant."

How can she know that?

The fuse is lit. Storming across the bedroom, her mother begs God to have mercy as she slams the door and stomps down the hall. Katie hears the glasses and plates crashing in the sink and decides it's time to go. *I'm outta here. I don't need him and I DON'T NEED YOU!*

The clock on her dresser blinks midnight, but it's been unplugged so many times there's no telling what time it really is. Hoping there are still buses running that can get her out of town tonight, Katie carefully slides open her window. As she climbs out over their garage, she eyes her bedroom door, wondering if she'll ever see her mother again and if she'll even care.

———

A tractor-trailer speeds by, blaring its horn. Flipping the driver off, Katie shuffles further up the expressway shoulder.

Fuck it, she thinks, tearing into the Butterfinger wrapper. *The baby's hungry.*

As she chomps into the candy bar, her thoughts drift to her mom for a moment. *I wonder if she's even looking for me.* Tears spill down her face. *I could be dead in a ditch somewhere, and she probably doesn't even care. Nobody cares.*

"No," Katie barks to herself as she drags a hand across her cheek. "Fuck *them.*"

With a resetting deep breath, she taps her belly, focusing on her plan. She's got cousins on her dad's side in Oklahoma City. When she visited them a few summers ago, Aunt Nathalie told her she was welcome there anytime.

Maybe they all knew how horrible my mom was, even back then. Maybe they won't even be that surprised to see me.

Either way, Katie knows they'll let her stay with them if she can just get there.

They have to. We're blood.

The cashier at the last rest stop said that I-40 ran straight across Arkansas. He told her she could be in Oklahoma City in, like, seven hours or so.

I'm almost there. I can wait till morning to eat.

She balls up the candy wrapper, hurling it into the grass, as she fantasizes about the huge breakfast her aunt will probably make for her.

Katie takes off her sweatshirt. She ties it around her waist, revealing the sleeveless white tank that most people refer to as a wifebeater. She hates that term, always wondering how it could be so popular. *Is it only a matter of time before some particular piece of clothing will start being referred to as a child-abuser sweater or date-rapist jeans?*

Ugh, people suck, she thinks, turning to face the oncoming traffic.

Josh always said she looked hot in these shirts, which will probably make it easier for her to hitch a ride. Katie extends her arm, signaling with her thumb, like they do in movies. She kinda digs how all the headlights accentuate her black bra.

A couple of cars pass, tapping their horns without stopping and Katie gives them the finger. As she crunches over the gravel, teetering backward along the blacktop, a large form appears in her peripheral. Spinning around, she spots a light-colored sports car parked on the shoulder up ahead.

Awesome, she thinks, approaching the trunk. *Oh, please let them be cool.*

The engine is not running, and there are no lights on inside.

Are they sleeping?

She peeks into the rear window at a backseat that's crammed with trash bags and stacks of loose clothes. There's a big cardboard box wedged against the door behind the driver's seat, so there's not really room for someone to stretch out. Continuing to scan the messy area, she can't see any recognizable body part.

There's definitely nobody back there, she decides, moving to the front passenger window.

On the seat, there's a road map underneath a crinkled Bojangles' sack, next to an unopened bag of corn chips.

Oh my God, I would kill for some Fritos right now.

"Hey!" a husky voice shouts from behind her.

She shrieks, spinning around to face a man standing in the shadows at the edge of the tree line. A huge black dog steps out in front of him, pulling at its leash with a grumbling snarl. As Katie steps forward to speak, a single booming bark explodes from the rottweiler's flapping jowls. She jumps back against the car.

"Quiet," the man yaps, silencing the dog. He wipes his hands across his pant legs as he moves out of the trees, glancing up and down the expressway. "What are you doing?"

"Sorry. I was just—hey, is this your car?" she asks anxiously. "I really need a ride."

He stops at the hood of the Challenger, considering the girl. His eyes scroll down her body, pausing at the tinted outline of her breasts peeking through her tank top. Without a word, he adjusts his ball cap, lowering the bill to cover more of his face, as he continues around the front of the car. He opens the driver-side door, ushering the dog in.

As panting quickly fogs up the window in front of her, Katie imagines walking along the expressway for another few hours, hungry and tired. She decides she has to act fast.

Mustering up some crocodile tears, she steps up to the car. "Please, sir. I'm pregnant, and I haven't eaten all day. I could really use some help. Please?"

Zeke slides in behind the wheel, starting the car. As the passenger window begins to slide down, he leans toward her, his face shielded.

"You're not married, are you?"

Before even thinking about her answer, the visual of that whore leaning against Josh's doorframe pops into her head. "Uh, no way," she spits.

CLICK. The passenger door lock shoots up.

"Oh my God," she gasps, hopping into the car. "Thank you, thank you, *thank you!*" Katie shoves her backpack onto the floor-board, pulling out a half-empty bottle of Mountain Dew. "I'm trying to get to Oklahoma City," she says, taking a swig. "How far are you going?"

The Challenger rolls forward, wobbling across the bumpy road-side gravel. Picking up speed, the right front tire dips into a tiny pothole, bouncing the whole car. As Katie clings to her door handle, she hears a muffled rattling inside the box in the backseat. From the corner of her eye, she thinks she sees its folded-in lid flinch up a couple of times. Glancing over her shoulder to be sure, she finds the rottweiler's muzzle just inches from her face.

As she carefully turns back around, Zeke taps a button on the console.

A voice begins to mumble from the rear speakers, "If you could go into the presence of God, unsaved, He would literally annihilate you. YOU'D RATHER BE IN HELL IN A HEARTBEAT THAN GO BEFORE A HOLY—"

"Oh, you really religious?" she asks, drowning out the minister's audio. "Yeah, my mom is, too." Katie eyes the bag of corn chips on the dashboard. "You're what she'd probably call a godsend," she mutters to herself with a touch of condescendence. Scoffing at her mother's cheesiness, she turns to him. "Hey, I'm Katie by the way. What's your name?"

As they merge into a stream of anonymity, he stares into the rearview mirror, nodding to the mask in the back window. His eyes slowly shift back to the red taillights speckling the long road ahead. And, with the quick twist of a knob, the volume rises from the back of the car.

"Ezekiel," the baritone voice says. "Sixteen twenty-five—*Thou hast built thy high place at every head of the way, and hast made thy beauty to be abhorred, and hast opened thy feet to every one that passed by, and multiplied thy whoredoms.*"

<<<<>>>>

ACKNOWLEDGEMENTS

Alaine Alldaffer is a brilliant, nurturing champion of artists everywhere. My gratitude is infinite for her unwavering belief, counsel and motivation. It is an absolute certainty that *Sinner* would not exist, in any form, were it not for her.

I am indebted to the many friends and family members who have, through the generous gifts of their time, experience, names, and individuality, helped make these characters more relatable and this world more real. I am truly grateful.

Drew, your ambition and the drive with which you pursue your goals, have been a constant source of inspiration for me and I am lucky to count you as such a steadfast friend.

Thank you to Marla Haut, Sue Gilad and KP Simmon. Through your faith, guidance and never-ending encouragement, you incomparable ladies helped grow a creative ember into a thriving flame.

Jared, you have walked me back from the edge more times than you will ever know. Your loyalty, friendship and respect are priceless to me.

Mom, as children, your love gave us the magical adventures of Stormy, Cloudy, and Sunshine to make our complicated world less scary. And all these years later, as a writer, your love has given me the confidence to make scary worlds less complicated. *Nothing Compares To You*.

And finally, to my selfless, supportive and unreasonably patient wife, I will never be able to thank you enough for all that you have brought into my life. But I will also never stop trying.

ABOUT THE AUTHOR

Christopher Graves is the creator and writer of the comedic web series, With Friends Like These and the feature-length screenplay, Sinner, which was named Best Psychological Thriller Script by the New Hope International Film Festival.

Born in the hills of Mt. Vernon, Missouri, his introduction to the thriller genre started early. At five years old, his mother abducted him along with his younger siblings and fled across the country. They were given new names, a new home, and a new beginning–until they were discovered and had to move again.

He lives in Manhattan with his wife, and their two judgmental Siberian cats.

Made in the USA
Columbia, SC
04 June 2018